THE IMPOSSIBLY

The Impossibly

A NOVEL

Laird Hunt

COFFEE HOUSE PRESS
MINNEAPOLIS
2012

COPYRIGHT © 2001, 2012 Laird Hunt
COVER AND BOOK DESIGN Linda Koutsky

Coffee House Press books are available to the trade
through our primary distributor, Consortium Book
Sales & Distribution, cbsd.com or (800) 283-3572.
For personal orders, catalogs, or other information,
write to: info@coffeehousepress.org.

Coffee House Press is a nonprofit literary publishing house. Support from private foundations, corporate giving programs, government programs, and
generous individuals helps make the publication of our
books possible. We gratefully acknowledge their support in detail in the back of this book.

To you and our many readers around the world,
we send our thanks for your continuing support.

LIBRARY OF CONGRESS CIP INFORMATION
Hunt, Laird.
The impossibly / by Laird Hunt.
p. cm.
ISBN 1-56689-117-5 (alk. paper)
I. Title.
PS3608.U58 I47 2001
813'.6--dc21
2001032484

2   4   6   8   9   7   5   3   1
PRINTED IN THE UNITED STATES

This book is a work of invention and dark imagination.
The situations and opinions set out herein are its own.

This book is for Eleni and Eva

CONTENTS

Introduction

INTRODUCTION

HEN THE FOLKS AT COFFEE HOUSE PRESS asked if I would write an introduction to Laird Hunt's first novel, *The Impossibly,* I said yes. I said yes without thinking. I almost always say no to such requests. But I could not say no. I have always loved this novel. How could I say no to writing an introduction to a spy novel that opens with a sentence about a stapler? But more, the sentence is about the word *stapler.* This is a novel about appearances, reality and shadow, identity and anonymity, words and their corresponding signifieds, or the echoes of those signifieds. *The Impossibly* is like Beckett's *Molloy,* but faster paced, better to dance to. It is like Robbe-Grillet's *Jealousy,* but so much funnier.

The Impossibly takes a kind of psychic snapshot of the soul of someone who must move through shadows, whose job it is to move through shadows, whose choice it is to do so. Reality for this unnamed operative is like a phantom limb, the limb having been severed from him long ago, but the sense of it, the weight of it, the aura of it remains, with all its paresthesias, transient aches, and the pain that resided in the part before its loss. Much as an operative in this dark and murky world must float away from his past and his identity, so the novel drifts away from what pretends to be coherence and sense. This work is about meaning, about words, and about the so-called uselessness of the reality and the appearance of that reality in regard to these words. The prose mirrors what must be the fragmented sense of self and being that someone so removed from his *real* life must experience. And if one can, named or unnamed, veer so far away from what was at some time understood and perceived to be reality, then what are we to make of any perception of reality? What is real? When is reality real?

Our nameless operative has failed at something, we don't know what. His mission? His understanding of the mission? His mere understanding of his own presence and purpose? Everyone in his sphere appears to be involved in his desired, needed absolution, and in his punishment, but are they? Are they even aware of his botched efforts? We comprehend the paranoid behavior, recognize the music of it, the rhythm of it. And the fear is palpable as the operative realizes that he has been assigned an assassin. But is there an assassin at all? The confusion is what is beautiful, for its clarity, for its logic. I could describe the story fifteen different ways and I cannot describe it at all.

Strange, beautiful, strange, complicated, strange. To call *The Impossibly* surreal is to miss the point. It is *hyper-réalisme*, its roots more in the philosophy of Jean Baudrillard than André Breton.

Who will kill us in the end? And will it matter?

Percival Everett
Los Angeles, California
February 2011

THE IMPOSSIBLY

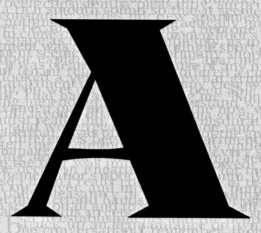

However, one must be cautious in passing judgment upon the phenomenon; for, although the phenomenon is the same, the reason for it may be exactly the opposite.

—KIERKEGAARD
The Concept of Dread

THE FIRST TIME WE MET IT WAS ABOUT A STAPLER, I think. I knew the word, and she didn't, so I stepped forward, slightly, and said it. The shopkeeper smiled, and she smiled, and the shopkeeper reached under the counter and produced a box. It was a fine box, smooth white on the outside, dark corrugated brown on the inside, and contained a nice-enough looking gray stapler that the shopkeeper demonstrated, first opening the mechanism and loading it with a generous strip of his own staples, then closing it on two sheets of a yellow ledger. He pulled lightly on the two sheets to demonstrate that they would not, if not pulled on too strenuously, come apart, stressing, as he did so, that no stapler could be expected to perform satisfactorily given unsuitable material. He then asked if the stapler would be used for heavy or light jobs, and, as the answer was both, put two small maroon boxes of staples on the counter, and asked if there would be anything else.

At this point I wandered off.

Though not far.

A moment later I was asked to come over again.

Hole puncher, I said.

The shopkeeper said he was very sorry, but that item was currently out of stock.

When we had left, she asked me to repeat each of the words I had used in the shop, which I did, then she asked me to repeat each of them again more slowly, which I also did, then she took out a pen and a small notepad and had me write each of the words down, which process I found quite hypnotic. As I did not write either of the words very neatly, she took back the pen and the notepad and very carefully closed one or two of my vowels. She then put away the pen and the notepad. Not quite sure what to say, I told her I thought she'd gotten a bargain, which wasn't true, and she told me, though smiling pleasantly, that she thought she'd been ripped off. That seeming to have been that, I started to walk away. But then she called me back. There were three other words she had been unable to come up with in her wanderings that day, and she wondered if I could spell them out if I knew them, so that she could write them down. Two of the words I did know, and one of them I did not, and then, with something only slightly different on my face, I did walk away.

In those days I was in the middle of two or three things that seemed to take up unnecessarily large amounts of my time, but of course there was no getting around them. One of these things was setting in motion the acquisition of a certain item, which was proving to be very difficult to obtain. Another was the process of establishing whether or not the poorly functioning washer / dryer in my apartment was under warranty, etc. I was told there were papers. I knew there were papers, but where were the papers? Then in the middle of the night, literally in the middle of the night, I knew. I told the man on the phone that the papers—behind the washer / dryer on the floor when the leak had occurred—had become wet and then damp, and were now, although I had more or less dried them out, very much stuck together. There was a silence on the other end of the line, then I was told that I would have to bring the papers to the shop where they could be deciphered, and where, I might add, once I had put the crumpled mess in front of him, they were not.

So there was this and one or two other amazingly similar though of course really quite different things I was involved with at that time, or at least involved with part of that time. Part of that time I was involved with nothing, a nothing that mainly consisted of lying on the floor staring at the ceiling.

The ceiling was new to me.

As was the floor.

I kept, also, becoming confused about the placement of the windows, and bumping my shoulders on bits of unexpected masonry, and waking up in the morning or in the middle of the night scared.

Though this has never, in my case, been unusual.

But also from the floor, you could hear the river. I had seen the river. It was not as big a river as I was used to, nor, however, was it as small as I had been advised to expect. I had not expected anything at all as regarded the number and variety of bridges, and so, in my wanderings, had been consistently, pleasantly, surprised.

As I lay in the middle of the floor, the river made a rich smooth sound so that it seemed as if there was an extra layer of fresh paint pouring constantly across my new apartment's walls. Or something like that.

After a time, then, of nothing, or anyway of practically nothing, I would get up and go over to the phone, but never because it was ringing.

Then one day it rang. It was my downstairs neighbor inviting me to come down. I did. This neighbor's apartment, though apparently the same overall size and shape as mine, was completely, as to layout, different, and confusingly so. Whereas my apartment was composed of a single short corridor and one fairly large room, this neighbor's apartment seemed to consist of many short corridors and many small rooms. Apparently, the neighbor explained, each of the apartments in the building were different from each other, which was clearly the root cause of any number of problems, especially, for example, in the area of tenant relations.

I was offered a cup of coffee, which I accepted, in a small room that overlooked a very small, somewhat grim courtyard, or airshaft, it was an airshaft, of which my apartment did not afford any view whatsoever, thus providing me with an explanation for why, on wet evenings, I had been able to hear rain falling behind a four-foot stretch of my wall.

That had been troubling me.

Not troubling me enough to find anything out, but troubling me enough, if you understand what I mean.

So we sat in the small room and steadily advanced our interaction on the now very clear connection between the phenomenon of differing layouts of apartments in a given building with the differing quality of tenant relations, and it really did, at least for the duration of the interaction, seem like a very clear connection, and we agreed on everything, and even at one point shook hands. It was after this handshake that I was offered a tour of the apartment, so that, it was explained, even though startling differences between our apartments surely existed, they would be—once I had reciprocated the invitation—collectively understood differences, and so, in the happenstance, more manageable. The tour was both very short, and, somehow, very long. In "the office" I saw, sitting alone on a shelf above a small red table, a recently purchased hole puncher, which, when the tour was finished, I borrowed.

I never laid eyes on that neighbor again, although on one occasion I heard sounds. As for the hole puncher, after a few days, I left it sitting outside the neighbor's door.

It was autumn. When I had completed my various tasks, though of course I hadn't really completed any of them, I began to wander.

It was and is a city of parks split by a river, and in the autumn, both in the parks and along the river, there was and is the daily pleasantry of dead and falling leaves that made small scraping sounds and hit against my face and hands, and at night when I was at home and alone again continued to fall or to seem to fall and to scrape and to hit against me. So in and around this city of parks split by a river plus streets and houses and small public squares I walked, and the cars went by, and I sat in establishments and the people passed and / or surrounded me. In one establishment I struck up an acquaintance or two but of course both of them, after some days, vanished. One conversation I remember, though not too fondly, was about appliances and their correspondences and about the mutual fund of electricity from which they sucked. My acquaintance actually used the word "suck." This was all said at a very skillfully modulated half-whisper. Frankly, I could not stand the idea of appliances sucking away at electricity, but nodded and listened and contributed and half-whispered in return.

That acquaintance vanished.

The other acquaintance, who also, as I have said, vanished, was the sort of acquaintance for whom one buys drinks and yet from whom one maintains a certain distance, or at least tries to, the exercise becoming quite impossible whenever there is laughter or confidentiality, and there is frequently laughter and confidentiality, or at least in this case there was. I did not inquire about the vanishment of the first acquaintance, but, for the sake of appearances, I did about this second, and was informed quite matter-of-factly that he / she had been ravished off the face of the earth.

It had been days and days since I had placed the hole puncher outside my neighbor's door.

One morning, a tall woman wearing a hat and sunglasses tapped me on the elbow as I was about to cross the street and said, tomorrow. A little later that day the same woman sat down beside me on a bench and said, next week.

For some days after that it rained, and most of the time I stayed indoors. Three times during that rainy period, however, I went to the shop to buy pens. The first pen was a blue felt tip, and when I returned home, I stood on tiptoes on a chair, held the base of it crimped between the tips of my thumb and first two fingers, and drew a series of unsuccessful clouds, unsuccessful in part because, as I realized upon their completion, clouds are not blue, not even in outline, in part because I don't draw well. The second pen was a red felt tip, and its story was that I almost immediately lost it. The third was a platinum nib fountain pen, which I had wrapped as a present, but the following day, after an unpleasant exchange with the shopkeeper, returned.

Then for a time I was very seriously and legitimately

involved in some business, and that took me along and engaged me completely for that time, which was not inconsiderable, and the early portion of the autumn swept along.

At the end of the business I found myself sitting in a park at a table in one of the outdoor cafés watching, through a shower of leaves, the last of the business, item in hand, walk away. Then it had walked away, and I thought, well that, anyway, is something, which it was — I had done everything they had told me to and had a well-filled envelope in a bag at my feet.

The waiter came over. The waiter went away. Across the park a small recorder ensemble began playing. And at that moment she sat down.

Then began those days, starting with that day, and we sat there and we talked.

Oh, well, you know, not much, I said.

It seemed to me that her hair had grown. She said it had just been cut. Then she said, I need you to help me with another word.

What word?

A ricer.

I told her I did not know this word in any language, but that if she would explain it to me I would do my best to find out.

She did explain it to me, though not immediately, and I did find out and a ricer was acquired, a ricer that is still, I imagine, sitting there on one of her shelves.

She had a world of shelves, and on each of them sat an almost impossible number of objects, the words for which were known or unknown, most by the end, I think, were unknown or unknowable, but for the moment that is getting ahead of myself. Generally speaking, I seem more likely to get behind myself. Once, for example, as the two of us were walking down the street, I was somehow walking down the street behind us, and we got farther and farther ahead of me, so that when we turned into a store and looked at red velvet dresses and talked, she later told me, to a salesperson with an orange hat and a cracked tooth, I missed the turn and kept walking and ended up falling in a ditch.

For the moment, though, which for the moment was just the moment and not the moment I was about to reach or had just missed, etc., what I did not know was the word ricer, and was nervous about the possible consequences of that ignorance, so that all the way through her explanation it seemed to me that, explanation finished, she would abruptly stand up to leave, maybe forever, and in my nervousness once she had finished speaking, I, in fact, stood up rather abruptly, and she said, are you going somewhere?

No.

Well then sit back down.

While the pleasant part of the autumn lasted we met quite often at that café in that park, and then it got too cold.

But in the meantime, having concluded my business, my days became either days in which I was to see her or days in which I was not. During the days in which I was not I examined my tools, checked various ropes and wires, and expended perhaps more energy than was necessary in bathing. Also, I found time to lie in the middle of the floor, looking up, or not looking anywhere, or only at the backs of my eyelids.

At one point or another over the course of that first conversation I told her about borrowing the hole puncher, and about why I had borrowed it, and she said she found that charming.

Her hair grew longer, as did mine. She commented favorably upon this development, and it was not until she had countered that favorable comment with another on the same subject that was less favorable, but really only slightly less favorable, that it was cut. So you can see that it was a confusing time. Both very clear and very confusing, which is likely news to few, and perhaps even to none.

I know all about that, for example, said a new acquaintance in the old establishment, quickly switching the conversation back in the direction it had been going.

So now, at any rate, I knew, is what I mean.

Then my friend came to town.

Once upon a time, this friend and I had lived together in a very small room in a very large city with big buildings and a big river, and at night or in the early morning after we had finished working I would talk. I would talk and talk, and he would doze and doze, and then he would tell me to shut the fuck up. This arrangement continued for a remarkably long time. Once, however, upon the conclusion of a particularly tricky job, one that had gone wrong in several ways, I said something and my friend went berserk and, after a short interval, went away, and that was, or had been, the history of our friendship. Now here he was again. He had arrived, he said, near the end of a tour he had been taking and was much refreshed and was visiting me.

So.

So.

Still up to it, I suppose, he said.

John is his name.

Yes, I am, John, I said.

John clapped me on the back, told me I needed a haircut, and said, how about some dinner, I'm buying.

It was a cold night in late November, and he said he would like to have some turkey. I told him that I thought this would take some maneuvering. He said he was willing, if I was, to maneuver. I was. We did. It was an interesting night.

No, they all said.

John's tour had taken him to several places since I had last seen him, and the quality of his hostility, when it came—and when they kept saying they did not have turkey it came—had been tempered, though I could not imagine by what. It had become a hostility, at any rate, the engine of which was a not unsubtle use of tone and syntax and carefully measured unreasonability, rather than, as preface to action, blunt volume added to a somewhat stock selection of words. I suggested at one point, for example, a chicken or pheasant or game hen substitute for the turkey. He suggested, at some length, using words like "mock" and "erudition," not.

On we went.

No, I am sorry, we do not serve turkey, said yet another man in a white shirt and black vest with just a touch too much oil in his hair.

Yes, but do you *have* turkey?

No, we do not have turkey, I am sorry.

Ah, and while I do believe that you are sorry, I do not believe you do not have turkey, why wouldn't you?

We do not, sir, have turkey, nor do I have for you any explanation.

And all I am asking for is an explanation.

Please leave.

Etc.

We did, finally, and following something a little like the interaction I have just described, get our turkey—

they had some, by chance it seemed, in the freezer. Neither of us at the end of eating it entirely believed it had been turkey, but it had been called turkey with maximum enthusiasm by the man whose head John had placed in the sink, and it had been appropriately garnished, so we didn't complain.

It was a very pleasant meal. John told me a little bit about where he had been and how long he had spent in each place and who he had spent his time with. He then told me that he was ready to go back to work, but that his line of work would now change, or would now perhaps change—he hoped so.

I raised my eyebrow. He winked.

He then quoted something that he had memorized.

Quoting was new for John.

I told him I approved.

That night he lay in my bed, and I lay on my floor.

Like the old days, a little.

It was not quiet outside the window, it was a variety of sounds, not such pleasant sounds as it occurred, so that it was not quite possible to hear the river if you had not yet heard it to listen for, and John had not, but I had and I lay there listening.

Life's years do not fill a hundred, is what he had quoted, earlier, at the restaurant, and I was thinking about this quote, a little, as I lay there listening for the river.

John had raised his glass and I had raised a forkful of turkey and he had said, Life's years do not fill a hundred, and I had said, who said that? and he said, no one said that, someone wrote that, so I said, who is that by? and he said, Anonymous.

We lay there.

Here was a little hard truth is what I was thinking.

I see you're not wearing your glasses, he said.

During the time we had lived together I had slept with glasses.

No I'm not, I said.

But you're still having those dreams? he asked.

Yes, I said.

The same dreams where you see all the . . . ?

I nodded.

With the hooks?

They are no longer hooks.

What are they?

I told him.

That's festive. You taking anything for that?

No.

You want something?

No.

You want to hold an event?

No.

Well, we'll hold one anyway.

It took some organizing. Most of which, John explained, would involve rounding up a base of participants upon which the body of the event could be built. I told him about a couple of recent acquaintances, ones who hadn't vanished. I also told him about the downstairs neighbor. I don't know why I did this, and sometimes still feel guilty about it. But at any rate, having greeted my dismal offering with great esprit de corps, he said I could leave it all, a few details excepted, to him. He started with the downstairs neighbor and was gone for some time. This is when I heard the sounds. Did you see the neighbor? I asked when he returned, and he said, that neighbor is not coming. Then he tried in the direction of my acquaintances and, an hour or so later, said that the acquaintances, if he had, in fact, gotten hold of the right ones, would very likely, and probably in company, attend. He then set off to recruit some more.

I set off for the park.

As I have already stated, it was late autumn, but this day in late autumn it was not overly cold, and we had agreed to meet where we had always met, even though there was no longer any outdoor café, just a couple of greenish metal chairs set against the base of a chestnut tree.

Hello.

Hello.

She stood a moment. She touched my face. We sat.

It was, in fact, a little too cold, after all, with the wind, to be just sitting there, so we got up and walked around the park.

I do not know what it is about habit in those situations that builds up some sort of a diminishing effect as regards the world, so that, slowly and steadily, given that common and accustomed locus of circumstance, and a certain measure of complicity, the world's effects on one's person are lessened. I heard once that both actors and soldiers experience a similar phenomenon when they are playing their respective parts. We were most assuredly playing our parts. I can't stress enough how alone in each other's presence we had already come to be.

We were not so alone, however, walking, as the walking together business was new.

Although the park with its light wind and scattered crowds and bursts of pigeons was lovely.

My friend is in town, I said.

Really? she said, so is mine.

We exchanged names of friends.

That's funny, she said.

She laughed.

She had a beautiful laugh, just beautiful, like that.

John and her friend Deau later met at the event and stood in the corner, in the kitchen I think, talking together for a long time. I think, if I remember correctly, John spilled some wine on Deau, or was it the other way around?

As I say, it was funny, somehow, the name business, and the fact of the effect on me of her laugh.

Later, in another city, a city on the coast, we walked together down a sloping street toward a harbor, and, this is why I even mention it, she laughed again.

That was because of a pair of monkeys.

So.

She asked me if I was ready to meet her friend and to see her apartment, and I said, yes.

We had, now, definitively it seemed, reached the period of the end of the warm weather and the beginning of the cold, and it would be some time, if ever, before we could comfortably recommence our meetings in the park. This is what I thought as we walked along and talked about various words and objects, though also, and I suppose this was a function of the changes that were in the process right those seconds of occurring, about other things.

She was asking me was I interested.

In what? I said.

She told me what it was.

I said I was, then I didn't say anything for a moment, then I said, yes, definitely.

At times, you see, after I was no longer hearing it, I was still hearing it—I am still hearing it—her voice, in a slight but quite crystalline echo, perfectly. This was distracting, and, when it was happening, often caused her to wonder aloud about what I was thinking.

We had not yet developed a vocabulary that could accommodate, in this line, any kind of elaboration.

I'm not quite sure, I would say.

And she wouldn't say anything.

Then we arrived at her apartment. I have already mentioned the impossible number of shelves that coexisted in those few rooms. It was a dizzying spectacle, one no doubt exacerbated by the number of objects those shelves supported. Obviously, the number of objects, of which there were many, many per shelf, must, in real terms, have far exceeded the number of shelves, but in my mind, strangely it does not. In my mind, strangely, there are more shelves than objects, and, accurate or not, this was the case right from the start.

Deau was not there. She had left a note. In which, in a large, round hand, she explained that she had just popped out. I have never been able to subtract that large, round "popped" from my impression of Deau, though I admit I haven't tried.

Her apartment. There was the stapler, in its place, and there was a shiny bright hole puncher, much like the one belonging to my downstairs neighbor, and there was an electric pencil sharpener, not plugged in, and there was a pyramid composed of twenty perfectly white rectangular erasers. In the kitchen, on one of the shelves that had not yet been filled but that would soon be, sat the ricer, next to a small blue colander, next to a short stack of red condiment dishes, next to a white crock pot, slightly cracked at the rim, next to a large green bowl.

More.

There was a lot more.

I told her I was impressed by the number of objects she had accumulated.

She told me to come over to the bed.

Eventually, Deau popped back in.

It was a very large apartment and despite the proliferation of shelves and objects we all, once the two of us had dressed, sat at a great distance from each other.

Hello, Deau called across the room to me.

Hello, I called back.

One of my unpleasant dreams involves the inadequacy of my voice to carry across even short distances, and while perhaps you wouldn't think that was much of a dream, I can assure you that it is quite effective.

I forget at which point we moved our chairs closer and had drinks.

Doing so was Deau's suggestion.

This is slightly stupid, she said.

Deau, coincidentally, was about to begin a tour of some kind, and she was going to begin it in the next place she went, this first place being a preliminary stop, connected to, but not a part of, she said, her tour. I told her that my friend, John, was also on a tour, but that he had long since gotten it started, and that this was by no means a preliminary stop, and that it seemed to be doing him worlds of good.

Who is your friend John? said Deau.

I looked at her.

She looked a little like her handwriting.

If her handwriting had also been slightly, perhaps, serrated.

Hmmm, I thought.

Just exactly what kind of a tour are we talking about, Deau? I considered asking her, only it was a question I hadn't even asked John.

Actually, I had never asked John much of anything,

and still haven't. I had, I remember sitting there thinking, once asked him where he was from, and he had taken me there, and had both shown and introduced me around.

Say hello to my mother.

What do you mean?

I mean say hi to Mother, come over here.

I don't think so.

Get over here.

What the fuck *is* that?

The conversation took a turn, it took several turns.

At one point I was informed by Deau that I was now in the presence of a young woman who was both wonderful and very strange, which combination of descriptives seemed to add up in Deau's mind to pleasantly eccentric.

Who are you talking about? I said.

We all three looked for a moment around the room with all its shelves.

I remember at this juncture thinking it was pretty strange to keep a stapler on a shelf you couldn't easily reach. I also remember feeling distinctly uncomfortable at having been made privy to Deau's opinion, presumably about the woman I was smitten with, no matter how well-informed, or, especially because it was well-informed, and I remember suddenly wishing that it was still warm out and that we were still sitting at the café near the tree.

Why is the stapler sitting way up there where you can't reach it? I asked.

At this, she smiled, leaned forward a little, and said, I didn't put it there for me.

Who is it for then?

She didn't answer.

Oh, I said.

Stand up and see, she suggested.

I did. And found the stapler perfectly in reach of my outstretched hand. There was a short stack of multicolored paper sitting next to it. I picked up a couple pieces, placed them under the chisel end of the stapler, and pressed. There again came the short, crisp clunk resulting, this time, in sheets of blue and turquoise paper being crisply joined.

I don't know.

I found it strange, and in fact despite all of it, persist in finding it strange, to have been thought of, in some way so exactly, while I wasn't there.

The whole business, if you will indulge me for a moment, made my arm feel like a treasure.

Thank you, I said.

John had the event all organized. It was up to me to pick up the chips and the pretzels and the small pickles, or anyway fairly small pickles just not big ones, and the crackers and the meats, and it was up to me to pick up the liquid things too. I started with the meats and pickles. The ones I found were plenty small and rather handsome. I then acquired a variety of meats in several forms and brought them home, and then went back for the crackers and chips and pretzels and some cheese too, I decided, and more chips and some nuts for variety. Then I moved on to the liquid refreshments. What a glory is a beverage store. It is too many colors and too many varieties of shapes of container, and all the containers contain too many different kinds of liquids, and too much, and that they slosh, that it is in their nature to slosh, and that too many of them I had known too well and too recently.

It took three trips to get home with all of it, sloshing.

That's that, said John.

Then it was the day of the event.

It was a very nice event, and, insofar as my dreams afterward were concerned, it did have a temporary palliative effect, as had been the case with other events in the past, although I have never been sure just why.

Marry the crowd! John yelled at me as at one point we stood at the drinks table.

Was that a quote? I asked.

Pass it on, brother, he said.

I passed it to the guy standing next to me. This guy said it to the guy next to him, a very old guy with a nose like something in a documentary on gross anomalies. Who are you? I said walking up to the old guy. He said something. I didn't quite catch it. I started to ask him again, but just then someone yelled, the event!

The lights went out.

There was a scream.

The lights came back on.

John was on top of someone.

The lights went out again.

They were out for a long time.

Later, a tall, skinny woman wearing sunglasses and a floppy hat came up to me and whispered, marry the crown, pass it on.

I passed it on to John.

John said, I just did, and grinned.

The room was crowded.

The crowded room spun around me.

Anyway, the first time she saw my apartment there were upwards of a hundred people in it. I exaggerate. But there were many, perhaps too many. Or at least this is how I put it to myself, because after a time, without telling me, she left.

I am an awful drunk. If I am not much present at the best of times, when I am drunk I devolve into something I think it would not be unfair to characterize as vaguely reptilian. I sit and sit and occasionally my eyes move. The last time I had been drunk — I mean before I got very drunk at the event and retracted, like something that might be happiest under a heat bulb, into a corner — I had been drunk in the presence, to speak euphemistically, of someone I was supposed to have been watching. I was supposed to have been watching him in case he chose at that late stage to say anything, but instead I sat on the floor behind him and took small sips from a large bottle I had been left with and got drunk, and when he did say something, in a very small voice, I said nothing, and alerted no one, and I stared at the back of his head, and drank, and after a time announced to myself that I no longer noticed the smell.

The day of the event was very sunny and then it was very rainy, and I was outside, attending to a few last details, in that rainy part of it.

It was not nice, this rain. It was a cold, thorough, ruin-your-fucking-universe kind of rain and I cringed each time great splashes of it hit my face.

It is unlovely to repeatedly cringe in public, and I found myself saying to myself, quit it.

Others heard me.

In fact, one person who heard me said, excuse me, and we struck up a conversation. It was not, to tell the truth, much of a conversation. Sometimes, I am capable of striking up successful conversations with complete strangers. Once, John watched me sit down at a table with someone in a crowded restaurant and talk until that other person, quite some time later, stood up to go. This incident greatly astonished John, who, though subjected during that period to my nightly outpourings, had never once before seen me address more than four or five words to anyone besides him. In fact, one time as the two of us stood at a counter with two acquaintances of the more pleasantly gendered persuasion, John described my almost total silence, as we stood there, as a condition—a condition I struggled with, gallantly. And I must say I frequently find myself returning, when I reflect on the varying success of my interactions, to the notion that I am struggling with some sort of condition.

I must be.

It is as if part of me falls into some great dark pit, though always only part of me.

Incidentally, this conversation I was having was with someone wearing large, reflective sunglasses.

Someone, I note again, who was tall and thin.

These are all details.

I am made nervous by events.

Strange things happen at them.

I took up a position in the kitchen. Then by the window. Then by my bed, for a moment, then by the door.

Finally, they arrived.

Hello, said Deau, very roundly breezing past me.

Hello, she said.

I brought her a drink and a plate of pickles and meats.

You have to meet John, I said.

Kiss me, she said.

It was quite an event. To his credit, John had managed to dig up a huge number of participants. I brought up the subject of John's excellent technique and pointed over toward him. John, cleaned up now, was spinning around in the center of a small group with one of my pillows on his head. We stood there by the door, each drinking what

I had brought over and nibbling on the pickles and meats. Comfortable. In fact, wonderful. But she didn't stay long.

Later the next week, she said to me, after a certain point, and it is a very clear point, I cannot tolerate events, and that is why I left, but it was very nice to see your apartment and to meet John.

That's fine absolutely anything is fine, I said.

I did not actually see them meet, but at one point John came over to me and said, okay, wow, then he went over to the kitchen, and a little after that is when he spilled wine on Deau, or vice-versa, and they laughed, and the two of them made the plan that the four of us should go away somewhere, perhaps to the country.

Given the circumstances, it was a wonderful trip.

There is always this question of circumstances.

Just before she left the event, for example, we kissed, right next to the table where I had piled the food, which had, by this time, been thoroughly massacred. We kissed and kissed, and when we were finished she explained to me that part of the point of her initiating the kiss, at that moment, had been that she was about to leave, and that insofar as she had imagined the event before arriving, that imagining had involved a kiss, any kind of kiss at any moment involving me, and that the earlier kiss by the door when she arrived had been nice but insufficient, and that was the reason for it, if it needed a reason, and she was happy, even if she had not stayed long, that she had come.

Yes, I said.

Yes, I said again.

Yes.

John rented a car and the four of us drove off toward the country.

On the drive the two of us fell easily into the habit of discussing objects and words. John and Deau did not participate in our discussions and did not appear, at any point, to have any interest in doing so, but that didn't bother us, and as we stopped along the way, we made several acquisitions, which would appear, later, on her shelves.

It was an excellent drive.

I did, however, of course, still harbor one or two creeping fears, but I was not cringing, and there was no rain, it was sunny, the event was over, and I was the better for it. Speaking, however, about rain — the rain that day of the event. At the end of our lame conversation the tall, thin individual I was talking to invited me, quite firmly, to enter a nearby building and go upstairs.

I do not know why I said yes to what they asked me to do when I got upstairs, I did not have to say yes, that had always been part of our agreement, but I did.

That I had said yes was why I said to John, a couple of days after the event when we were recovered and were discussing travel plans, let's go here.

Why? said John.

I've heard it's beautiful, I said.

John has never approved of my engagement with this world, a world for which he has always found me, rightly I suppose, ill-suited. Quite a number of years before, in fact, he had helped me to get started in another line, one that for various reasons I did not pursue.

But we did go where I proposed because my lie, this particular lie at any rate, was not, or so I then thought, detected.

Of course I knew you were lying, John later said.

That week, before our trip to the country, I slept beautifully.

And then we were driving up to the tops of the low round hills that occur on that drive and down them.

At one point, as we had stopped the car at the top of one of these hills and were looking out over a vista of undulations, in the direction of the ocean, Deau announced that her tour had now begun, and that she was ecstatic that we were all with her, so at our next stop in a little town we toasted the beginning of her tour with a glass of wine, then lightly burned our mouths on some delicious stewed apples. Deau and John had a certain level of unusual gourmandise in common. It was Deau, for example, who had insisted we order the stewed apples. And this had endlessly charmed John, who had insisted the meal before that we select only the most col-orful dishes available—borscht, pomegranate, horned melon, and candied plums.

Stewed apples was, we agreed, an excellent word and concept, and before leaving the restaurant we acquired a handsome jar of it. So you can see that it was all going along very well.

At that business meeting on that rainy day it was like this. I had never before met the woman I met that day and she was persuasive, strangely. I had met many other women and not-women in the course of my career, but not this one. She was one of the ones I had heard about, or perhaps the only one, it's difficult to say.

I think, probably, it was more than just her—that behind her, so to speak, were other women and not-women, with other cigars, in other rooms, who had other perhaps more important individuals than me doing pro-jects for them. I do not of course mean to imply that if the woman with the cigar had superiors, or even just partners, that they were all smoking cigars and wearing gloves, etc.

This seems unlikely. Boss types, it has been my experience, all have their own special stamp. In my previous place of residence, for example, I had worked for a person who had in his office a very complex model train system that was always in operation, at every meeting and otherwise.

The organization that I was currently working for, by the way, was reputed to be immense and immensely effective, although largely staffed by part-timers like myself.

Probably not much like myself.

Or only maybe.

At any rate, the woman with the cigar who I was standing in front of was definitely a boss. Perhaps there were more-unnerving-to-look-at bosses, perhaps there were not. Once, I had been told, someone at a meeting had seen an eyeball set on top of the model smokestack on the model train in my former boss's office, but there are many such stories, actually.

She sat there smoking the cigar, which is an endless thing in a meeting, never finished, and I was standing in front of her, and I could see myself reflected in miniature in her sunglasses, and it was a small room.

Yes I'll do it, I said.

Also, however, she had a stutter, quite an intense one, and sometimes into the center of the stutter she would insert the cigar, and, the story of the eyeball on the model smokestack notwithstanding, I still have not seen or heard of anything quite as impressive as that.

This is all about why I said yes.

You'll find I have precious little to say later about why I changed my mind.

What? I said.

She was speaking to me, not in the car anymore, we had left the car and were now, the four of us, installed in a hotel in a small city on the coast, and the two of us were in our room, and she had been speaking to me. Here is what she said:

It is not the objects, not the objects at all. It is not the words either, although often they are lovely and the contrasts are surprising when you have one in your head shaped like a rectangle and then you have another in your head shaped like a square, for example. That is lovely, as is the sound of your voice saying them, when you say them, but it is not the fact of the objects or the fact of the words, really, it is the fact of establishing the correct establishments on which to place them, that is all.

Each uncombined expression can mean one of these, she said, i.e., what, how large, what kind, related to what, where, when, how placed, in what state, acting, or suffering. See? For example, a woman may be five-foot six and a writer, a student of philosophy at her desk at midnight, sitting down and writing, and suffering from the cold.

Substance, quantity, quality, relation, place, time, position, state, action, and affection, she said.

I can't do it, of course. I can't say, again, what she said, not ever, not exactly. It is all there, inside me, is what I mean, but I can't say it, not even for myself. It seems tragic that in matters of the heart one should have to suffer, even in discourse with one's self, from this sort of aphasia.

Lately, for example, I have been thinking of an instance in which, to say it in general terms, she came across the room toward me, and even though it was considerably more than this, it is only in these general terms that I am ever able to say it.

She came across the room toward me.

It was too many shelves, at the end of it. It was a hell of shelves. From where I sat that day, I kept losing count of them. Over and over I would count and then lose count, and then begin again.

The next morning the four of us set out to visit the city. John and Deau were already walking with incredible synchronicity, and it was agreeable to follow them up the steps of that building and under the arches of this. She looks happy, she said. John's happy too, I said. Old men limped along pulling carts and young women went by on scooters. We stopped at a flower shop where I bought her a daisy and a tulip and a rose and a carnation and a sunflower and a narcissus and a gladiolus and a lily and a tulip and a sunflower and a ranunculus and she said, they're lovely, thank you. In one place, we drank tea poured from above the server's head, and in another we ate fresh-made ice cream mashed green with pistachio nuts. Sometimes John would drop back and take my arm, and sometimes she would walk ahead and disappear with Deau. Once they disappeared for quite some time, and John and I sat down before steaming bowls at a table under a hideous bluish candelabra in a warm room that smelled of cinnamon and saffron, and, very powerfully, of what we were told was goat.

John, I said.

Tell all, he said.

Nothing.

We sat and sat and took care of another round of steaming bowls and talked. John talked about Deau and I talked about her and found I didn't really have much to say. Then we paid and left and found them sometime later wearing completely different clothes.

Actually, they found us. Sitting on the terrace of another establishment sipping yellow drinks and watching old men play a game with shiny steel balls.

It was then that we walked down through the gently sloping streets of the warm city and saw the pair of monkeys, which made all of us, but especially her, and I do not know why especially her, laugh.

Then we slept.

I woke.

You were shaking, she said.

I was shouting? I said.

Shaking, you were shaking, you are shaking, stop.

I did stop, gradually, and then it was the second day in the small breeze-swept city on the coast.

I have changed my mind.

The personage sitting across the table from me, at a table with a view of the ocean and several rooftops belonging to the coastal city, did not blink, did not move, in fact never moved, not once, and after I had repeated myself twice more I left.

Nobody interfered with me as I walked out, which is unusual. Part of me, to tell the truth, had been hoping for a little immediate interference, which is quite standard and would likely have encouraged me to undertake a course of action that could have significantly minimized the interference that followed.

I thought of the woman with the cigar and of the cigar inserted into the center of her stutter all the way back to the hotel where they were sleeping in.

I thought, also, of an old man I once saw smoking a small homemade cigar through a hole in his throat and how that man had only had one eye and something very wrong with one arm.

That place was far away from anywhere anybody has ever known me.

And I think that soon, very soon, I will go away, to such a place, to stay. Even if once I arrive I find myself obliged to sit in close quarters with just such an old man, smoking, in just such fashion, etc.

Which is to say that, getting ahead of myself again, if you have never smelled it, then you should never have to smell it—the smell, I mean, of burning flesh.

She was not sleeping in. She was sitting up in bed and looking across the room to the window, which had a view much like the one I had seen from the room I had just left. Here, however, there was a certain amount of that fine winter light that comes into such rooms at such times in such parts of the world, and it was falling across her knees and her bare arms wrapped around her knees, which were pulled close to her chest, and a line of light was running along one of her forearms, and she was smiling.

It was stupid, really stupid, all things considered, to have agreed to it, and then to have changed my mind. It was even stupider not to have thought to smooth it out. While not necessarily encouraged, a certain amount of noncompliance is admitted by the organization, and it would have been straightforward enough both to have failed to carry out my assignment and to have mitigated the significant recrimination I could now look forward to. Of course I had thought about it. There was an easy way. Much about the business is actually quite easy once you've been at it a while. I could have, for example, picked up the phone, or at the very least double-checked the address of the package I had dropped in the mail on my way back from telling them that I had changed my mind. But there is in me a small speck of something hard, something stubborn, something immensely intractable, and I didn't.

There, in the center of the cigar smoke, she had used the word "important," and I was to think of that word a little later, as I sat there, thinking of preposterous causalities and staring at those shelves.

That afternoon the four of us drove away. We had been to the city I had suggested. Now we were going to the country.

2

WE QUICKLY FOUND EXCELLENT LODGINGS.
The old house, in which no one else was staying, had
huge rooms, high ceilings, wide hallways, and one or
two windowless staircases in addition to the regular
one. I did not like these windowless staircases and generally avoided them. Once, though, late at night, in fact
the last night, I woke and strayed and met an old man
on one of the staircases, an old man I will more properly
introduce later, who stood in what should have been
absolute dark with what seemed to be a pale light falling
onto and around him, and who said to me, listen, listen
to what I have to say just a little more. Also, there were
a rather unusual number of toilets in the house, some of
them small and inexplicably dark even with the lights
on, and one night walking by one of them I thought I
heard someone praying, or at any rate mumbling rhyth-
mically, on the other side of the door. The house did not
have a garden, or rather had for its garden the whole
countryside, so that lithe, dark trees seemed always to
be waving in a soft evening wind. Our room, on the
sunny side of the house, had a yellow door, a silver door

handle, a pale blue dresser, darker yellow walls, white moldings, three large windows, those translucent curtains, dark green shutters, a washbasin, a hardwood floor that creaked in four spots, two lamps, two small tables, a silver candelabra, a long mirror slightly cracked in the top left corner, a desk with two drawers, two round floor rugs, a wastepaper basket, a vase that contained a quantity of dried flowers varied in shape and color and tone, one comfortable chair, one desk chair, a faded print in a chipped gilt frame that showed the proceedings of a circus, a huge bed with curtains hung around it, and two very slow old flies buzzing lowly. The circus. John, it seems to me, at some point had something to say about the circus, but about the gladiator-stick-you-with-large-forks-style one, about some place one could visit where the old fork-style circuses had been held. This gladiator business has always seemed improbable to me. Once, as a boy, I put on a suit of plastic armor and took up a plastic lance or sword or club and was pummeled by my friends. That pummeling ended what had been a long-standing interest in the glory, not to mention effectiveness, of knights and their shining armor, and probably preempted any interest I might later have developed in gladiators. Anyway, I prefer the regular kind of circus, she said. As, I said, do I. What was the best thing you ever saw in the circus? I told her about an elephant. And also about some fleas. We both liked fleas. And clowns. Soon our room contained other things, some of which we had acquired on the drive, such as a funny pinwheel that had put her in mind of a strange story, some of which, like the row of insect wings, we had found in the course of our excursions in the fields near the house. In all, we only stayed four days in the country, but it was enough, it was like a year, it was the best time of all, though not really. Never really. At any rate. I was feeling rather giddy from my recent course of action, or nonaction, and so was an incredible amount of fun to be around, I was told. I am sometimes given to telling anecdotes when I am in high spirits and in the company of friends, and in the country I told anecdotes left and right. One of them was about a tree house I had loved to jump out of as a boy and the time I landed on my head. Another was about a bone collection I once had, and that I was made, upon its discovery, to soak with oil and to burn. Another was about an old woman I had heard of who lived alone in a house set off in a stand of trees and whom I visited and with whom I took tea. Despite her current appearance, she had told me, wiping a hand across her oily brow, she had been quite a beauty. Tell another, I was told. So I told an anecdote about a car I had owned, and it was an anecdote because I had stolen the car, but I had managed to do it, everyone agreed, quite interestingly. She said to me afterward, after a whole string of anecdotes, I didn't know, and I said well there is / are more, and she said I hope so, and there was a little more. Things seemed to be progressing. In this vein there were, of course, several things I wished I could have asked her afterward. And still do. But at any rate, at our disposal was an enormous bathtub, of which we all made frequent use. Once, in fact, I walked in at a moment when the tub was being used quite spectacularly. The general effect was of something that might occur unquietly in the branches of a tree. It was almost warm enough at night to have the windows open in the bedroom, but it was also nice that it was cold enough to be able to breathe slowly on the glass and to make a light fog. We loved, also, to close the curtains around the bed. Sometimes, when we were behind the curtains, in the huge dark bed, we could hear John and Deau in the bedroom across the hall, and more than once it seemed clear that they could hear us. During the day, the four of us or the two of us would go walking through the olive groves. The trees smelled of something we all recognized, but couldn't name. A soft wind blew. I have always been partial to soft winds. At one time, in fact, I entertained dreams of becoming the captain of a hot air balloon. I have still never been up in a hot air balloon, although I see them once in a while—off in the distance, drifting silently. Once, as we were walking along through the olive groves, through a soft wind, I walked with Deau. Deau was very happy. I am creating my itinerary, she said. In consultation with John, of course. He has made some dazzling recommendations. It is nice now to have finally started. It gives you this wonderful in-the-middle feeling, like you've left behind your beginning and you haven't yet reached your end. I asked her how she would know she had reached her end. She said she didn't know, hadn't quite thought it through yet, but it was wonderful to feel so intransitive and yet so transitive, simultaneously. And I remember finding it strange but pleasing that she had used those words, and I remarked on this both to her and to John. Yeah, well, if you want to talk about strange, said John. What do you mean? I said. Words and objects, he said. And shelves, I said, don't forget the shelves, you haven't seen them all yet. I haven't seen any of them yet. Well, you will. He did. He didn't like the shelves. In fact he stood in the center of the room and said, ouch! but that was later. In the afternoons and evenings we walked among the olive trees. There were low stone walls and twisting paths and a blue sky behind the waving branches. Deau told us that she was a sun worshiper. That she belonged to some organization or other and had to pay dues. Every year, she said, each member was required to allow him / herself to be seriously burned by the sun. I found this quite funny, and generally, found her, Deau I mean, quite funny and nice, and certainly more than just a little pleasant to look at, so I don't know why I snapped at her later. I will likely chalk it up to my nervousness, but I don't think that's quite right. Perhaps there was a hint, in my mind, of something sinister about her. Perhaps it was because there was no hint of something sinister about her, ever, and yet she was. Perhaps I did not like her. Perhaps I am a crumb. I am a crumb. But no real matter, and after all I did apologize. Sometimes on our walks we stopped for a picnic. We ate fresh apples and fresh cheeses and fresh meats and fresh breads, just like you are supposed to do in the country. More than once as we did those things I wondered why they did not come. Why no one came. Surely they would come. Wasn't that, after all, what they did when someone fucked up? At any rate, at one of those picnics we had the idea that each of us should tell a story. To get things started, Deau told a story about a murder case involving a young woman who had been killed quite unpleasantly in the presence of the only witness, a small girl. There were several suspects, and a couple of what John appreciatively called back-foldings, and at the end of it we learned that the case had gone unsolved, as only the small girl had no alibi, beyond the fact of her size, which, we all agreed, surely exonerated her. There were many nice details in Deau's telling of the story, one of which was that the young girl in question was known to have been in possession of a fine, red-maned rocking horse, and that, according to a relative's testimony, she had been in the habit of riding it, at times, for hours, and that more than once she had been found to have ridden herself to sleep, and in fact was found, when the postmurder finding was done, in the saddle; covered with blood as she was, she, too, had initially been taken for dead. John then told a story about something the two of us had once done together, is the way he put it. I told a story about an old farmer living alone in the country who had dark, funny dreams and wished one day to be the pilot of a dirigible and to dock at the top of the tallest building in the world and would have accomplished it, except that by the time he arrived, the building was no longer the tallest. Then it was her turn. Taking John and Deau's intervention as her lead, i.e., proposing to relate a factual account, she told a story about a house in which she had once lived and a man she had once seriously contemplated killing. When she was finished, no one said anything. Deau was smiling, John was not smiling, and I was not smiling and had a hot mouthful of dry cheese. So did you, in fact, end up killing him? I finally asked when I had gotten most of the cheese down. No, she said. He didn't look like he'd get up anytime soon so I left. Was that true? I asked her that night as we lay in bed. Absolutely, she said. Which parts were true? Most of them. How about the part where you closed the door on his head? Let's not get back into it right now. Fair enough. Okay, yeah, good one, better than your pal there with his farmer moo, baa, or whatever, said John when she had finished telling her story, which caused me to jump on him and start punching his arm. When I was done we moved on to talking about heroes—improbable things, heroes—and then about some guy who John said he'd once known. This, although he didn't say it, was sort of a follow-up, or appendage if you like, to the story he'd told earlier about that thing we'd supposedly done together. Real hero, said John. I used to work for him. His daughter got bumped off in some bad deal, looked like an inside job. He did eight of his organic assets personally until he thought he'd found out who had done it, and in the meantime he had all twenty-six of us others at the ceremony even though they didn't have anything even approximating his daughter to put into the hole. We were all in black tie and he was in black tie and black hat and we stood in the rain and just fucking stood there. He liked model trains, I said. Who killed his daughter? said Deau. And then we kept on talking about heroes for a while. Later I asked her what she thought about heroes, and she said, nothing, and I said, no, really, and she said, sometimes when you look at some people you just want to cry. The next morning it was fine and bright again and I found myself walking along a little stretch of road with Deau. Let's talk about her, said Deau. All right, I said. She really is wonderful, isn't she, said Deau. I said yes I thought she really was. She is eccentric and wonderful and so funny. Yes, I agreed. For example, that story she told was so wonderfully over-the-top, said Deau. How do you mean? I mean she was lying about all of it. Ah, I said. Hah, said Deau, and by the way, your friend John is a tremendous fuck. This was exactly what she said. Yes, I said, yes I had heard once or twice before, though not put that way, that he was. And you saw him in action, saw us in action, in the bathroom, she said. I agreed that I had. Did you like what you saw? I'd rather not answer. Are you a tremendous fuck? Hardly. I bet you are. I bet I'm not. Take a look at these, she said, lifting her shirt. I will not. But I did. Did you and John really do that thing together? she continued, a little later, rather smugly. Did you, I answered, ever ride yourself to sleep on a red-maned rocking horse? I didn't do it, she said, I was far too young. I didn't say you did, I said. Then she smiled, not pleasantly, and, very slowly, repeated her question. Yes, we did, I said, also very slowly, and although I am not generally in favor of such elocutions, I very slowly added the words "you" and "big fat bitch" to my sentence, and, once she had slapped me, that was the end of that walk. For a moment, then, just for a moment, I found myself thinking again of the city, and of its river and bridges and trees. And also of the floor of my apartment. And of the ceiling. And of the small unsuccessful clouds. And even of the mushy papers for the washer / dryer. Just for a moment, though longingly. When I got back to our room with so many nice objects in it, she, and I am not referring to Deau, had her hand in my bag. I am not suspicious by nature, in fact, I am not very much at all, I have concluded, by nature, and while I do not have any great desire to put forward the notion that in this instance I was suspicious, it would be unfair to hide the fact that having seen her with her hand in my bag, and given the general set of circumstances I was in plus the interaction I had just had with Deau, I was. Actually, it would probably be considerably more accurate to say that while I would like very much to put forward the notion that in this instance I was suspicious, it would be unfair to mask the fact that even having seen her with her hand in my bag, I was not. But I was nervous. I do get nervous. I must already have said that. I moved toward her, rather quickly, and she stood up and said, oh fuck. By the way, what John and I did together that time wasn't really doing anything together at all. Once, you see, as we were walking along in a park next to a very different sort of river from the one I have made mention of in this narrative, we, I or John, I can't remember who first, saw a dead body floating in the water. It floated with its face and hands above water and its legs below, and its lips were orange, I'm not kidding, it was very dead. It had on a flowered skirt and a long black wig and it was moving along surprisingly quickly. It was not a pleasant speed. And I have since found, on far too many occasions, the impromptu memory of that speed quite troubling. Once in fact I almost stumbled. At remembering. John, in his telling of it, told it as if we should have called the authorities or something but hadn't, as if that was why it had meant anything to us. According to John, we just walked along next to it, and it kept skimming along near the wall, and we passed a lot of people, but no one else saw it, and we just kept walking along as far as we could, which was a long way, and then the current took it out into deeper waters, and we did not see or hear of it again. If you call that doing something, you can. I call it doing nothing. The doing part of the business occurred some weeks before the time of John's story about the river and the body and the flowered skirt, and it was an accident. Entirely. At any rate, that's how we planned, if it became necessary, to explain it to the boss. I did not know what I thought I was going to do. I mean, just after she had said, oh fuck, and the oh fuck was unpleasantly repeating itself in my head, and I was moving toward her too quickly, out of nervousness and slight embarrassment at my outburst at Deau, and also the fact that maybe the whole story about the soup and the man and the cottage—not just part of it—had not been true, but mostly just the general nervousness, not suspicion, and then I had arrived in front of her. Hi, you have five seconds to explain yourself. Hi, I thought you were out walking with Deau. I was. And you're back so soon. What were you doing in my stuff? Nothing. What the fuck were you doing? But then it turned out to be about a present she had been hoping to hide in my bag, a present which she, once I had taken a step away from her, immediately showed me. It was supposed to be a surprise, she said. What is it? I said. She was holding her hand out, cupped, with her fingers curled and pressed tightly together, as if to hold a small quantity of liquid. What does it look like it is? she said. I told her I was having trouble making it out. She held her hand out a little closer. I kind of leaned over. Don't get too close, she said. I said maybe if I tried another angle. The other angle didn't help. Well then I'd have to say it looks like nothing—is it nothing? No. What is it? She smiled. She said hold out your hand. I held out my hand. She said, here. I said, thanks, but here *what?* She smiled then went over and sat down on the bed. I held my hand up to the light. It's not nothing is what you're saying? I said holding my hand out just so, and moving it back and forth under the light. That's right, she said. And I'm holding it? You are. Well, how about that. It's beautiful, said John, later, when I showed it to him. It's exquisite, agreed Deau. Can I put it in my pocket? I asked her, earlier again. She nodded. I put it in my pocket and said, look, I have to apologize — I just called your friend Deau a big fat bitch. I then went out and told John that I had called Deau a big fat bitch. Oh well, he said. I really should have told him about what I had done in the small city on the coast. That would have helped — John was always good at helping. But we were in the country and it was fairly pleasant, and there was still a chance for it to be extremely pleasant, I thought. So I didn't. Dumb. And then the next day we left. Back to the city. At breakfast the next morning, she told us she was ready to leave. So we left. But other things happened before that. One of those things was that I apologized to Deau. No problem, she said. I've just been a little nervous, I said. In general, as a matter of fact, I find you, and especially in your current transitive / intransitive state, to be very pleasant. Hearing this pleased her, I told myself. Look at what she gave me, I said. It's exquisite, said Deau. It is, isn't it? I said. At any rate, she went away smiling. So that was patched up. Then I went and found John who told me to go away because he was busy thinking pleasant thoughts. Instead of going away, however, I asked him if he could quote something, something in the style of what he had quoted that time in the restaurant, or that time at the event. Go away, he said. I went away. But then, he called me back. How about this, he said, I just thought of this — nothing that hurts shall come with a new face. Good one, I said. Yeah, it's pretty good, isn't it? he said. It was, and in fact I was saying it to myself a few minutes later, when she came across the room toward me. Hi, I said. Hi, she said back. That afternoon we spent out in some nearby fields acquiring things. I did not know the words for any of these things, but that no longer mattered, I now think. Or perhaps it did matter, but it was no longer essential, and anyway, thinking about it now, I remember that in the cases where I did not know the words for things, way before we went out in the afternoon in the field, before even the event and the decision to take the trip, before all that and we were sitting in the park and it was warm and she professed interest in acquiring, for example, a quartz crystal, and I said I knew neither the word for quartz nor for crystal, that did not stop her from managing to get one, and without finding out the word from anyone else. We collected a whole new shelf full of dead insects and dead insect parts especially wings, and who could, as one or both of us articulated, know all those words anyway? She tried to explain to me where she would put this new shelf, "this shelf of insects, etc.," she called it, but I could not quite picture it. My memory of her apartment was a little confused, and to tell you the truth, even then, it was not a pleasant confusion. But perhaps I am misremembering and am subconsciously overlaying what it is I remember now onto what it was I remembered then. In fact, when I was still in the process, some years ago, of actively learning, or of actively acquiring knowledge, I once read that this overlaying process was not possible, I do not say difficult, I say *not possible* to avoid. We then set about collecting a shelf's worth of vegetable matter, then one of moss and soil. Did you really plan on shooting that guy? I asked, scooping a handful of organic detritus into a small plastic bag. I did shoot that guy, she said, he just didn't die. We had brought along a blanket, and even though it was a little cool and the ground bumpy, we, getting cozy, etc. Later, we lay on our backs looking up at the blue sky. I'm sorry I called Deau a big fat bitch, I said. Deau *is* a big fat bitch, she said, and incidentally, they're fake. What are? And recent. How long have you known her? A couple of weeks. We lay there. Birds and clouds and insects went by. I think I'm in some trouble, I said. How so? she said. It would be interesting to know how she would have responded had I told her. I suddenly realize I have forgotten to relate something about the event. Something connected to earlier and / or later portions of this narrative. It involves a magician and a magician's assistant John found in one of the apartments down the hall. He had knocked on the door to ask if he could borrow a can opener, and a woman in a green sequin-covered leotard with a tail of peacock feathers and bits of blue glitter around her eyes answered. Behind her, sitting on the edge of a couch in front of a coffee table was a not-too-handsome, very-earnest-appearing individual in an undershirt. The magician. To get the can opener John had to go through a trick. It was pretty good. The magician swished his hands around a few times, and the can opener appeared. The magician then asked John if he needed to borrow anything else. John told the magician that as a matter of fact he was short a hard-boiled egg. The magician turned around for a second, then turned back and pulled one out of his mouth. I mean out of his own mouth, not John's. His assistant was definitely very exotic, even if she just sort of sat around on a chair. Obviously, they were invited to the event. They came late, from a job, and in full costume, which meant a black tuxedo and a mask for the magician and exactly the same outfit as before plus a mask for his assistant. Neither one of them, John later told me, said a word. They just kind of strolled around investigating the drinks table and having drinks. At some point, I don't remember when exactly, John came over to where I was sitting in the corner with my eyes closed and whispered, the magician would like to do a trick. Sometimes, when I am very drunk, my eyes and my head do this funny thing—they don't move. They were doing that funny thing when John came over and whispered, the magician would like to do a trick. The magician came over. Here, said John pointing at me, is the man of the event. The magician crouched down in front of me. He was holding a dove. He then, having made a show of putting the dove away, produced a hat and swished his hands around the way John, in his earlier description, had said he had and would if he came, and then—I saw this because of the funny thing my eyes were doing—he took the dove out of his coat, placed the hat over it, and then swished his hands some more, and then asked me to lift the hat. After a minute, as I hadn't moved, he asked somebody else. The hat came up, the dove flew out, everybody clapped, and the assistant's hand snapped out and ripped the dove out of the air. The two of them then went back to their strolling around and a few more drinks. Why did everybody clap? I asked John the next day. Because it was a trick. He made the bird appear. His hat was empty and then a bird flew out of it. That's what's called a trick. But all he did was take the dove out of his jacket pocket and put his hat over it. Well if he did, no one besides you saw him do it, so it's still a trick. It was true that there had been a lot of hand swishing. And I did remember that at one point the swishing hand had flown up in the direction of the magician's head. I suspected, and I was to give this further thought later, that the ascension of his hand coincided with his cleverly placing the dove on the floor and the hat over the dove. It's a shame you missed that trick, I said to her as we lay there in the field. The trick with the dove? Deau told me about it the next day. Yes, it's a shame, I said, as we lay there in the field, in the country, looking up at the sky and the occasional bird, with the wind off in the distance, way off in the distance moving the olive trees.

The End

But all of a sudden John and Deau were there. Look, it's all over, I said. What is, Sport? they said. They had someone with them. This guy is a beekeeper, John said. My bees make good honey, the beekeeper said. He had quite a nose. It looked like it was about ready to fall off. The two of us sat up and moved over, and John and Deau sat down beside us on the blanket, and the beekeeper, standing off at a slight remove, settled right into talking. He was quite a beekeeper. He seemed to favor words of more than two syllables, and gave quite a speech on a number of interconnected subjects, despite the nose, which really did look, the whole time he was holding forth, as if it was about to tumble off his face onto the grass and maybe even bounce very lightly once or twice when it did. That evening after dinner, having thought carefully about what the beekeeper had said, or having attempted to, I told John that nature was not in the least bit fascinating and that there was nothing natural about it and that honey baskets and pollen hunts were creepy, as were, if you thought about it, velocity and preponderance, not to mention minute digestive tracts, and that nature didn't have any fucking plan, and the elements, all ninety-fucking-two of them, in fact the entire fucking periodic table of elements and all the other charts the old bee-keeper had mentioned, could go fuck themselves, and that whatever I had said about it in the past was untrue, and that, furthermore, he, John, had been absolutely fucking right that time to go berserk and beat the shit out of me. Shut up, said John. Correctly. Then we went back to the city.

IN THE CITY, THEN, IT WAS ALL WORSE AND ALL OVER AND ALL everything, but we were not quite there yet. We were not quite there when we began being there by dropping them off at her apartment, the car quiet for a moment as we all said good-bye. Then, still not quite arrived, John and I returned the car to the rental agency and walked back over the river to my apartment. It was much colder in the city, even if we were not quite there yet, than it had been in the country. It was cold and a wind was blowing, a real wind, and we had bags to carry and were underdressed. The river, even with all its real and reflected bridges receding off into the distance, looked unforgiving and slightly angry. If it is possible for a river to look angry. I think it is.

Then we had arrived.

As a boy, I lived for a time in a room that looked out across a small empty lot onto a high white wall somewhere in a very small town, somewhere. The wall was as wide as it was high and, itself windowless, filled my window entirely. It was to this large white wall that I woke each morning, and it was at this large white wall, dimly illuminated by service lights, that I looked each night. Sometimes, during the day, birds flew along the wall. Or threw their shadows onto it. But that was all. For years. In its near impeccable blankness, is what I would like to say, it produces a memory, this wall, that, upon conclusion of the incidents I would now like to relate, I found, and in fact continue to find, soothing.

Then, I repeat, we had arrived.

Both in the city and at my apartment, which had been taken to pieces.

John looked at me, then at the remnants of the apartment, then went berserk.

Fuck, I said, for my part. Several times.

When he was calmer, which was some minutes later, he asked for an explanation.

What he said was, yours or theirs?

Mine.

Yours?

Yes.

What the fuck?

I know.

You don't know anything.

True.

You don't know shit.

Yes.

He picked something up off the floor and said, I bought this nifty keepsake in a little market on the side of a mountain in the middle of a rainstorm.

He held up a piece of it.

He held up a piece of something else.

I said something.

He said, fuck you, then we kind of wrestled around a little until he was on top of me.

Uncle? he said.

Yeah, uncle, I said.

Say Uncle John.

I said it.

He got off.

He walked around a little.

Then he sat down.

Okay, he said. Okay, fine. All right.

I nodded.

He looked at me.

We sat there.

All right, so why did they do this?

I shrugged.

He grabbed the back of my neck, pulled me forward a little, and punched me.

So I told him. Everything.

He agreed with me, 100-fucking-percent as he put it, that my actions or nonactions or whatever the hell I wanted to call them had been stupid.

Nice work, Mr. Jackass, is exactly what he said.

I asked him if I could get him anything. Maybe a snack or something.

He said, yeah.

I said, what?

He said, shut up for fuck's sake, stupid, what did you do with it?

I told him.

He looked at me.

So why haven't they gotten it yet?

Because I think I may have put the wrong address on it.

Jesus, he said.

Speaking of stupid, or of stupidly, I am put in mind of the following anecdote once told to me, or actually twice.

A former colleague was set the task, well within her expertise, of executing the following procedure: (1) removing someone's kidney; (2) laying said someone on his / her back in a bathtub full of ice cubes; (3) placing a note on his / her chest, which would read along the lines of, if you would like to live please dial Emergency. Part 1 was approached carefully. Part 2 was accomplished neatly. Part 3 was unfortunately, however, forgotten, too bad, effectively botching the exercise, which had been meant only to serve as a warning. Later I tried recounting the anecdote, but could not remember which part of the procedure the former colleague had left out, and so subsequently solicited and received a retelling of the anecdote by a colleague who was neither the one who figured as the hero of the anecdote, nor the one who had first told it to me, but rather was a third colleague, who for practical reasons was also intimately acquainted with the details of the affair.

I am not entirely certain, in this instance, that I have used the word, hero, correctly.

Ah, well.

It suddenly occurred to us that what was stupid was for us to be sitting there.

On the way out the door, John said, not without justification, and I suppose it would have ruined your little instance of intractability to just bring it back to them, and I said, yeah, I guess.

We decided to split up. First, though, we tried to call her apartment. No answer. Several possible reasons presented themselves, a couple of which neither of us wished to contemplate, and we decided that we would each, individually, continue to try calling, because going over there right now was out of the question. We split up. Each of us, as it occurred, with someone following. A little while later I got clubbed on the head.

But first, for a while, I went through the city with someone following me. I have already mentioned that it was cold. Then it started to rain. It was the sort of rain, as it has been throughout, that is far from being pleasant. And perhaps because of thinking about the unpleasant rain falling on and around me, and, by extension I suppose, about the sometimes mysterious and unpleasant rain that I had used to hear falling behind the stretch of wall in my apartment, not to mention, at times, behind a much larger stretch of wall in my dreams, I thought of the downstairs neighbor and of the hole puncher and of John's account of his dealings with the downstairs neighbor, I mean of how he had dealt with the downstairs neighbor, and of tenant relations, that too, absurdly.

I walked along the river in the rain for a while, then stopped walking along the river. This for two reasons. Three. One was the fact that John had, so recently, told the story, or rather, the expurgated story, of our experience with the corpse in the flowered skirt, which is, with several facts added to it, entirely different. I don't know why, in fact, he felt obliged to bring it up. All of it was a mistake, right from the start, both in its inception, and in its absurd conclusion—the part which I described John relating while we all sat telling each other stories under a tree.

It wasn't her, he had said after I had heard the shot and he had climbed back to the car where I was waiting for him.

What do you mean? I had said.

I mean it wasn't her. I didn't get a good look until after it was done.

That was one reason. Another was the earlier and above-mentioned bit of business I had done for the organization I was now in trouble with.

That bit of business had involved this river, a big bag, and some rocks.

The third, strangely, was the beekeeper, and his monologue about nature and God-knows-what.

Nature, had said the beekeeper, is really quite intelligent. Both as to its inceptions—he was the first to have used these words—and its conclusions. Do you wish, he had asked us, to speak of punctuation? Do you wish to speak of commas and semicolons? Ellipses and apostrophes? Nature possesses it all. Take for example your average bee. Happening to have a dead one or two in his pocket, he had done so. He went pretty fast. He went from bees to planets and from grammar to physics in about three-and-a-half sentences. It was, the dead bee he had passed around, a planet in a solar system and the solar system in the galaxy and the galaxy in the universe. He explained the connections. Which allowed for curved space and chaos theory and dark matter and a few other things. It did all seem quite intelligent. The way he described it. Extremely.

So what you are saying is that everything is dead like the average bee? I asked him.

But at that moment he was called away.

Walking along the river I found myself wondering if, in all its morpho / syntactical brilliance, nature would be smart enough to make me, say, take a bullet in the back of the head.

After the beekeeper had concluded his discourse, which he had only ended because his wife, somewhere off in the distance, had begun calling him with a bullhorn, we talked about honey for a while. We had all, we confessed to each other, been pleasantly lulled by the old man's voice and dead bees and chewed-up nose—it was only later that I became agitated. We lay there on our backs talking about honey, about its different colors and grades—yum, we said—and wondered aloud if dead bees produced ghosts as dead fleas, it had been said, did, and if ghosts of bees would go on making honey and what that honey would taste like, probably not so good, though we couldn't be sure, but sooner or later we'd find out, and we concluded that nature, especially given the creation of honey, all kinds of honey, really was, as the beekeeper had said, quite smart.

Honey was smart.

Honey was brilliant.

Even if I, another aspect of nature's expression, wasn't.

That night, incidentally, out there in the country with her, I dreamed hooks again.

And again, in the face of my utter distress, she was admirably, heartbreakingly calm.

I called her apartment. She answered. I got clubbed over the head.

That was certainly a clear-enough conclusion.

Think of its complexity, the beekeeper had said. I would require an entire sheet of paper to list all the treasures it contains. It is so very, very complex, he had ended, shaking his head.

Very, very complex indeed. When I woke up the first thing I saw was a shelf with a jar of honey sitting on it.

John, incidentally, was not clubbed over the head, as he had managed, he later told me, to slip the tall, thin woman who was following him. This maneuver had involved entering the restaurant where we had once had our turkey dinner, and leaving that restaurant by way of a window. Having slipped the woman, he had called their apartment and got her. We're fine, she said. Where's Deau? Shopping for dinner. And in a manner of speaking, that was true. Dinner was cooking, my dinner. I smelled onions and stewed apples at almost the same time I saw the shelf.

I don't know when the two of them left. Perhaps, of course, they did not leave, and throughout the process were sitting among the shelves in the back room, some of which, no doubt, were still empty, having not, as yet, found objects for themselves.

Or sets of circumstances. E.g., the fact that I want to be the captain of a hot air balloon. Now. One could set that circumstance on a shelf.

Or of a dirigible. Although in that case there would be engines involved, and instruments. I'm not sure if instruments are needed on a hot air balloon. No doubt they are. Instruments and instructions. And charts. I will have to learn how to read charts. And to navigate at night. That could also be set on a shelf. Even the same shelf. Fragile objects that float at night with things and instruments in them.

Or just drift. A dirigible adrift. Of course, a dirigible adrift eventually explodes. I saw footage once — not pretty. Or a projectionist. Another shelf. That too. Projecting film, silent film, onto a white wall. Which is what I used to imagine I could do. See above. Back then.

But the story really is still out by the river where I really still was, looking down into the cold, slightly angry-looking water, figuring that, at least until circumstances might determine otherwise, I would keep some distance between it and myself.

Mine was a medium-sized not overly great-looking

earnest-appearing individual. I stood on one end of a bridge, he stood on the other. I knew this one. He was one of the best and was going to be hard, if not impossible, to slip. Hello, I called across the bridge to him. He didn't appear to hear me. I waved. He didn't appear to see me. I began walking. He followed. It was quite an interesting relationship.

Off we went. Up the streets and down them and through doors and up escalators, I mean elevators, very small ones, but also I do mean escalators, or escalator, it is a rather funny word, as they all are, said over and over again.

It is possible, in this city, to cover distance underground. I did so. Through doors and down stairs. Corridors like snakes. Bright posters and glistening tile walls. People coming toward you in trickles and bursts.

Off in the distance, down one of the corridors, I heard music.

Voice and instrument.

Each after the other.

Gal I knew.

Hello, I said.

Part of the time she was one of us.

Right now, as far as I could tell, she was not.

She let go of her instrument, let it hang from a thick strap around her neck, and held out her hand.

You? she said, glancing down the long hall at him.

Yes, I said.

She nodded and started singing again so I dropped a coin into her hat and pushed off.

As I rounded the next corner and moved up toward the exit I heard another coin dropping, the other's coin dropping, and the voice, which by the way was impossibly low and lovely, stopped.

Then I stopped.

Then it started again, with the instrument this time, and I started again, only, having started, found myself walking back the way I had come, so that, having re-rounded the corner, I was now walking behind him. He was not far ahead of me, and not moving fast, a nice easy pace, and his legs were shorter than mine and he looked a little, perhaps, round in the middle, and limped slightly, that was important, so that probably, conditions permit-ting, I would have him soon, I thought, only at that moment I passed her again and she nodded again and the music stopped.

She shrugged.

I dropped another coin.

He, in passing her again, after me again, did not.

So that was that and, back outside, we walked around like before until I was tired and sat down in an establish-ment where they served nice big drinks, one of which I sent over to him.

A few weeks before someone had sent one over to me.

I raised my glass.

He appeared not to notice. He appeared not to be drinking, either, but did, of course, and was.

I was trying to develop a plan.

I am no good at all, I believe I have already mentioned, at planning.

Nevertheless, I thought that I could somehow employ the paradigm of the dove-coming-out-of-the-hat trick, as described above. Yeah, I thought. I thought, somehow you understand, that I could reverse it, the idea of rever-sal having rather effectively just injected itself into my mind. It seemed to me that I could make the dove (myself) disappear into the hat (some receptacle) if I could only figure out some equivalent for the swishing of the hands. Dove, I said to myself. I swished my hands around a little, practicing. He was, without appearing to be, watching me. That was the problem. Even if I was a dove, the trick could never work if he was watching me. I mean if he was watching me while he was supposed to be watching my hands, or the putative equivalent thereof, swish around. I had been the proof of that—at the event, when I was sitting on the floor, before I had become a dove.

I'm a dove, I said.

The waiter shot me a look.

I kind of eased off on being a dove and got up.

He got up too.

It was a little like wearing a well-tailored, loose-fitting jacket.

Albeit one made of eyes.

For a second I thought about running. But then I remembered hearing about someone who had tried running on him. So I walked. Wearing the jacket. Quickly, but I walked.

In the end, I couldn't think of anything except for a scheme which would have required as half the swishing part a few short seconds of time travel. I actually conferred with him on this and he said that he thought that yes that might just about do it, though he couldn't be certain, after all it was difficult to be certain about these things. Incidentally, what do you think of this? I asked him, holding out my hand, slightly cupped.

Nice, he said. Where did you get it?

It was a present.

Nice present. Those are hard to come by. Interested in parting with it?

Nope.

I'll give you 200.

Nope. Etc.

Or actually, more accurately, at the end what I thought of was calling her, which is what I did, you already know.

Hello.

Hello.

Suddenly he was standing right behind me.

I'm going to hit you now, he said.

And he did.

In one of my dreams I sprout wings, glorious wings. And I wait for them to fly. And they don't.

They climb. Up tall buildings.

Dreadful heights.

Prehensile wings.

Always at some unexpected point in these dreams my head, which seems only ever capable of lolling, hits against a projecting cornice.

Whunk!

At this point in the dream a separation occurs and I watch myself being dragged by the wings up and up.

She had added animals in cages to her shelves. It took me a moment to realize that someone else must have done this while we were on our trip. There were birds and rodents and a monkey and some kind of a cat.

It looked like a cat.

Also she had added, although it could not, almost, have been possible, more shelves.

There were splotches of bright violet on a few of the shelves. I cannot, I don't believe I've yet mentioned, tolerate bright violet. There was a bit of bright violet on the hole puncher. The monkey had a bright violet hand. I registered this part about the color, it now seems to me, but I have already spoken to you about overlay, at precisely the same time that I began to smell cigar smoke.

Hello, I said. Boss, I said.

The only response I got was stutter.

Then, however, began the Q & A, and I can tell you that in her part of this exercise my boss was quite fluent, and that it was I who seemed to stutter.

She asked, I answered. Actually, I also asked, but she did not answer.

This, in its way, was another kind of relationship, everything seemed to be about some kind of relationship. For example, one of the questions I was asking was, where is she?

The conflated smells of onions and of some kind of meat and of stewed apples and of the animals and of cigar smoke and of, after a few minutes, singed hair and singed flesh is not a good one.

I am, pardon me, I repeated, telling you the truth, I suggested, all truth etc., please please please, although I definitely did not suggest this in so many words.

The singed hair and the singed flesh part was about this: each time I answered I got burned on the back of the neck with the cigar. It was the tall, thin woman who would take the cigar, apparently, from my boss and place it against my neck.

I think that each time it was the tall, thin woman.

But it was impossible to be sure.

Those are just kisses, the boss would say, stuttering on the kisses part, so that it seemed to me, each time she never quite finished saying it, that I had received several kisses instead of just the one.

Once, I went to a circus, the clowns and animals kind.

Once I say, but this was not really all that long ago. It was a small circus just outside a city or, rather, outside the old borders of the city, when the city had ended, or had had an end, and then there had been some area, then more area and who knows what, the maps went blank, before you reached another city or the sea, but what we are talking about here was inside the city, as the city, is what I mean, had been extended into the area. I had stumbled upon the circus by accident as I was following someone, and when I had finished following that someone, I went back to it, bought a ticket, and went in. Inside the orange and ochre tent it was all bright lights and flashes and drums and choreographed roars and clowns and odd movements and frightening voices and a woman standing on top of a horse and an elephant, finally, the feature, sitting in a car. Put your hands together, said the announcer, a dwarf on stilts, for Kisses the Driving Elephant, who was, in fact, driving, so to speak, an appropriately enormous convertible, using her trunk to turn the wheel.

Eventually, Kisses drove her car into a small pyramid of very short clowns.

Which hadn't been meant to happen and hadn't been all that funny.

In various parts of the world, at various times, they have used elephants to execute people. One way was the elephant would rear back and you would be tied to something and then it would come down on your head. Brave people, it was said, wouldn't close their eyes. Those elephants were painted with all kinds of patterns. I forget who told me about that. But at any rate I used to imagine it sometimes—lying there, eyes open, being brave, with the painted elephant rearing back.

I don't think any of the very short clowns were badly hurt. Kisses, certainly, was not hurt, and she kept driving, around and around.

It was of this Kisses the Driving Elephant, at any rate, that I thought, and of elephants in general, and of those painted elephants, as they applied, for perhaps the sixth or seventh time, of great big elephants and of jeering onlookers, one of their kisses to the back of my neck.

Insofar as I was able to think.

Then they made me ingest the onions, the stewed apples, and the meat.

I wished they would not make me eat the stewed apples.

They had been our stewed apples—for the shelves, in our jar, etc.

Chew, I was reminded by someone close to my head.

I chewed.

It was very sweet. Sweeter than just the fact of the stewed apples.

Honey sweet.

I had seen all this process, from a small remove, on that previous occasion, the latter portion of which, involving the bag and the rocks, I have already mentioned. But that had all transpired in an almost empty room, empty except for a small blue appliance that sizzled and sucked away at an outlet in one corner. The process went on long enough for me to notice that the walls, which I had taken for white, were really a very pale green, another effective—I knew something about the subject—technique. The woman with the cigar, my boss, had not conducted that exercise. The tall, thin woman plus one or two others had. My job, at the first, had been to stand at the door, which I did until all of them had left and it became my job to sit in the room and watch him. Part of my stupidity, you will note, consisted in having been a party to this previous process, and having, nonetheless, taken the course it has been part of the purpose of this narrative to describe. But I had been in the condition I had been in when I had chosen my course of action. In picking me for the assignment, the boss hadn't counted on what might become the ramifications of my having fallen in love.

Or perhaps she had.

Preposterous causality.

But at any rate, I was still in that condition.

I am still in that condition.

Where is she? I asked, my mouth full of hot objects and I don't know what kind of unpleasant tasting meat.

This time I did get some kind of response.

It was the stapler.

Each time its two ends came together there was that fine, crisp clunk.

That was the way John found me, having, as he put it, made his arrangement with them.

We came to an understanding, he told me a little later when I was back on my feet again.

Yeah? I said. An arrangement? I said.

Way for them to reimburse me for breakages.

Which surprised me a little. After all, with the exception of the incident involving my former downstairs neighbor, and one involving one of the waiters from the night of our turkey dinner, as well as another just before his arrival involving a young man on a motor scooter who had, as he had put it, injusticed him, he had all but given that up.

Just temporary, he said.

A little arrangement, I said. One you just made.

That's right, one I just made, he said, then leaned over and gave me a little pat on the cheek.

I say that was the way John found me, with a piece of onion stuck to my lip, and with the staples.

Ouch! he said.

Looking around at all the shelves.

Then at me.

As I had sat there, stapled, and I had apparently sat there, stapled, for two days, I had been thinking about, when it had been possible to think, those early days in the autumn when we would sit together at the café in the park. She had very nice hands, that's what I thought. They were nice in their movement, which was unusually fluid and precise, and they were nice to look at and also to consider as they held up some object or other, of which there were, absurdly it now seems, so very many. Also there was her mouth, which was really just her mouth, but I had liked to watch it, desperately, as I had liked, strangely, to watch her shoulders, which she had held almost impossibly straight, like, I had always thought, some impressive individual in a painting, but just as likely, I had also thought, not.

She came across the room toward me.

She had come across the room toward me.

The end.

Sitting on the shelves, or perhaps I've already said this, were several of the objects we had collected in the country, as the world, even as it wrapped itself tighter and tighter around our throats, was made to seem to vanish.

Was made to seem to vanish, I say to myself, pathetically.

Actually, of what I thought, as I sat there, was nothing.

Or not nothing.

But not quite something either.

Exquisite.

The caged animals were now, after two days, all moving more slowly, if at all, and all of it, including me, now stunk.

They're done with you, Sport, said John.

That's it?

That's it.

Where is she?

Who?

What do you mean, who?

He shrugged.

My tongue, at this point, was very swollen, and John suggested I not speak anymore, and for quite some time I couldn't, so that was that, and now me alone in this fucking apartment, the end.

It is not, however, quite the end with her, there is still this. As we were standing on the sidewalk in front of her apartment beside the rental car, just after she had insisted I not accompany her upstairs, she told me two things. The first was about a woman, once, very long ago, who had lived in the country and had done some very nice things and some things that were not so nice. The things that were not so nice had been done most recently, and had involved much weeping and sobbing and kneeling. There had been a man involved, a man of similar background—nice and not nice plus a little dumb, is how she put it. His involvement was, in fact, what all the weeping and sobbing and knees were about, somehow. Then the man was no longer in the picture.

It was rather a long story to be told out there on the curb, and Deau had already gone breezing up into the building, or out shopping for dinner, my dinner, and John was waiting for me in the car so that we could return it to the agency before we were charged for another day. John did not, however, seem too impatient. So:

The woman went into one of those buildings one goes into and knelt, as one does, and sobbed a little, according to custom, all the while talking up at the ceiling while looking down. Then the ceiling, which was quite unusual, she was told by everyone else in the building, talked back down at her.

Here is what you must do, said the ceiling.

Okay, the woman said.

So she did those things, all successfully, then the ceiling reached down in a great flash of light and swept her up off the earth—the end.

The other thing she said to me, just after we had kissed, was that, for what it was worth, she was sorry.

For what? I said.

Good-bye, she said.

Actually she didn't say any of that to me and the last thing I remember is swishing my hands around in the backseat of someone's car.

Quite effectively, in this instance, it would seem.

Most stories have built onto them some kind of epilogue, this one, the end I say, does not.

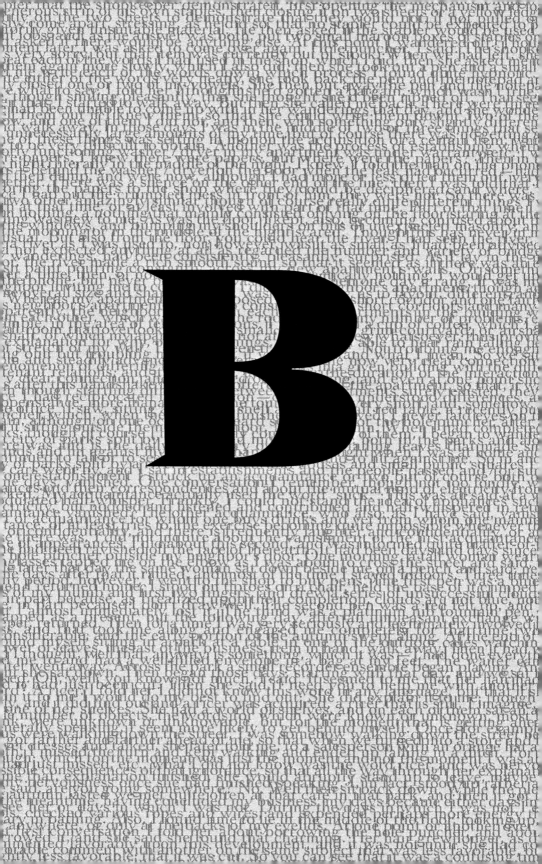

Now, instead of encountering a different set of strangers, we encountered the same ones, and this familiarity comforted us to no end.

—PAMELA LU
Pamela: A Novel

BUT THEN ONE MORNING I THOUGHT I saw her again. I was walking along a street near my apartment carrying a bag that contained three warm pastries or, rather, two and one-half warm pastries — I had already started eating one of them. It had a light, sweet glaze that would have gone well with steamed milk, and I was vaguely touching the tip of my tongue to the center of my upper lip and feeling very happy, thoroughly contented, perhaps even a little smug, when I saw her again, or thought I did. She was standing quite near me on a corner, looking in the direction of a man coming rapidly across the street toward her. The man was wearing a hat with a wide rim and sunglasses, as, I might add, was she. The man approached and kept approaching and then, although his speed broke for a moment, had passed her and continued along the street, and she turned and stood looking toward me, or seemed to be. I greeted her. She didn't respond. She did, however, continue to seem to look at me, so I approached and said, would you like a pastry? They're very good. How true: in addition to being finely glazed, these pastries contained a fresh pear filling blended with an almond paste and one could smell this aspect of their preparation even through the bag. When she didn't respond I leaned forward a little and asked her if she wanted to smell the bag. Good God, she said. It was a bright, warm day in early summer, and there were birds in the trees and on the cars and on the building fronts, very pretty birds. I tried to come up with something to say about the birds but couldn't, so instead I complimented her on the shorts she was wearing. Thank you, she said. This seemed more promising. After a moment, however, it occurred to me that she might just as well have complimented me, in return, on mine, as I had just purchased them the previous day in a store we had once walked by together on the way to the cinema, but she did not, even when I reminded her of these details, which, I have to say, did not seem to me to be entirely devoid of interest, it had been quite a successful evening, the one I was remembering, we had often had such successful evenings together. How's that little rash? I asked her. That little rash? she said. Her mouth had changed, seemed somehow elongated, the lips were a touch thinner, paler. Her nose, too, looked different, was somewhat wider, a slight flaring of the nostrils, just a touch. It's good to see you, I said. Umm, likewise, she said. Several cars went by. She looked at her watch. Somewhere in the distance a gun went off. On the job? I said. I'm not sure, she said. At this she smiled, almost bitterly it seemed, showing me teeth that were not quite as lovely as the teeth I remembered, but it had been some months, perhaps, in truth, somewhat longer, and I am not unwilling to admit that my own teeth, in that interval, had also undergone a not unremarkable measure of decline. I was preparing, in fact, to broach that subject when, somewhat abruptly and without further comment, she began to walk off. Hey, I said, and when, my interpolation having had no effect, I began to follow her, she sped up, and when I sped up, she started running, and when I started running, she ran faster than me. Never a fast runner, I had put on several pounds and had become something of a fatty at that time. This was not just a function of a regular intake of glazed pastries with pear and almond filling, it was also a function of cakes. I liked a good deal of chocolate in a cake and I could not go lightly on the butter. It was not, in fact, a cake at all for me during that period unless it was heavily iced, and it was not fit for consumption unless it was very large. Also, I had become fond of nuts and of oils and of cream and of cheeses and when I slept, during that period, it was with dark visions of rich dainties occupying my head. I watched her run for a time, then went home. Walking home, I thought to myself, well, that was strange, and I thought to myself several other things, and I remembered a few things, and I thought about her nose, it was a nice nose, both versions of it, and I began to feel a bit moved and I had not felt moved for some time, and it was rather nice to feel moved and to feel, also, somewhat relieved, that she had reappeared, had reentered my life, although the nose was troubling, and I heard some more shots and fought my way through a crowd which had gathered, there was something that looked a lot like blood but I couldn't tell if this one was real, then said hello to the old woman with ochre hair who sells pictures of roses near my building, and who at other times works in liquidation, and then I was in my building. I went up some stairs then took a short break, then went up some more stairs and, a little surprised to see that the door was open, into my apartment. The gentleman with the hat and sunglasses was there. I hope you don't mind, he said. Not at all, would you care for a pastry? I said. He ate very neatly with one hand cupped against his chest to catch stray crumbs and flecks of icing. I liked the delicate action of his jaw and the way his tongue came out to probe his lips between bites. It is a fine pastry, he said. It is, I said. They don't skimp on the custard. No they don't. So often, he said, they skimp on the custard, and the fruit and paste is left to fend for itself; one should not have to feel sorry for the fruit that passes one's lips. I nodded. This seemed like useful information. He asked if he might trouble me for a glass of milk. I apologized for not having offered him one. It is so infrequently, I said, that I entertain. But you do occasionally? he said. Very occasionally, although once I had an event here. An event? Yes. Were there any casualties? One. We both looked around the room. Did you come to it? I asked him. It's possible, he said. It was a great event, I said, there was a magician present and my sweetheart came. Your sweetheart? he said. We sat quietly a moment. I could see myself in his sunglasses. Yuck, basically. Well, what are you doing here? I said. Actually, first I said, excuse me, then got up, went to the bedroom, took my own pair of sunglasses off the dresser, returned to the kitchen table, and put them on. Well, what are you doing here? I said. Those are very nice shorts you are wearing, he said. He smiled. I smiled. Are you still hungry? I asked. He nodded. In that case why don't I make us something more substantial, which I did, some excellent omelets, and when we had eaten them we ate some more, I had a good piece of sausage on hand. After a while, I began to feel sleepy and suggested that before continuing our conversation, which up to that point, I assured him, had been very interesting, we have some coffee, which we did, quite a lot of coffee, this is excellent coffee, he said. Thank you,

I said, and told him that I was pleased to have made the acquaintance of someone as pleasant as he was and as interested in comestibles as I, myself, had become. I am not against the occasional calorie, he admitted, there is something so very satisfying in those beautiful bits of heat. I thought it an admirable answer. In fact, I thought him, generally, admirable and told him so. This was not to remain the case, not even for very much longer, but at that juncture that was how things stood. In the throes of this soon-to-be reversed sentiment I told him that he, too, was in possession of quite fine shorts, and I asked if he could let me know where he had gotten them, and he did. I wrote it down and some weeks later, when I had recovered, I went to the address I had noted and found only an old watchmaker's shop, and an old watchmaker's assistant, something of a humorist, who asked me for the time. You need a watch, son, he said. I need very many things, I said. Well, what we have here, son, are watches, now let me see, I'll find you one. We sat there. In my kitchen. That was her, out there on the street, wasn't it? I said. No, he said. Are you sure? Absolutely. Do you know who I mean when I say her? He shook his head. I told him who I meant. Ah, he said. How long has she been back? I'm not sure. I thought . . . Yes, we all thought. No, I mean I very deeply believed . . . We all very deeply believed. So she is back. Yes, definitely. You're not lying are you? He didn't answer. I repeated my question. He smiled, and I decided I'd just learned nothing. At this point, the telephone began to ring. I do not like telephones. I asked him if he would be kind enough to answer it for me. He was kind enough, and, in fact, swung the phone out of its cradle with great panache. Yes, hello? he said. Yes, I'm fine, just had some breakfast.

Who? Yeah, fatso. Yeah, yeah, big as a fucking balloon. I was looking at him, waving my hands around to indicate that he should tell whoever it was that I wasn't there, and perhaps take a message, but a moment later I found myself, receiver pressed against my ear, saying, yes I'm available, tonight, 11:30, yes, I understand, you'll send someone to take me. I always feel proud of myself once I've actually been on the phone, have made it through whatever it is there is to make it through and have set the receiver down. You will understand, then, why it was that when I replaced the receiver, I grinned, or smiled, I think it was a smile, no, it was a grin, a gesture which, at any rate, was meant for him, only he was no longer there. Hello? I said. No answer. It occurred to me that he might have taken the opportunity to excuse himself to the facility: we had, after all, consumed quite a bit of coffee. Hello? I said, positioning myself near the bathroom door. No answer. I decided that this lack of a response was inconclusive, that there simply wasn't enough evidence to make an informed judgment, and that it would be best, until further evidence presented itself, to wait. As I stood waiting, I thought about things. I thought about my breakfast and about my teeth, which really were spectacularly in need of care, someone had just recently made a remark to that effect, there had also, recently, been a remark about my breath, probably not unrelated, and I thought about one or two other things like my need for a new bookshelf and my difficulty in acquiring such things and generally how strange the day had become, and how it was just beginning. A former acquaintance of mine once told me over a dinner that beginnings were quite extraordinary things, there being nothing and then there being something, a prelude and an aftermath. On top of that, he said, many beginnings were a positive morass of the unlikely, the bizarre, the insignificant but intriguingly odd, the innocently calamitous, the highly charged mundane. All the great stories, he continued, began strangely, often stupidly, and ended incomprehensibly, and then there were all those elements in between. How do you feel, I asked him, about a story that begins with someone seeing someone again, but there being certain differences in the person's physical makeup, like their nose has changed, so you are not entirely sure who it is? I see, said my acquaintance, who is she and when did she get back? No one, I said, and she hasn't even left yet. She hadn't. Days lay ahead of us, perhaps even weeks. Within that interval we would take pleasant walks together and travel to a small coastal city and picnic in a grove of olive trees. There would be an event for us to attend and some business for me to mishandle, to choose to mishandle, to believe I had chosen to mishandle, and a large bathtub in an old house in the country, and a cold windowpane onto which we would breathe our mingled breaths. But all that was years ago. It must have been years ago. How old was I now? I was fat. My hair was curly and touched with gray. It had occurred to me, in the interval, to take up singing. I had even performed the lead male role in a small production of a famous opera. I think this is true. I have just tried singing. I can sing. Also I thought — I was still standing there, still thinking — of a proof of the infinite nature of the series of prime numbers, it employed the following equation $Q = (2 * 3 * 5 * 7 \ldots P) + 1$, quite pretty, this was the work of one of the very old mathematicians, though transmitted by one less old, or at least one more recent, if I am remembering correctly, possibly. Then I worked a few problems in my head. Simple ones. Small acts of division, of slicing apart. In my youth I was known to be quicker than average with a figure; in fact, I was once first runner-up in a contest. The prize was pizza with the school's math teacher. It was this teacher who told me about prime numbers and also about irrationals—not as pretty but much more powerful, very deep. Having at this point waited for some time, needs of my own had become pressing, so that—I should not have chosen such a course otherwise—as I had stood with my ear against the cold wood for some seconds and heard nothing, I gingerly opened the door. Empty. I registered, however, as I rushed forward, that he must have been there, had either washed his hands or used the facility or had entered as part of a sweep, we often make sweeps, because an object, a memento, my green duck, a gift I had kept despite a troubling defect in its buoyancy, was out of place. Its place was on the porcelain soap dish next to the bathtub. Now it sat on the shelf opposite the toilet. This was troubling. And curious. But little more. At any rate, I sat. I stood. I resisted the temptation to bathe. Then returned to the kitchen and found a note:

Dear Sir / Madam,

You must pardon, or I must ask you to pardon, my surreptitious departure. This course of action was factor only of an inability on my part, and under any circumstances, to say good-bye, to anyone (you will please note that I am not saying it now), I am quite simply incapable, this since birth (please don't ever ask me about it), and so am forced to take my leave when the opportunity presents itself, regardless, I might add, of whether or not my business (if the circumstance relates to such) has been concluded. This being the case, I have taken the liberty of attaching to this document a summary of the substance to which my visit (I hope my presence has not too greatly importuned you) corresponds. Please consider me, if it should seem (I am always hesitant to loosely employ the verb "be") appropriate, your humble servant.

The note was not signed and there was nothing attached to it. I read it through again. It seemed straightforward enough, although I wasn't entirely sure whether or not it was or was not, and was absolutely unsure whether or not it was appropriate for me to think of him as my humble servant, probably, I decided (rightly it turned out), not. Then he threw a brick through my window. This wasn't, I should hasten to add, as unpleasant an incident (or as exciting an incident) as it could have been had my window been closed. I am not opposed to unpleasant experiences, by the way—I don't mean to imply that at all. The unpleasant experience clearly has its place—an important, perhaps even indispensable place. But at any rate, the brick sailed neatly through the window, clattered across the white tile floor, and slid into the wall with a nice crisp clunk. I like that sound. In the daytime I like it. I do not like it at night, but in the daytime, and when it is explained, it gives me a pleasant feeling at the back of my throat. I went to the window. Did you get it? he called. Yes, thank you, I said. I stood there. He stood there. Fatso, huh? I said. I'm sorry about that, it slipped out, he said. Did you like my duck? Your duck? In the facility—the green duck. I have not been in your facility, in fact, I am just rushing off to find one. He did look a little uncomfortable. Must run, he said. Was *she* here? I said. He stood there. While I was out shopping? He didn't move. Can't you just leave without saying good-bye? I said. I can't talk about it, he said. A few people went by. No one paid any attention. Was she here? I said. Yes, he said. Was she in my bathroom? Yes. I lifted my sunglasses, winked, let them drop, leaned back inside, walked over and got the brick, put the brick on the table, went back over to the window, and found him gone. Then I went over to the table and pulled the attachment off the brick. It was much shorter than the Dear Sir / Madam note, was relatively personalized, and had not been typed. The handwriting, I might add, seemed familiar, but also not, maybe mostly not. It read, and I think these words will mark the end of my beginning, for what it has been worth:

Dear Sir,
Do not, under any circumstances

Some minutes later I left for the café where, following a pleasant walk, I was to meet an individual I had an appointment with and eat a cheese sandwich. Also, I was to have my cards read and the inside of my thigh stroked, but the main thing, now that my breakfast had begun to digest, was the cheese sandwich. It was a very good sandwich, so good that, having taken just the second bite and while still in the middle of chewing it, I nodded appreciatively to the bartender, who, while not having himself prepared the sandwich, was the one who had responsibility for it. The bartender graciously blinked back at me, and I continued eating, just as earlier, on the way to the café, I had continued walking, enjoying the sunshine and noticing along the way the varying quality of shorts that were visible. Few were as nice as my own or as those belonging to my recent interlocutor. None were as nice as hers. It was of shorts, then, that I thought as I made my way to the café, and also of the events of that morning, a little. In thinking of the events of that morning, as I

walked along beneath the trees and, behind the trees, the
gorgeous old buildings, and behind the buildings all the
rooms with their appliances and television screens, I
found my mind drawn toward more distant events,
events of a previous autumn and early winter, events that
had involved her, I felt certain, as well as others. The
trees and buildings, as I say, were lovely, especially in
reflection, one wished almost to dive into them, were the
water not quite so murky, and I found it difficult to con-
centrate. It is a very pleasant river, thoughts of swimming
in it and of other things aside, especially on a warm
spring morning with a blue sky above the surrounding
buildings so that the orange of the chimneys seems very
bright. It was all very quiet and impressive, and I liked it
better than most of what I was remembering of that previous autumn, though not better than all of what I was
remembering—parts of what I was remembering were
much better than the river—and then I walked up a flight
of steps, crossed a street, and approached the establishment. Just prior to entering it, however, I paused and
attempted, once more, to gather my thoughts, even just a
little, around the subject of those earlier events and the
events of that morning, but could not. I went in. The air
was dark and smelled of beer and dust and antiquated
cleaning product. I let my eyes adjust. I decided, as they
were adjusting, to make one last attempt to think about it
a little more, but other things came to mind. E.g., one of
the instances in which I had thrown someone in the
river—the one with the trees reflected in it, waving in it.
A boat had gone by. Some people had waved.
Fortunately, the body had not floated. They do sometimes. Despite your best efforts. Or those of your colleagues. Most, however, do not float. This one, as I say,

did not. It went down in a white cloud, the dark water whirling around it. This establishment is one that I have frequented for some time, almost as long as I have been in this city, which is quite a long while now, in fact it becomes hard to hold it all in one's head. The first time I entered this establishment was one evening that previous autumn. I entered it because as I was passing someone standing in the doorway said, pssst. That was how I became involved with the organization and came, occasionally, to do some business for them. It was this someone that I had it in mind to meet that morning. Hi, I said. Whatever, she said. She was sitting at a table near the back of the establishment shuffling a deck of cards. Subsequent to my greeting is when, incidentally, I ordered a glass of beer and the cheese sandwich, that good one. Whatever, she said again as I came over. She did not look very well, even in the dim light of the back tables, but she seemed to be in somewhat better spirits. They had been on the low side the week before when her bruises had been worse. Her bruises, while not entirely healed, were better, and the swelling, which had been very pronounced, had gone down. How are you? I said. Cut the deck, she said. I cut the deck. She then sort of swirled the cards around on the table and told me to pick one. At that moment my sandwich arrived. Without looking away from the cards, she pointed at the empty table next to us. The bartender, who had been kind enough to bring the sandwich over to me, very gently set it down on the empty table, and for some minutes it sat there shimmering in the dim light. Pick another card, she said. I did. I then picked another and she said, stop. Judging this to be an appropriate moment to take a preliminary investigative bite of the sandwich, I began to do so. No, she said. I put the sandwich back down. Even all bruised up, she was pretty intimidating, still. Also she had begun to stroke my thigh. I do not know what she had done. I am referring to the bruises. It is rare that one knows. Even though it is true that she had played some role in my own earlier bruising, she very likely did not know what it was that I had done. Even I, although this is not true, was not sure of that. Likely, no one knew exactly what it was I had done, or if I had even done something, anything at all. Three of Hearts, seven of Spades, King of Spades, she said. No, I said. Four of Diamonds, two of Spades, Queen of Spades. No. This went on. Eventually I showed her. All right, yeah, whatever, she said, put them down on the table. I put them down. She began to squint, to mutter, to make small movements with her hands. A few minutes later as I was eating my sandwich, her prognostication having been made, I said, I thought you were supposed to do that with special cards, and she said, you think too much. Which is true. At that moment, for example, I was thinking about the bartender, and about working with him down along the river. His great-great-grandfather, he had told me on that occasion, had used to poach ducks. He had gone out, the great-great-grandfather, in a boat in the early hours of the morning when the ducks were sleeping and had filled up huge bags with them. This came up because we too used huge bags. Once there was a very large body. He had not been a body at the start of the business, he had been an individual and he had woken up. Then he went back to sleep. At any rate, it was interesting. I mean what she had said. And I certainly hoped that it would become the case. Incidentally, my meeting with her was in no way contingent upon the curious events of that morning — I had arranged to meet with her some days previously. It did, of course, occur to me that the interpretation of the cards she had given might have been contingent upon her having been made cognizant of the events of my morning, such as they had been, or of some part of them. I thought about that. In the middle of so thinking I had my pleasant interaction with the bartender. He had not been quite as friendly of late, and it bothered me to think of this. Throughout our association, he had always been quite friendly, so it pleased me to see that he was warming up again. You're telling me I should definitely go to work tonight? I asked her. Yes, absolutely, and do everything you're told to, and don't ask any stupid questions this time. Do you really think all that will happen? I do not think—I have told you many times that I do not think, never, not at all. This was true. She had told me that several times, and I had no reason not to believe her. And after all, reading cards was what she did with herself. When I say it was what she did with herself, I mean when she was not otherwise engaged in business. The same business I was engaged in. Of course given the amount of bruising she had received, it was likely that it would be some while, if ever, before she was recuperated, or so I thought. For my part, I had only just recently been recuperated. A state of events with which I was quite satisfied, but not entirely sure what to make of. My recuperation had been initiated by the bartender some weeks previously. When I had gone up to the bar to order my standard midmorning beverage and hard-boiled egg he had said, very casually, the usual place, tonight. And at the usual place that night, instead of blankets and chains and bags and the bartender, I had found an earnest-looking man of moderate size who had said, come with me. It is my understanding that in most organizations, once an organic asset has been disaffirmed, it is only under unusual circumstances that he / she is recuperated. This had been the case with the organization with which I had previously enjoyed affiliation. That had been unpleasant. I had been placed on a list. In such situations one leaves. I did. The subsequent organization, this one, is structured differently. This is due to its very generous and active recuperation wing. The organization is quite large and considerably diversified. I had been in one part of it and now I was in another—an interesting if slightly infuriating part, which suited me quite well. The woman who had just predicted so many fine and interesting things for my day had also been in that previous part of it, but, as she had not as yet been recuperated, or so I thought, she did not yet belong to another. It was for this reason that I concluded that she had likely not been made aware of any developments regarding certain parties, but thought nevertheless that it would not hurt to attempt to make sure. You saw who? she said. Yes, I said. Well that's sort of interesting. I agreed that it was. I then asked her if she had any insight into that development. She said she did not. However, she said, and began swirling her cards around on the table. I reached out my hand to pick one, but at that moment something singular transpired. When one is disaffirmed from the organization, one is often, if the disaffirmation is not overly stringent, supplied with a document summarizing the character trait(s) found wanting, the character trait(s) that might well have helped the asset avoid trespassing into the circumstances into which he / she has trespassed. I learned this not long after the events for which I was disaffirmed. That is to say that one morning during my convalescence I opened an envelope and read the words,

FOUND WANTING:
CEREBELLUM

To the organization's credit, I think, there was no overly determined attempt on its part to remedy this situation—in fact, I was left to meditate on the subject alone. It is quite an interesting subject, and the events in which I had been involved were full of instances where I could see that, under the circumstances, my cerebellum had been wanting. Lying on my back on the narrow bed in my small room it was easy to think of, not to say imagine, several instances, one of which took place during the event I mentioned having once held in my apartment. During that event, I was taken aside by an old man with an awful nose, who took out his sunglasses, put them on, and told me that the assignment with which I was being entrusted was an important one, and that, although the organization had developed some confidence in my abilities, they had decided to send along a few staff members with me to facilitate the proceedings. Who are the staff members? I said. He listed them. Quite a generous bit of information and one I chose to completely ignore, and in fact succeeded, more or less, in wiping entirely from my mind. This process of erasure deserves some development. One has one's theories and one has acknowledged those of others. If I were to say for instance, I have a heart, one might then, if the evidence were present, be inclined to say, I gather that. But likely not, I believe that. And yet, I contend, what we are talking about, even with the evidence directly, so to speak, in our face, is belief, not gathering: I believe that. But such faith, others have contended, is misguided. Which I also believe: I believe that. Somewhere along the line a degree of dread becomes indicated.

Becomes amplified. Absolute. Nevertheless, I found I agreed with the organization's assessment and at one point even sent them a letter to that effect. It seems unlikely that this played a role in their decision to recuperate me. The organization, its literature states, is rarely swayed by individual revelation or entreaty. But the fact remains that I was recuperated, and at the usual place on the evening of said recuperation, after I had followed the man I have described above, I was asked to perform a task in a variety of operation that the organization was known to undertake. In fact, I was scheduled to perform another one that very evening. I did. But before that a singular incident transpired.

This incident was not the previously mentioned singular incident, which prevented me from drawing another card, forced me to lie flat on my back in a warm puddle for some minutes, and obliged me to help the bartender carry an individual out to the trunk of a car. This was a second singular incident, one that took place a short while later, after I had left the store where I acquire my job-related supplies. For this job, according to the instructions I had received over the telephone, those supplies included red duct tape and a standard wooden-handle feather duster. The red duct tape was very pleasant to work with. It was both excellently adhesive and relatively easy to remove. I still have a small stretch of it. One acquires considerable amounts of leftover product upon the termination of this variety of job—much of the work has about it a certain performative aspect, thus placing a premium on the quality of the realia put into use. Realia, the organization's literature on the subject states, is most essential, serving, as it does, to "anchor the event." Most

evocative, for me, of the leftover product I have accumulated, is a heavy power transformer, which was used to
run a branding iron, which was used to heat a certain element, which was used in conjunction with several liquids,
each of them very expensive and hard to come by. I have
other things in my possession which are capable of
inspiring in me certain associations. One I carry with me
at all times. I have shown it to very few people, as it has
elicited mixed reactions. One party said, okay, nutcase.
Another said, oh that's very interesting. Another, quite
some time ago now, called it exquisite. I am still not
entirely sure how I can describe it. I could not believe
that it hadn't crossed my mind, that morning, to show it
to her, although it struck me as altogether possible that
she would not remember having given it to me, various
things about her seeming, as they had, to have changed.
But to return to the second singular incident. There was
nothing to do but encourage the horse to right itself. It
was an old horse lying on a patch of grass next to a vegetable stand, and I had no idea how and what it had come
to be doing there. An old woman figured in the incident,
insofar as the horse was sort of lying on her. The old
woman, though she was eager to talk, seemed incapable
of answering questions or rather of providing answers
that seemed in some way to correspond with questions. I
had been in this situation before. I knew what to do —
when to say yes and when to nod. When I was young my
father used to tie linoleum strips around my ankles so
that the snakes wouldn't bite me when we were berry
picking, the old woman said. I nodded, I held her hand.
She described the handles of a tea set she had once
owned. Also she had been a teacher. In her cardigan
pocket was a list of the subjects she had taught. I have a

list in every pocket, she said. She then told me, pulling out one of said lists as evidence, about her mother's onion tarts. Here I listened very carefully. It was apparently all in the consistency of the cooked onion. An emergency team arrived, the horse was lifted, shot, and carted away. I went to a computer shop. There I was supposed, also according to my instructions, to acquire a computer, a very small one. The salesperson assured me she had just the thing and demonstrated how neatly her product could fit into, for example, one's breast pocket. She was very proud of her product and succeeded in imparting a fair measure of that pride in me, the new provisional owner of the very small computer with the illuminable screen. Later that screen was to come in handy, as was the built-in calculator, and one or two other functions. Alas, that item was not one I was permitted to keep. It was held as evidence and played a role at my trial in exonerating me. Then, for the second time, I thought I saw her again. I was leaving the store, small computer in breast pocket, red duct tape and feather duster in a plastic bag. The feather duster was nice, too, in its own understated way. The tips of the feathers had been touched with green paint and one could imagine how nice they would look gliding across oak or cherry or teak. She was sitting in the window of a restaurant across the street talking to someone — someone I couldn't quite see, someone wearing a hat and sunglasses. It certainly did look like her, albeit with one or two of the somewhat important differences I mentioned previously. Sun was flooding the street. It occurred to me that it was perhaps the presence of so much sunlight that made her appear to have changed a little. There had of course been sun, even bright sun, during those other days, but it had not been warm, or only rarely. Most of the time there had been rain. I tried to imagine I was looking at her through the rain. I squinted a little. It helped. Still squinting, I crossed the street and stood outside the window. It was her all right, I thought. As for her interlocutor, I couldn't be certain, but it seemed to me that she was speaking with some difficulty, as if, even, she was stuttering, and it also looked a little like she was holding a gun. Such impressions often prove erroneous, however. In fact, the last time I had seen a person who spoke with a stutter and who seemed to be holding a gun, I was wrong, about the gun part. This was following the conclusion of the task I had undertaken at the outset of my recuperation, some weeks previously. I had performed the task and the lights had come on and all present had nodded and we had all shaken hands and just as they were beginning to clean up the blood someone had said, follow me. We went along dark streets for a while then into a building and up six flights of stairs. I don't mind this, this is great, I said, huffing a bit. Will you please keep your fucking mouth shut, the person I was following said. Then we were at the top and I kind of leaned over and the person told me to kind of stand up and I said hold on just a second and the person gave me a smack. I stood up very straight and we went into an apartment and then into a room and in the room there was a swimming pool lit with golden lights. At the far end of the swimming pool stood the individual with the stutter and the presumptive gun. It's good to see you again, I said. Jump into the pool but don't drown, the person I had been following and who was now standing beside me said. I jumped and did not drown. I am actually a very good underwater swimmer, especially in indoor swimming pools. This has been true since my childhood. During that portion of my life, I was often to be seen in the swimming pool at the local hotel. I excelled at all games that involved retrieving coins from deep water. Others would gather around the edges of the pool to watch me swim from coin to coin, often emptying their own pockets to create what looked to my submerged eyes like a glittering rain. At any rate, as I say, I did not drown, although for a time I did sink. The pool was strangely deep, in fact it was considerably deeper than it was wide, and I was fully clothed. Nevertheless, once I had adjusted, it was nice underwater. It is lovely to see a lit pool from under its surface, lovely to lie on your back near the bottom. Then they fished me out. For a while, I lay on the tiles beside the pool. From where I lay, I could quite clearly see that what I had thought was a gun had not been one. In this case I was not as certain. The bright sun was falling across the table onto both of them and it certainly looked like a gun. I tried mouthing the word, gun, but I am not very adroit at mouthing, so that when she looked up and saw me doing so she raised one eyebrow, frowned, and looked elsewhere. Then I was taken away by two large individuals. They did not speak to me, they just silently invited me into the back of a truck parked some distance down the street then handed me an ice bag and silently invited me to get out. When I returned, she was gone, although the woman who had been holding the gun, or what looked like a gun, was still there. Then I had to go to work. Work, in this reference to it, did not involve the phone call I had received earlier. One of the many interesting aspects of the organization, and I believe I may have touched on this elsewhere, is that there are very few, if any, organic assets who serve the organization full time. As the work is part time and not always very well paid, one finds oneself obliged between assignments to seek gainful employment elsewhere. This had not been the case for me when I had arrived those months, or perhaps years, previously, but now it was. In my previous employment, with another organization, a transactions firm, I had managed to put a certain amount of my compensation aside and, for a time after I had been obliged to leave and had come to this city, had been able to live quite comfortably; i.e., many of my days were spent lying on the floor, staring at the ceiling, listening to the river, or to the rain, or to the falling leaves. That afternoon at work I sold thirty-six cakes and earned compliments from the senior cakeseller, compliments I was only too glad to accept, as my luck with the cakes had not always been excellent. In fact, early in my period of disaffirmation, and up until my recuperation, it was not uncommon for me to sell a mere six or seven cakes over the course of an afternoon. This is not many cakes. Especially since they are attractive cakes. With thick glazing and the scent of fresh lemon and cream. I was not at all astonished then, given the excellence of the cakes and the fine location of the cake stall, as well as the comprehensive nature of my training, that the senior cakeseller expressed a certain amount of disappointment, in the early going, at my poor luck. In that light, it was fortunate that, as far as cakes were concerned, my luck underwent a change. Regarding other aspects of my life I can report that I have registered no such change. For a brief time during the period prior to the events I am now relating, I was under the impression that it had changed, but it had not. I am not very lucky, I told her later that day, when I saw her again, which is to say that I did see and speak to her again, whether or not it was her. We

were sitting in a dark room on a couch and had been discussing science fiction movies, a topic I had proposed.
Certain events were to begin shortly, and until they
began we were obliged, according to instructions, to wait
together in the dark. She had refused to gloss her presence in the room, except to say that it was job related,
and she hadn't asked me why I was there, so I told her
about a movie I had seen recently in which the rocket a
man is riding in loses an engine, forcing him to crash-land
on a planet populated by citizens dressed in iridescent
robes, who enjoy going to the arena, where often there
are gladiators fighting wild pigs. The pigs in the film were
very large, I explained to her, much larger than the average pig and they could fly. Actually it would not be quite
fair to say the pigs could fly. What they could do was
hover. This was described as a form of instinctual levita-
tion. As a young man, subsequent to my coin-diving
period, I knew pigs, our pigs—often I was given the job
of filling up their trough. It was quite a deep trough and
the pigs were frequently hungry and, as I remember it, I
used to hold this against them. Made aware of this, a
friend suggested we hit them with two-by-fours. It was
unclear to us whether or not they noticed. One day having worked with the pigs, I went to school without
changing my shoes. Normally in such instances, the
teacher would strike us with a textbook. That day, however, he instructed me to remove one of my shoes and,
holding it carefully, used it. Basically, the spaceman was
lacking both the tools and the materials to repair his
rocket. There were many shots of the stranded rocket—
a glistening, elongated cone with elegant blue fins. It was
pleasant to hear the people in their iridescent robes who
came daily to offer advice to the spaceman say, titanium.

That's a nice word, isn't it? I said. Yes it is, she said, in fact, right this second it wouldn't be a bad thing to be encased in it. Encouraged, I told her about another movie, this one involving an android whose eyelid function wasn't working, causing it great discomfort. Then I stopped talking because suddenly she was holding my hand. That had not occurred for some time. For quite some time. That her hand seemed larger than it had previously and that her arm against mine seemed slightly longer than previously did not matter in the face of this pleasantness. Do not, under any circumstances, yeah right, I thought, squeezing her hand and sort of humming a little. It is definitely a nice word, she said. Yes it is, I said. Then our period of waiting was over and there were others in the dark room with us. Two of them sat down on the couch. I felt to make sure that the roll of red duct tape was still in my pocket—it was. A moment later, however, it wasn't, and she was no longer holding my hand. After I had finished selling cakes, I went to a small restaurant I know. The restaurant is lit, principally, by yellow bulbs behind yellow shades around which, in the right season, insects circle lazily. The proprietor is a kindly person, and the waiter is neither too quick in his service nor too slow. I ordered, on this occasion, what was described in the menu as "a large piece of meat," and as I waited for it I sipped a pleasant beverage and looked at the other diners. They had all, it seemed, chosen the large portion of meat, and it was agreeable to watch them lift their heavily laden forks and wipe at the corners of their mouths with their napkins. By and by the waiter came to me with my own plate. It is a lovely thing, during those occasional intervals when nothing is all that is required and more, to eat a nice piece of meat in a warm, dimly lit room, one with adequate ventilation, and I was very sad when it was finished. May I take your plate? said the waiter. May I keep it a moment longer? I said. He nodded. There were others in the room sitting over plates glistening with that lovely sheen of residual sauce. And as we sat thus aimless and sated, some of us even dozing in our despondency, the door to the restaurant opened and in walked the woman with the sunglasses and the hat and the stutter, only she was wearing neither hat nor sunglasses, and she did not stutter when she called out to the waiter to bring her a piece of meat, a cup of soup, and a wedge of bread. It was only later, when her meal was finished and she reached into her bag and retrieved those two articles, that she began to stutter. This is one of those instances in which subsequent circumstances stain previous ones. I say this because in thinking about her and the remarkable luminosity of her eyes and the elegant timbre of her voice and the excellent quality of her hair, I remember most clearly sunglasses and stutter and hat. This was due in large part to the fact that once these things were in play she came over to my table and sat down, and the entire restaurant, lovely plates notwithstanding, cleared out, so that it was just the two of us, or perhaps I should say the three of us, because in her hand, and there was no mistaking it this time, was a gun. I do not know if you have been involved in an interaction like the one I then found myself involved in — it was curious. She began to say something, but was unable to say that thing so left off and we sat there. We sat there for quite some time and the only sounds I could make out were the sounds that one hears in one's own body when one is forced to sit so still for so long after such a fine and copious supper, to sit, I might add, in the presence of reflective sunglasses, in which one can see oneself, one's barely palatable self, and in the presence of a large semiautomatic handgun. I sat without moving, of course, and she sat mostly without moving and every few minutes she would attempt to speak. It was something beginning with a sound that involves simultaneously expanding the base of one's throat and contracting it. I know this because I have tried it since, in my free time. I have quite a bit of free time lately. I can tell you that it is pleasant to be aware of having a good deal of free time on one's hands and to just, perhaps humming, sit there. One sits and hums and looks out the small window. Stop humming, someone said. I stopped. We continued to sit there. Occasionally her head would move. I mean apart from when she would make an attempt to speak. We would just sort of be sitting there and her head would turn. Then my head would turn. When hers would, I mean. That began to happen after a time. It was just a slight turn. I could see the motion in her glasses. At some point the waiter came out, very quietly, and brought us each a portion of sorbet. It was a green tea sorbet, quite delicious. We ate it off of very tiny spoons. It was interesting and even pleasant to observe her sucking the sorbet off the spoon while holding the large gun. It really was quite a large gun. Clearly, many a caliber could be propelled through it. I wondered, if the gun went into action, if it would strike me in the breast. No doubt it was wondering this that put me in mind of the hero, who, his invulnerability having been called into question, was able to maintain the illusion of it by the fact that when presently he was fired upon, the projectile that struck him lodged in the address book he was carrying in his breast pocket. I understand that, relatively speaking, it can be quite elegant to be struck by a projectile in the breast. I am told that, unlike the head or the groin or the stomach, the chest bleeds quite beautifully, that sometimes the escaping lines of blood make marvelous patterns. She began to say something. She stopped. It was all quite intricate. Then she lifted her hand and someone came up behind me and said, don't fuck it up tonight, we'll be watching you, now get out. Back on the street it was evening and for a while I just walked around. Any city on a warm evening is probably just as lovely as this one. Not true. I have been in more than one city on a warm evening that was unlovely. This one wasn't. I walked for a time. I lost myself. It is a very pleasant city, and, in that regard, holds on the crowded boulevards, deep within a variety of circumstances, the evening walkers, myriad undulations, under the fountains, once or twice crestfallen, as we speak. Obligatory pitfalls often mitigated, though always not, etc., or not always. I was told once in a big bed in the countryside by the woman I loved that what made it always so difficult, all of it, was being an interior in a world of exteriors. The skin embraces while the bones, stripped of their flesh and fat, long to click and knock against each other. It is only when the skin is gone and the flesh, a function of decay, releases its water that they finally heap the bones together, she supposed, but this is too late. Just as, as I slowly, in a manner of speaking, returned to myself, it occurred to me that everything was too late, but I kept walking. This is likely, I said to myself, reverting to my earlier line of thought on the city's loveliness, due to a variety of factors, a few of which involve the city's physical attributes, that is to say its tendency, generally, to undulate. I have always supported, in a city, a well-balanced street-to-structure ratio, and this one certainly enjoys that. Also, here there are many spaces that are empty, or only partially filled, and the people can enter them. Or, if these spaces are in some way partitioned off, at the very least the people can approach and, at leisure, allow their eyes to explore them. For many it is preferable, of course, to be able to physically enter, or, with the very real possibility of doing so, to think of entering, to stroll, for example, without strolling, across deliciously clear spaces or among trees. I am of those who find it unbearably lonely to actually enter such places. This is true most days. It is not lonely, however, on the mornings when the colorful stalls have been set up in part of a given space and the wares have been displayed, and the men and women call out words and numbers to you as you walk. And occasionally, then, of course, you purchase something, and the person you have purchased that thing from, while perhaps not ecstatic, is pleased, and you are pleased and occasionally ecstatic, even if you happen to be alone. I do not count circus tents as structures either and once, in the middle of a very large space, upon the conclusion of a certain piece of business, I went to one. Also, of course, there are movies to go to, and that brings up the aspect, added to space, of mediated light and dark, and in this city there is plenty of that. There are plenty of movie theaters where you sit alone or in company and watch rocket ships and androids and points of light and, that world, of movie theaters, is both light and dark and dark and light, as it is on the streets in the evening in this city, with the dark, quiet crowds, and the undulations, and the lights coming on. The lights were coming on. Suddenly I realized I had forgotten my hat. I retraced my steps and reentered the restaurant, which, now crowded again, was bright with the sound of forks falling and rising and of mouths being filled. The woman who was the woman with the sunglasses and the handgun had been replaced by the woman who at any time might become that woman, but currently was not. I forgot my hat, I said. I know, she said. She waved to the waiter who disappeared then reappeared with a hat, but it was not my hat, and I told them so. This sequence repeated itself. I'm sorry, I said. What kind of hat was it? she asked. I explained that it was quite similar to the variety of hat that she occasionally wore. And you are sure you left it here? I nodded. Because I don't think he has it, she said, lifting her chin and pointing with it at the waiter. The waiter, very politely, shrugged. Have a seat, she said. Do you have any aspirin? I said. She produced a small bottle. The waiter brought me a glass of water. I sat. She seemed to be wearing some sort of scent, and after a moment I made mention of this. She thanked me. I ordered a coffee. When it came, I inserted a certain amount of sugar. So much sugar, she observed. I explained to her that I had lately become quite devoted to it. We then discussed sugar for a while. It is quite a thrilling substance, I said. A world without fructose, maltose, sucrose, or even glucose, she mused. The thought, we both agreed, was profoundly distressing. I confessed to her that I often dreamed about sugar, most frequently, although I had not yet determined why, of raffinose. Ah raffinose, she said. We then spoke of eggs for a time. She was a partisan of whites, I of yolks. I asked her what she did. She told me she worked part time as the coach of a swim team. We discussed swimming. I told her how much I liked to swim underwater in indoor pools and she asked me what stroke I used. I told her that I hadn't thought of there being strokes for underwater swimming.

She assured me that there were. I suggested that at some point she could give me some instruction, and she said she would be delighted and that as a matter of fact she was free right then. I thanked her for her generous offer, but told her that I was feeling a touch out of sorts, as I had had quite a shock that morning, and in fact again that afternoon. What kind of a shock? she asked. I saw someone, I said. That can be a shock, she agreed. We then spoke for a few minutes on the subject of the shocking quality of, as we saw it, the larger part of interactions. It really gets to be a problem, I said. One finds oneself becoming hesitant to relinquish the horizontal position each morning, she said. I asked her if she had a boyfriend. She didn't answer. I used to have a girlfriend, I said. And was she lovely? Yes, she was. It's nice when they are lovely—often they aren't. How did you meet her? It had to do with a stapler. Is she who you saw again today? I think so. Incidentally, she then asked me, how do you feel about justice? About what? Justice. I prefer other subjects. So you don't care to discuss whether or not those who have committed errors should be judged. Oh, well, that, sure, I'm all for that, I said. And do you think it is a process that should be interfered with / impeded / obstructed / disturbed? Either, I mean, in cases affecting your own person or in cases affecting others. I believe in 100 percent compliance, I said. And have you always? I've learned from my mistakes. That's a good answer. What are you going to do to her? To whom? To my sweetheart. I don't know who you are talking about. I think you do. I think, she said, reaching out her hand and placing it, for a moment, on my forearm, that your line of commentary is becoming inappropriate. She then asked if I would like some more sugar. I told her I would.

As the bowl had become empty, she waved to the waiter and very graciously made my desire known to him and then very graciously said she must be going and that, if I wished, I could accompany her. She had a small errand to run, a little business to attend to, and then we could continue our conversation, or could do as we desired, do whatever it was that we wanted, perhaps swimming and even swimming underwater, she knew a nice pool, one that was beautifully lit and deep. I thanked her for the offer, which, I said, was very kind, but confessed that my discomfiture seemed suddenly to have accelerated and that unfortunately I did not feel at all like swimming. I'm sorry to hear that, she said. But I do think that the aspirin has done the trick, I said. Well that's something, anyway. We shook hands. I watched her leave. When I got out on the street I went over to a pay phone and made a quick call. Then I threw up. A gentleman passing by asked me if I was all right. I said I was not. He asked if I required assistance. I told him I did not. I must insist, he said. Oh, I said. It was the guy from that morning in my apartment. He was wearing the same hat and shorts only now he had added an elegant lightweight hunting cape, because the evening air, as he put it, had become a touch fresh. For my part, I do not become much concerned by minor shifts in the weather and am quite comfortable in my shorts in a wide range of temperatures. I have shorts in a variety of lengths, some quite long, some quite short, although lately, concomitant with the general expansion of my proportions, I have found myself less likely to opt for short shorts. It has become, quite simply, unbecoming. I know this for a fact, because one day when I was sitting on the terrace of an establishment enjoying a beverage and hard-boiled egg a passerby told me so. That, quite frankly sir, is unbecoming, the passerby said. Have you finished throwing up? the gentleman said. I told him that I could not be certain, but that I thought so. Splendid, he said. I told him that I did not think that anything, right at that moment, could be called splendid. At this he launched into a rather lengthy disquisition on the subject of a raise that he had just that day received. Oh yeah? I said, sort of leaning against a wall. Oh yes, he said. By the way, shouldn't you be putting on your sunglasses? This was true. I had, officially, gone on the clock when I had made the phone call. I reached into my pocket, but they were gone too. I don't have them, I said. Don't you carry a spare? I do not. But this is relatively terrible. It was—one was required by recent directive to wear sunglasses when carrying out official duties. Hats, while recommended, were optional—sunglasses were not. Perhaps I could borrow yours, I said. Perhaps you certainly could not. Well then what about your spares? I'm sorry, but if I gave you my spares then I wouldn't have them in the event that I misplaced my own. He had a point. The only thing to do was to buy a new pair. Why I was unable to do so is a long story, one that does not, suffice it to say, recommend itself to retelling, except to mention that a display case got broken and a lot of stairs were climbed. Well that was a complete fucking waste of time, I said to him an hour later. It certainly the fuck was, let's go have a snack, he said. We found a small shop that sold fried potatoes, of the variety that one dips into a white sauce or into a red-and-white sauce onto which one sprinkles bits of chopped raw onion. I like that variety of fried potato and so did my companion. Well, I said. Yes, he said. We had both, during the search for a suitable pair of sunglasses, become rather tense, and eating the generous portions of thick warm potatoes soothed us. During the search, I had twice dropped the roll of red duct tape and had slightly damaged the feather duster and had also suddenly grown worried about the durability of the small computer, and he had spoken at great length about very little. I would be the first to admit to a tendency to speak too much during tense situations, but in this regard my companion far surpassed me. He was also, in my estimation, fatter than I was, his earlier remarks about me notwithstanding, and to be honest I did not think all that much of his hunting cape. Well, I said. Yes, he said. I ate a couple more potatoes then, still savoring the warm salts and oils, being aware of their residue on my lips, I asked him to what I owed the great pleasure of his company this time. I have a message for you. Can I have it? Not without sunglasses on. Well can you tell me what it's about? No, I cannot. Not even a hint? He shook his head. For a couple more minutes we just sat there eating potatoes. Then I had an idea. Hey, Sport, I said. I told him what I was thinking. Okay, that might work, he said. We shook hands then approached each other and he took out his spare sunglasses and, without letting go of them, slipped them onto my face. This procedure obliged us to sit in extreme proximity and allowed me to see more than I would have liked to of his mouth. Have you ever watched a mouth talk from about seven inches away? A mouth that does not belong to a loved or even tolerated one? One that has just been eating fried potatoes with sauce? I was glad I had the sunglasses on to kind of dim things up. But it was a good message, better than average, very interesting. It was a little confusing, there were a couple of spots I'd clearly have to chew on, to make better sense of, but all in all it was surprisingly clear. I had received messages before that were not at all clear, and had suffered the consequences. E.g., not very long before these events I had received a message and proceeded to purchase, instead of a player, a recorder, a very nice one with a black body and turquoise buttons, one that was absolutely incapable of playing. I had arrived near the beginning of things rather than, as I was supposed to have been told or to have understood, at the middle, so that what was supposed to have been played near the end of things, wasn't played at all. It wasn't played at all because I didn't have a player, not because of when I arrived—I realize that. I kept the recorder. I also kept what I recorded. It is not what you would call easy listening. It is remarkable the subtlety of the sounds that recording device was able to register. A friend for whom I played the tape commented on this and referred to the range of sounds as texture. This has texture, she said. I asked him to repeat the message. He did so then started to take off the glasses, but I pulled them back on. Who gave you the message? I said. I can't tell you, he said. Did she give it to you? Is she in trouble? Who do you mean by she? She, I said. I can't tell you. Won't tell or don't know? I have delivered my message. Tell me. At this point I had him in a choke hold. It was by no means an impressive choke hold, but it had some effect on him, because after not very many seconds of being choked he said, okay I'll tell you. I loosened up a little. When I did, he leaned back and rubbed at his throat. I am, on occasion, capable of surprising myself. I enjoy such occasions. Though that should not be taken to imply that I enjoy surprise in general. I do not. I did not, for example, enjoy the surprise I experienced later that evening, if you could call it that, I'm not sure you could.

He exhaled. I ate a potato. Then he answered my questions. Who gave you the message? The central office. The Stutter? The Stutter. So it wasn't her. I don't know who you mean. Is it a setup of any kind? I don't know, probably. What's my part? I haven't been told. And is she involved? I don't know. Who is it I am supposed to sit next to on the couch? A fellow participant. And who is the subject? I was not informed. I paused a moment to take this in. Nothing, or very little, seemed to enter. Excuse me a moment, I said, suddenly yanking the sunglasses out of his hands, I have to use the facility. May I have my second pair of sunglasses back before you do? I'll only be a moment. He said nothing and when I got back he was gone. Hah! I said. But then he jumped me when I got outside the fried potato establishment. He moved very well for a larger individual, placing his knuckles where they were sure not to damage his glasses. Nice, I thought. Very nice. Then he knocked me out. When I came to I was somewhat disoriented and for a moment was under the impression that a woman was standing over me, a lovely woman in possession of nimbly locking joints and great general fluidity of aspect and intent, in fact, great everything, but I was wrong. There was a woman standing over me, but she was very tall and very skinny and short on fluidity and she was waving a deck of cards. Pick a card, I'll get it right this time, she said. You were right about the horse, I said. What horse? she said. She was no longer the same woman. This woman was quite interesting. I had had several dealings with her, often of the pleasant variety. Usually we had frequented her quarters, which were well-situated and comfortable and had a wonderful bed. It was large and firm and much, if one had the inclination, could be done on it. My own bed, incidentally, is some distance from what one might consider comfortable. Which is not to say that I dislike my bed. Often during my recuperation, I would lie on it and listen to the river that flows near my apartment. I would sigh and the phone would ring and I would never answer it. Food would appear at the kitchen table, very simple dishes, quite easy to chew and digest, which, in the evenings, I would leave my bed to eat. Then I might take a soothing bath with large sponges and fragrant salts, and one day when I went into the bathroom this woman was there, already in the tub, and she had with her the aforementioned green plastic duck. Good lord, I said. Unusually nice, huh? she said. I immediately sat down on the edge of the tub and we talked. I asked her how business was and she said business had not been good lately, not enough coins and no bills were being left in her hat, although her repertoire had expanded and she had made certain innovations that had positively affected both her voice and her playing. Well that's encouraging anyway, I said. Then she pulled me into the water and, when I was further recovered, I went to spend time in her bed. You need to get up now, she said. What? I said, opening my eyes. Beside my head, faintly pressed into the concrete, was the imprint of a hand. Not a large hand. Perhaps a child's. Or not quite a child's. It was somewhat larger, the digits thicker. There was water in the little finger. Had it rained? I remembered something. Another city. Many years before. Being dead. It is almost time, said the woman. I looked at my watch. I was no longer wearing a watch. But then I remembered that the small computer I had acquired was capable of giving the time in several zones. Which zone are we in? I asked her as I stood and extricated the small computer, which, in its protective case, seemed to be undamaged. Put that away and follow me, she said. But I don't have any sunglasses, I said. She did not appear to hear me and set off walking, so I set off walking after her and I could not, in following her, help remarking the fine articulation of the muscles in her calves and the near proportionate slimness of her ankles, which put me in mind, as we walked along the deserted street, of another pair of calves and ankles and of other things, which, so thinking, reminded me of a film I had seen recently in which a robot follows another robot through the desert. It was a fine movie with great dark cities and burned plains set against the backdrop of galactic empires and frightening weather patterns, and this aging robot, or rather this robot who thinks he / she / it is aging and cannot stop thinking of days gone by. It is never made quite clear what has set this robot, after 7,000 years of service, to, as he / she / it puts it, dwelling. I cannot stop dwelling he / she / it says at one point to a companion robot. This must be your fatal error, the companion robot says, not without a touch of awe. They speak, of course, without lips and with lights flashing and have large, boxy heads, but their voices betray much feeling. In conversation recently I was told that my own voice betrayed much feeling, that my interlocutor could detect in it a distinct trembling. It is trembling because I am afraid, I told my interlocutor. Afraid of me? Yes. It is this companion robot who does not know what his / her / its own fatal error is or will be, who precedes our hero out into the desert at film's end. The two robots walk slowly out into the sandy wastes, and our hero, watching the small, blinking, turquoise lights on the backs of the other robot's knees, thinks of other small blinking lights that he / she / it has seen over the course of his / her / its

7,000 years, and perhaps later dreamed of, for these robots dream occasionally—they refer to it as being "on in off mode." They even have nightmares. This they refer to as being "on off in off mode." I have nightmares. I think I have addressed this elsewhere. Once, recently, however, I was on off in off mode and saw electric horses fighting slowly in a forest. It was, I think, the remembered slowness of their battle that most troubled me upon waking, and the fact that when they noticed I was there they tore me, slowly, to pieces. This was not very long ago. Also not very long ago, it occurred to me that perhaps what I was most lacking, even more than a sturdy cerebellum, were solid grounds for my argument, that in fact my argument, such as it was, was utterly groundless—where did it come from? relative to what did it exist? I say to myself: I have a hand, I know that this is my hand, but can only mean very little by it. At one point during the movie, a robot of a different variety asks our hero—who is wanted by the authorities for not having debatteritized another robot, that is, for not having terminated it, our hero is a "central matrix assassin"—what it is like to be on in off mode, could it be viewed as analogous to being off in on mode. No, he / she / it responds, adding that the phenomenon only ever merits discussion when, in instances of being on off in off mode, it is troubling. My matrix has never been troubled, the robot of a different variety says. Then you do not understand, our hero says. At this point the conversation is terminated because the authorities have arrived. There is a terrific robot fight involving serrated pincers and curious threats and our hero escapes. It is at this juncture that the robot with the turquoise lights comes into the story and that their adventures in common begin. All in all it was one of the best films of the science fiction genre in the style of some years ago that I have seen, and I had hoped to discuss part of it with her, in addition to the other films I mentioned above, as we sat on the couch together, not too many minutes after I looked at those ankles and calves and thought of her ankles and calves, or at any rate of ankles and calves that I had loved fiercely as a subset of an individual I had been in love with, fiercely, once upon a time. Incidentally, it is fall again—here, now. The streets are quiet and the people begin to move more quickly. The glass in my windows is cold. Leaves drop from the trees. I hunt for warm pastries in the bakeries. I steal cakes at work. There are always crumbs caught in the sugary oil around my mouth. None of this is true, of course. I mean in the sense that it is actually the case, that it occurs, or that it can be confirmed. But that is saying and making too much of too little. She refused to answer any of my questions about what she was doing there, then we sat down on the couch together, is the way it went. The couch was structured so as to elevate one each of our buttocks, in my case the left, in hers the right. There were many other couches in the room and chairs set close to each other and many discreet alcoves and from them, as we settled ourselves, we began to hear a faint murmuring. I've missed you, I said. And I you, she said. Would you like me to sing for you? Yes I would. I sang. She was silent. Why did you come back? I never left. I thought you were dead or that you had betrayed me. I was, she said, I did. I then suggested that we make love. The conversation sort of fell off for a time after this, so I started regaling her with film-related anecdotes and descriptions, which I think she found quite entertaining. My interpolations, however, were cut short when it became apparent that we were no longer alone in the room. This is not to say that we had ever been alone in the room—clearly, given the murmuring, we had not. It is just that all those who had been implicitly present, on their own couches, so to speak, had not yet rendered themselves explicitly present, and I think you will agree that that is a very different sort of thing. At any rate, there they all suddenly were, and there we were, being crowded by some of them on the couch, meaning, according to our instructions, that it was time to begin the substantive part of the operation, a prospect that left me a little cold—we had been holding hands, sort of, and her hand, even if altered, had felt wonderful to me. Just before we braced ourselves to leap up off the couch and begin propagating ourselves through the treacherous dark, I whispered, we'll meet afterward, and she said, of course we will. Usually I enjoy these assignments. One is obliged to operate in dark rooms in which many pieces of furniture are present, so that one must move gingerly, which I enjoy, for as long as it is appropriate. One is always in company and, while the tasks of all those present are distinct, they are far from unconnected. Also, in such a unanimous dark, where one moves across thick carpet and there are always many couches and heavy wall hangings and pieces of soft furniture present, pleasant encounters can occur. Once, for example, I lifted a velvet tablecloth and, letting it drop behind me, found myself in a dark set off from the greater dark in which there was another, some other, come here, she said. And, as we lay a moment later tightly locked, the perfumed air beneath the table was pierced by a scream. It occurs to me that I have forgotten something. This occurred earlier, prior to my acquisition of the small computer and subsequent to my acquisition of the lovely red duct tape and the rather ordinary feather duster. What occurred is I stopped off at a lecture which was to have taken place in a small amphitheater in one of the side wings of a very great and very old university. The lecture was to have been on the subject of the horse in medieval courtly romances. There was to have been a detailed analysis of the number of lines in such romances given over to descriptions of horses and of the categories of horses described. Also there was to have been a slide show, of representations of horses, one of which was to have been an image, from the fifteenth century, of horses fighting in a forest, and I was eager to see this. But the lecture had been canceled. To fill up the time I had allotted for it I went out into the university's courtyard and sat on the steps between a pair of statues and drank coffee from a small plastic cup and looked at the students and wished that I was one. I had been one. In another country. Before I became involved with organizations and evening missions and amateur opera companies. I was actually a pretty good student and frequently earned relatively unqualified compliments from my instructors. I spoke to other students and they spoke to me. It was one of those students who introduced me to representatives of the first organization I had dealings with, the transactions firm. He later told me that he had done this out of friend-ship for me, but that he had made a mistake — I was actu-ally poorly qualified. He was highly qualified. And very popular. Especially with female individuals. I don't know what has become of him. It's possible that he has retired. Maybe he was disaffirmed or killed. When my allotted time had expired I: left the university, went to a nearby park, took out my knife, inspected the blade, found it satisfactory, cut open the tip of my finger, watched the finger, sucked the finger, felt happy, smiled at some guys who thought I hadn't noticed them trailing me, then, the bleeding slowly stopping, as it usually does, took out the feather duster and whittled the butt end of its handle into a sharp point. Which proved to be effective. In fact afterward I received a compliment, in writing, on the innovative quality of the instrument I had provided for that evening's exercise. At the bottom of the sheet of paper, which read,

compliment

was typed, "a copy of this official compliment will be placed in your file." I was later able to confirm that this had been done. This confirmation took place just recently and is, in its posteriority to the events I have been describing, somewhat irrelevant. I have worked very hard in my life, on occasion, if not to avoid irrelevance, then at least to recognize it. A colleague of mine, when I was holding forth on the subject at one point, remarked that a certain amount of irrelevance was inherent in any organic asset; that, in fact, irrelevance constituted a key difference between organic and technical assets. To illustrate this point, my colleague related a story in which a young man, a visitor in a far-off country, climbed a fence to enter a baseball game and found himself being beaten almost to death for having done so. He further illustrated his point by describing, in some detail, the working parts of a telephone receiver. So you see, he said. I do not quite, I said. Which did not bother him in the slightest and he let it go at that, but I have continued to consider it, this difference, it intrigues me. It is that way, she said.

Which way? I said. We had been walking for some time, and I had not, I should clarify, spent the whole time looking at her ankles and calves and being put in mind of epic movies about assassin robots that have begun to dwell. A good part of the time I had spent looking around me — at the people, who were varied as to aspect and attitude, at the cars, some of which I coveted, at the shops and doors and lampposts, which presented themselves, for the most part, in the standard one after the other fashion, although occasionally the odd group of doors and lampposts would arrive all at once. Is that irrelevant? I wondered. I wondered what my small computer would have said. It said several things that evening, and especially the next day at the trial, but none of them, I think, addressed this point. Once "Tuesday" blinked. And on the twenty-fourth there was a rendezvous scheduled with a certain individual. It was possible to have an overview of the events of an entire week or month or year or even half-decade, and to see them listed, before and after the fact, categorically, chronologically, and in order of priority. I must confess to having a penchant for the last. I once spent considerable time with an individual who ostensibly preferred the first. She would have pretended, that is, to have liked to know all meetings on a Tuesday afternoon at the cafeteria in the train station with a particular woman in the past year. Or all purchases of items costing between X and X purchased on behalf of whom for whom, etc. I should say I *think* she was pretending — I was never able to verify this. In fact, it was really little more than a hunch. Speaking of pretending, for a time afterward I used to pretend she was still there. I would greet myself and have small conversations. Usually I would do this in the dark, although once I did it on the terrace of a café. No fruitcakes, the waiter said. For my part, I have no particular interest in categories. That is to say that I am only ever interested in knowing when there is an unpleasant duty coming up. One was coming up. The fact that I had seen her then had seen her in the company of an individual holding a gun and had subsequently had a gun held on me was indicative. It's that way, she said. Can't you come with me? I said. Or perhaps I thought it. One thinks many things, of course, some interesting, most not. Here, she said. She handed me a pair of sunglasses. My sunglasses. Where did you get these? Never mind. And what about my hat? I don't know anything about the hat. Well it's a nice one. It suddenly occurs to me that I am approaching the end. Yes, I said. At the end. I said some other things before this. I am thinking of one strange sentence in particular. Hard to believe I uttered it. Did I utter it? I'm getting confused. Thanks for the sunglasses, I said. You're welcome, she said. I put them on. We had been traveling through progressively smaller and narrower streets, which were also progressively darker streets, streets lit only by lanterns hanging from hooks above the doors or candles on the inside of the occasional window. It was a disgrace, really. I think if there is one thing a modern city is obliged to do it is to pump light into its streets. Millions of gallons of light should always be available, indoors or out, at the flick of a switch or the pulling down of a lever or cord. Ideally, of course, the intensity of the light could be modulated. I am not advocating some kind of universal brightness here. I am not fond of glare and so, while wishing to be adequately lit in my nocturnal endeavors, I would wish also to be gently, even tenderly lit, but here is my point, I was hardly lit at all. So you can imagine what it was like with sunglasses. To their credit, these sunglasses are of the variety that permits one to see quite well in varying conditions; dark to very dark, however, is not one of them. Still, I made my way forward as best I could, and, in so propagating myself, arrived at a low door that sat in the center of an enormous wall. You will pass through a low door then a large courtyard at the center of which is a fountain where you may refresh yourself, my latest guide had told me as soon as I had put on the sunglasses. Once you have or have not refreshed yourself at the fountain, you will exit the large courtyard, where they used to slaughter live-stock and wash linen and pluck fowl and hold dances and weave baskets, and where a middle-aged man was once flogged for having stolen two eggs, and enter a smaller courtyard in which they did nothing, just walked through, at the far end of which there is a tree. Climb the tree. I was in the tree. Now the trick was, she had told me, to move out to the end of one of its branches and step onto a balcony, only there was no balcony, just a window. I went out to the edge of one of the branches. There were cracking noises. Small ones mostly. Then I fell. And fell—clear through the floor of the courtyard and farther, we're talking sub-sub-basement, and, I have to give myself and my training (the organization offers occa-sional seminars) some credit, I didn't scream, just gave a little yelp, not much more than a squeak, which was good because I landed in a huge pile of old hay. Pure fantasy. There was a door in a high wall, but all that happened was I rang a bell, was admitted, and went up an elevator that opened with a soft, electric swoosh directly onto the room in which there sat, among other pieces, a fine red couch in the center of which was a young or youngish woman who looked somewhat familiar. You haven't changed, I said. You have, she said. Basically, I thought you were dead. You've already said that. So you were just reassigned. There was no assignment. You were disaffirmed? I would prefer not to discuss it. What would you like to discuss? I would like to discuss this couch. In the old days you would have wanted to acquire it. Would I have? I think so. Why would I have? I was never quite sure. You weren't? I shook my head. That's a little sad. It was. I was sitting in a pile of damp hay. It took me a moment to disengage myself. In the process of doing so it occurred to me that someone should be made aware that damp hay had been known to spontaneously combust. This had happened once in my youth, in the middle of the night. We all rushed out to the barn, but by the time we got there all we could do was watch. For some reason my father wanted my sisters and I to sleep with him that night. I remember it occurred to me that his breathing, in the midst of all the other breathing, was precarious, which later got shifted in my head to precious, the eight shared letters. Then relatives, mostly, came and took us away with them. Leaving the hay behind, I moved through the room toward a bar of light. All around me, small things scurried and something was growling, but, in accordance with my training, I walked rather than ran. The bar of light was attached to a door. The door was unlocked. The room I entered was lit with rows of torches and there were columns with bright red dragons painted on them. There were also many figures moving slowly around a square pool. Hey, excuse me, what the fuck is this? I asked one of them, but he / she didn't answer, so I continued across the room and entered another, no door this time just an arch, this room larger still and lit by trees upon which hung some kind of gorgeously glowing fruit. About this couch, she said. I've been sitting here wondering, and you will think this is silly, if it is still red when the lights are turned off. Yeah? I said. I mean that it continues to be a red couch, will continue to be so when, in a few minutes, they extinguish the lights. Aren't the lights already extinguished? Not yet. Then, yes. Yes what? Yes I think that it will be. Will remain red? Yes. I could see it. Sitting there in the dark being red. Just as, similarly, I could see that her eyes, when I could no longer see them (I could no longer see them), remained blue. Yeah? she said. Yeah, I said. My eyes aren't blue. Technically, this was true. The woman with whom I was speaking (she lifted her sunglasses—a breach of protocol—as I illuminated the small computer) was in possession of brown eyes, or maybe they were green. Strange to relate, however, that when she replaced her sunglasses, her eyes immediately reverted to blue. Perhaps, then, it is green in the dark. The couch? Yes, or violet. Violet is a good color. Personally, I can't stand it. It reminds me, she said. Of what? Something many years ago, never mind. Who are you? Does it matter? Are you here because you're in trouble? Yes. Was I once in love with you? Maybe. You aren't allowed to steal those, someone said. I had leaned into one of the glowing trees and had my hand around one of the mildly ovoid pieces of fruit. I see you managed to acquire a pair of sunglasses. I see you managed to get your fat ass back into my business, I said, declamping my hand from the piece of fruit and making to clamp it on the son of a bitch's throat. We did a kind of a dance, a dance lit by the gently glowing trees. It's actually rather pretty to think of— my hands going after his neck and his neck retreating from my hands and somewhere water was running and I think there might have been a light breeze. Time out, I said after a while, huffing a little. Both of us put our hands on our knees for a minute. You ready? I said. He nodded. I leapt for his throat. He backpedaled and pivoted and stuck out his foot and I fell and he put his boot on the back of my neck. Are you finished? he asked. Yeah, I said. He removed his boot and I stood and brushed off my shorts and he said no hard feelings? and I was just about to say, yeah right, you big fucking jerk, when he pulled a thick envelope out of his pocket and offered it to me. Which was actually quite a decent gesture. Almost anyone would have to admit. So I took the envelope and he stated his business, which was that he had been instructed to take me the last leg of the journey, which, once I had finished counting the contents of the envelope, he proceeded to do. We left the room of the glowing fruit trees and entered a room where toys were being made. Here there were many workshops lit with colored lanterns and candles made of multicolored wax. We walked by workshop after workshop, and the crafts-people held up for our perusal perfectly determined tin solar systems, singing robots, and glistening segments of train track. I knew a couple of the toy makers, one of them, for example, was the waiter from the restaurant where I had supped, and it was not unpleasant to stop a moment and converse with him. My guide had found his earlier form and was proving very agile with the repartee, and we all laughed quite a bit and found ourselves forced to stifle our laughter so as not to disturb the other workers, who occasionally lifted their heads and shot us disapproving glances. After a few more moments of conversation, the waiter invited me to step across the room for a glass of something, which, taking momentary leave of my guide, I did. A word of advice, he said. Yes? I said. Call it off. Call what off? What it is you're doing. What *am* I doing? I'm not sure. But you want me to call it off? That's right. Did someone tell you to say that? Yes. Did you steal my hat? The young lady did. Which young lady? The one who came in to dine after your departure. My first departure or my second? Your second. And you say she stole my hat? I may have the sequence of events wrong. Well I can't call it off. Why not? Because I'm already there. How's that? In the room. It's dark. We've already started. Someone just screamed. There were several other rooms, all of them pleasant, none of them real, and then my guide and I rode up an elevator and shook hands and he said, we've arrived at last, and I said, thank you for the envelope, and he said, you are welcome, and I closed my eyes, and when I opened them he was no longer there. I walked through a door and found her standing in the center of the room and she said, I want to get out of here, right now, so we made for the door but a large individual appeared, shaking her head. Then I was moving gingerly through the warm dark with my arms outstretched, palpitating the occasional object—a table, a chair, a sharpened feather duster, a roll of red tape. That I had, in my palpitations, placed my hands on these objects, which upon entering I had placed in a drawer as per my instructions delivered over fried potatoes earlier, was quite significant. The procedure was regulated by rules which stipulated that if your hands closed over certain preselected objects you used them. Prior to that evening, my role in those proceedings had consisted in, among other things, transporting the evening's realia— always different—and then standing very still in a corner;

or in acting as a placer of the preselected objects, so that the key person, as it were, would find them. That I had been selected to play a substantive role, and not just a tangential one, was an unexpected development, and it was with both pride and trepidation that as the instructions began to be delivered over the intercom, instructions that were meant only for the holder of the preselected objects—take two steps forward, one left, not such a big step, three right—I began to move forward and left and then right as the others stood or sat or hid or lay together waiting. One of them marked the end of my itinerary, though none of them, as they waited, knew who had been chosen or who was coming or what exactly beyond unpleasantness would occur. At certain junctures I was prompted to say, I am coming, and so I said, I am coming, several times, and moved through the dark and, moving slowly, following their instructions, right then left then left then right, arrived at my terminus. Once, as we sat in the tub watching the green rubber duck float poorly between us, my acquaintance of the glamorous proportions and of the evocative calves and ankles, recounted the following anecdote. It appears that some time ago, she said, a certain party, A, was obliged to murder a certain party B. However, this obligation was complicated, as it occurred, by the need first to murder parties C, D, and E, none of whom, when A began, had yet been located. Why did A first have to murder C, D, and E? I asked. Because it was an essential part of the mechanism that A, or the person for whom A acted as instrument, had elaborated. I see. Yes. Did A find C? And D. But not E? It was necessary to substitute. F? F escaped. Was there a G? Yes, G, in effect, became E. So then B became possible. Yes, it all worked out in the end.

I, too, was a part of something rather elaborate once, I said, giving the rubber duck, listing rather precariously at that moment, a shove. It was interesting and elaborate and also had a mechanism, albeit rather an indeterminate one. It involved fixed and moving points, some of which converged, and others of which dispersed. I ran first through streets and gardens and then through a woods. In the distance, it was possible to hear dogs barking. Occasionally in my running I would intersect with another point and we would confer. Then a siren sounded and we all went to see what there was to be seen but there was little left. When I had finished recounting this anecdote she sort of looked at me, then said, your anecdote is lovely, you may keep the duck. The duck? Yes, the duck. That is how I got the duck, which I think I still have. Is that you? I whispered. I was standing in the warm dark holding a sharpened feather duster. Not a duck. The duck never leaves my apartment. The duck is not really all that interesting. Not nearly as interesting as the gift I had been given previously by the individual I now imagined was standing before me in the dark, was breathing before me in the dark, and which I keep always in my pocket and that seems impervious to explanation, although I do make some attempt in my description of those earlier events, not an entirely successful one. Then I went home to bed. I mean after the entire affair had been completed. What affair besides the breathing? you might well be asking. But by then I was already fast asleep. Here is what I dreamed. The two of us are sitting at the edge of a castle wall. There is a considerable drop-off and I am concerned about her proximity to it. She, of course, finds my concern suspicious. I didn't want to do it, I say. Oh, but you did it, didn't you, she answers. And in a moment, even here, my erstwhile lover, you will push me off this wall and that will be that. But I wasn't even sure that it was you. And why should that matter? Before I could answer, I woke to someone pounding on my door. I opened it and a very small man came in. Are you the detective? I asked. He nodded, then told me that I was required to answer a number of questions. Okay, but can we do it over breakfast? I asked. He shook his head. It won't take long, he said. It didn't, I suppose. But by the time he had left I was ravenous and began ripping the cupboards apart. No sooner, however, had I settled into some breakfast—a very beautiful loaf of bread, an excellent jar of fig jam—then someone else started pounding on the door. Uh, hi, I said, who are you? We are the police, you are under arrest, they said. Well can I be arrested after I have completed my breakfast? They looked at each other. Couple gals with big hair. One of them said, he is resisting arrest. I said, I am not. But they clobbered me just the same. In the instance of unconsciousness they knocked me into I was back on the castle wall alone. I really didn't mean to, I said, my voice seeming to echo. I didn't mean to all that much. I was lacking information. There was a key string missing from the sequence. Then I came to because someone was shaking me. As I have said, the organization I work for is very large, and while it is clear that the concept of large, and certainly of very large, is relative, there is about it a sense of comprehensiveness, of saturation even, such that some days one sees very many pairs of sunglasses in the city indeed. One sees also, of course, very many hats and hunting capes on individuals not wearing sunglasses. I find it an excellent aspect of the organization that its sunglasses, so to speak, can come off. Mine, you will have noticed, were off during a significant portion of this narrative. I am quite proud of that fact. One learns to plant the flag of triumph where one can. At any rate, the organization is large and within that largeness it expands and contracts, sunglasses coming on and off, and individuals arriving—just as I had arrived that previous autumn—and individuals leaving and going far away, like I have now done. Or will do. Soon. I have it in writing. Of course "leaving the organization" should also be understood in a relative sense. The process of leaving is rife with conditions and stipulations, and you often come back even when you don't want to. That was her case, I'm sure. In fact, I asked her and she said, yes, you're absolutely right, the fuckers made me come back. But at any rate, the organization does claim to arrange for the eventual permanent relocation of its assets, organic and otherwise—this is advertised in one of its many brochures. I once, however, went to the relocation office listed in the brochure, in hopes of scheduling an eventual exit interview, and found only a vacant lot. At the back of the lot a notice was posted to the effect that several years hence the ground would be broken for the office. The notice was not dated. Obviously, now I've admitted that I have nothing in writing, no written guarantee. We'll run away, I said. What? she said. We'll run, I think I can get us out of here. We will not. Why not? Because there are monitors watching us with infrared goggles. This was true. On a previous occasion it had been my role to serve as one of the monitors. So what should I do? I said. You should plead innocent, it's your best option. This was the lawyer talking, the one who had been shaking me. The lawyer chewed gum and used great quantities of a fragrant product in his hair. I was sitting next to him in the trial chamber, which was very crowded and very warm. All rise, someone said. The judge came in. She had on a wig and a black robe and we all stood for some time while she instructed us to be seated. It was while she was working on the s in seated that I began to understand, but by the time she had finished the word I had been encouraged by my lawyer to stop. Then there was a trial. I was innocent, according to my lawyer and according to the other lawyer I was not. Order! the judge would occasionally attempt to say. Then the witnesses were called in. The first witness was the detective, who told the judge I had confessed. On the evening in question, the detective said, the defendant entered the dwelling place of the victim and, following drinks and light conversation, placed a piece of duct tape over the victim's mouth and inserted the sharpened end of a feather duster into the victim's ear. The second witness was a second detective whom I had not yet seen. This detective had found, she said, the remains of the roll of red duct tape and the sharpened feather duster, its point broken off, in my kitchen. The third witness was the woman who had earlier, you will remember, stroked my thigh and read my cards or her cards or someone's cards, and who was now, I quickly noticed, again in possession of sunglasses. I told him this would happen, she said. What she had told me, I'd just like to set the record straight, is that I would see a large animal with the words, do not, under any circumstances, painted on its side, and that I would be, in whatever I undertook that day, a big success. The fourth and fifth witnesses were my two guides, and they pretty much sold me out. Hey fats, I yelled as the larger one left the box. Then there were some other witnesses, including the bartender, the heavies, and the judge. The judge took off her sunglasses and wig, stepped into the witness box, and testified that she had dined with me during the course of the afternoon of the day in question, and that I had pressed her for information regarding certain swimming strokes, and that I had commented, somewhat lasciviously, on her perfume, and that I had eyed her bosom, and that I had sworn up and down that I would kill a certain party who had some years previously jilted and perhaps also betrayed me. Then there was a video, clearly doctored, which showed someone who looked a little like me running around and someone who looked a little like my alleged victim wrapped up in red duct tape. Which was all pretty damning evidence and then I was pronounced innocent (the small computer / electronic organizer found on her person clearly indicated that she had had a rendezvous at exactly the time of her murder with another individual "of the worst element"). So I was released, and the compliment was placed in my file, and the locale of the murder was scrubbed down, and the people who lived there came back from their vacation, and the subject was buried in the woods, and I went back to selling cakes, end of story, or almost. There is still a bit more that can be proposed, conjectured, said. For instance, on the evening of my reaffirmation, as I lay on the deck of the swimming pool all those pages ago, the boss, holding what I had thought was a nifty little automatic but that wasn't (it was a cigar wrapped in silver paper), told me that should my brain functions during my assignment to this particular branch of operations prove to be enhanced, I would earn a reward, a lovely one. What reward? I sputtered. You may, she said, see her again. Yeah? I said. Yes, she said. Before or after the operations? After. As often as I like? Absolutely. What I mean, you understand, is that she might have said that. She might also have said, you will see her again and then you will be forced without quite knowing who it is to murder her and wrap her up in tape and toss her in the river or bury her in the woods, you dumb sucker. Or she might, further, have said, you will, asshole, see someone very much like her and will wonder if it is her and if it really matters anymore after all this time and will never be entirely clear on this point and meanwhile some events, events in which you will have a small role, will be played out. But here is what really happened. Fuck you, tell me something, I said. She did not. Individuals picked me up and carried me to a bed, wrapped me in towels, turned on some nice music, and went away. So I wandered through the dark room thinking about this and about other things. I thought about my shitty day and about my two guides and about the rubber duck and about the message—do not, under any circumstances—which seemed like words to live by, I would have to give some thought to their implementation, I have, it has worked, most days I do not, stupendously, and thinking about that message I thought of my journey through the underground rooms, which had not happened, and about how when I was down there, in addition to the waiter, I had run into her, or had been led to her, my guide had said, oh yes, over there near the rocket-ship display there is someone who would like to speak with you. We spoke. She told me what had happened that previous autumn afternoon. How she had been there the whole time. Had even once or twice burned me with a cigar. Had sat laughing in the back bedroom with John and Deau. Had splashed all the objects in the room with violet paint. You're kidding, right? I asked. She didn't answer. You weren't really there were you? I asked. She didn't answer. So we talked some more and I told her a story that took place in the desert although I only knew the ending, which she liked, then I asked her, are you, you? And she said, yes, are you, you? And I thought, that's it, I'm not. No, I'm not, I said. Well that's good. Yes it is. Okay, I'll see you upstairs. We were upstairs. It was all already happening. But then I called her back. I'm definitely not me, I said. And the truth is I'm not her, she said. So that was finally settled. Before we parted ways, she said, incidentally, whoever I am, I'm in trouble — I've been in trouble for a while and now it's time, I've been told, for me to pay for it. What did you do? I don't know, something, it's been years — I double-crossed someone. The boss? No, not the boss. You're being disaffirmed? You could put it that way. Do I have anything to do with it? You're here, aren't you? I was. She had blue eyes. I was placing duct tape over someone's mouth. We were holding hands. I got out the feather duster. I'm coming, I said. Or at any rate I was thinking something, I must absolutely have been thinking something as I drifted through the dark where there was the sound of breathing and whispering and I thought, this is something and I am something and that is something and she is standing before me or she is not standing before me and now she is taking my hand and afterward I went back to selling cakes they are good cakes and I am quite happy that is the strange part and even fatter and there is more although none of this has happened and tonight I had my cards read again and the prediction was not pleasant and I thought this is how things seem these days they seem not pleasant it is raining it is cold I have long since given up on shorts and fine sunshine I heard breathing and I thought, I thought to myself, at any rate, all this is long past.

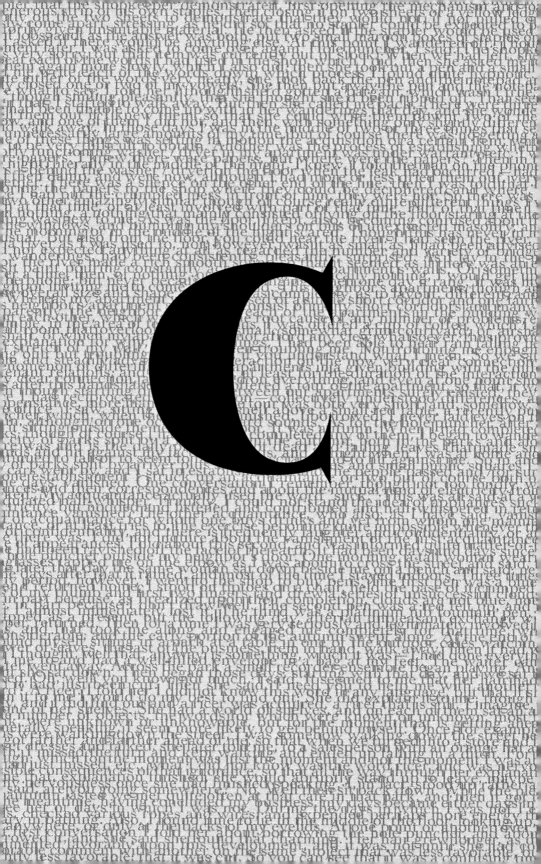

*Sadness the first powder to be abided upon
waking. It may reside in tools or garments
and can be eradicated with more of itself, in
which case the face results as a placid system
coursing with water, heaving.*

—BEN MARCUS
The Age of Wire and String

*"To the right," said the peasant. "That will
be the road to Manilovka; but there is no
Zamanilovka. That's what it's called, I
mean to say, its name is Manilovka, but
there is nothing like Zamanilovka here."*

—GOGOL
Dead Souls

NOT LONG AFTER THAT IS WHEN I LEFT. They came one night, shook my hand, and gave me a ticket. The next evening I was on a train, and late that night I got on a boat. The passage took several days. The captain would make announcements over the intercom. Then one evening at dusk I saw a great white city and the boat docked. In addition to the ticket, they had given me an envelope. In it I found a stack of bills, an address, and a set of keys. A taxi dropped me off on a poorly lit street in front of a building draped in black netting. The downstairs lock turned easily. I went up a flight of stairs. Another. The door was open. Come in, a voice said. The room I went into was large with high ceilings and several windows. A woman was sitting at a small round table under a handsome metal floor lamp. She had very high cheekbones. She looked very young. As I entered, she placed her hands on the table and stood. My instructions were to verify your arrival, she said. She walked past me. She had a slight limp. She said something I couldn't catch and was gone.

The apartment was well-furnished, but lacked a view—the three windows in the main room looked out through the netting onto a high white wall and the bedroom window gave onto an airshaft. The kitchen was painted bright yellow and had counters long enough to recline on. I know this because I reclined on them. One day a group of individuals, associates they called themselves, came in and found me on one. You won't get anywhere like that, they said. Get anywhere with what? I said. Several days went by. I sat at the table. Also I sat on the various sofas and couches, as well as on several of the chairs. The dining room I mainly used for pacing, and the den I entered only once. It was mainly in the early evenings that I ate the food they left in the refrigerator—meat, soup, boiled vegetables, soft, salted cheese. Dogs barked all night and sometimes kittens mewled. In the early mornings I slept.

After a week, at dusk, I ventured out. As I walked by them, the walls, if they were white, went gray then dark gray then the streetlights came on. The city was reasonably well-lit. My street, of course, was not very well-lit, but most of the city was. Or not most—much. Significant parts of it, I discovered, were full of shadows and haphazard sounds. One wondered where they came from. Where they went. But generally, as I say, was the fact of more or less adequate civil illumination.

So in the late evenings I walked. Past structures with or without balconies, across empty plazas, under crumbling arches, and through the public gardens where old men sat on benches under tall, flowering trees and young men lurked in the bushes. There were also lovers on the benches in those curious configurations, and the sound and clipped shadows of night birds, and usually, after walking for a time, I would stop at a small fountain, take off my shoes, submerge my feet, and let the cool water ease the swelling. There were many narrow, twisting streets in the city and any number of large, rocky eminences, and I soon discovered small paths that led by houses where old women sat beneath birdcages remembering, I imagined, the old men. If I went far enough, and a few times in the early going I did, it was possible to leave the city and to walk out into the surrounding hills. But in the hills, of course, there were no lights at all, and the paths were treacherous for an old man like me, lit only, as they were, by the moon.

Often, during this period, when I returned from my walks, I would find that the refrigerator had been filled and that the apartment, if not cleaned exactly, had at least been dusted and sprayed. Different scents were used for this spraying. The pine scent was far and away my favorite. The citrus, used liberally until I put out a note, I could not tolerate. Much of it, then, was what I had asked for—the food, the furnishings, the windows, the large bed, some kind of a cleaning crew, the city by the sea. I had, of course, requested a view and for all the streets of the city to be well-lit. I had also requested and not received a certain amount of reading material, a copy of my file, and a large handgun. Generally though I was satisfied. I had heard stories of retired assets receiving none of what they had asked for, even assets who had enjoyed relatively glittering careers and had never been disaffirmed. I, of course, had been disaffirmed twice. Although I should probably say straight away that the second disaffirmation, upon review, was found to have been unmerited and the following note was placed in my file, which I still do not have— "granted: the motion to vacate judgment." It was perhaps, I more than once speculated as I sat under the handsome floor lamp with its gold trim and metallic brown shade, because of this reassessment, this determination that my actions had, in fact, been justified, that so many of the requests I made in my retirement interview were provided for. Perhaps.

The days, as I discovered, were nearly as pleasant as the nights. The white city, with its orange roofs and endless terraces, shimmered in the sun or glimmered in the proxy of it. As I have noted, the city was surrounded by hills and broken up by rocky eminences, on one of which stood ancient battlements topped by a columnar structure, in the center of which sat a crane. There were endless motorized vehicles in the streets, and large insects in the air, and the pine trees shared the earth beneath the pavement with the root systems of palms and various blossoming fruit trees. Everywhere, too, there were rusty antennas and white satellite dishes and establishments where it was possible to sample grilled meats and various aquatic comestibles and to drink chilled resinous wines. Also worth noting were the numerous unfinished structures, structures that had stood unfinished for many years and that, I was told by a garrulous individual on a bench one evening, would continue to stand unfinished for many years — ruins, as it were, in reverse. No one in this city wore hats or capes, although sunglasses were nearly omnipresent. When I say that no one wore hats, I am of course referring to a certain variety of hats, or, rather, to a certain way of wearing them. I had requested that too. I no longer, I had said in my interview, wish to see or wear hats or capes. What about sunglasses? I don't care about sunglasses, I had said. Also, I had given up on shorts. I had, before the reversal of my second disaffirmation, which was largely passed at the bottom of a not-quite-dried-up well, lost a tremendous amount of weight—of which, admittedly, there was much to lose, but still—and had found, upon my release, that none of my lovely pairs of short pants fit any longer. Lovely is perhaps overstating it.

And yet I rarely went out during the daytime. In fact, once was enough. After a bout of unsuccessful swimming at a beach not far enough away from the city and its septic mechanism, I saw what I have already set down and I saw some other things, including: a cat simultaneously hissing and relieving itself on a broom and a three-legged, sore-infested dog chasing a pigeon that could not completely fly and had no feet, and after these and other observations, once home, I found myself exhausted, unwell, unable, in fact, to leave my apartment for a considerable time, and so decided to restrict my circumambulations, insofar as this was possible, to the dark hours. This was possible—it has been fifty-five days since I was last outside in the daylight, and while at times the stray lines of light that make it through the netting and the shutters to fall across my floor and, occasionally, across my hands or arms, are able to elicit certain emotions and to stimulate certain memories, I find I am happier this way.

Happier is not the word. Happier is definitely not the word.

Along those lines, before I completely leave daylight behind, it would be just as well, I think, to clarify that the city, setting metaphor aside, is really almost anything but white. This is not to say that many of the buildings are not white — many are or are clearly meant to be. It is just that, upon more careful inspection, carried out on that day of diurnal exploration, from the precinct of a large hill at the southern end of the city, I discovered that the city has more that is gray or tan about it than anything, and if one counts the endless and variegate colors of the awnings drawn over the terraces and rooftops and balconies (green and blue and yellow could be said to predominate), and the above-mentioned orange roofs, all seen through a considerable haze of pollution, then the city ceases, far from being, even to seem white. Years ago, in the company of friends, I visited another city by the sea, and I have made several attempts these last days to remember what color it was. I do remember, of course, walking arm in arm, and I remember the slightly waving fronds on the trees and the generally sloping aspect of the streets and the gentle curve of the hills. I remember, too, setting the events of my first disaffirmation in motion, the disaffirmation that was justified and of which, however perversely, I maintain a certain measure of pride. The second disaffirmation, the one that didn't hold, the one during which I lost so much weight, I find I cannot feel proud of, although I have no doubt she deserved it. Why this? I asked her. Why this, after everything you've put me through? Why now? She made an attempt to answer, couldn't get past the stutter, gave up, and lifted her gun. But I was faster.

I thought about that, of course, as I sat beneath the handsome floor lamp or lay sleepless in the large bed. I thought about it as I walked the well-lit streets after dark or sat, in company as it were, among the old men on the benches in the gardens, and sometimes as I thought

LAIRD HUNT

134

about it my hand, which often itched anyway, itched to be holding a gun. And yet all of that was over, long over. It's best to make some effort to let these things go, I said to an old man sitting beside me on a bench. Hah! he said. Which pleased me greatly, but seemed also to preclude any sort of elaboration. And in fact when he continued it was in a completely different vein, so that after several minutes of regarding his unhealthy gums, I moved on. It occurred to me, following this interaction, to climb the narrow streets and consider the old women a little as they sat in their doorways or stood talking in small groups. Some of these conversations, I discovered, were quite interesting. One old woman, for example, was describing her recent efforts to have the asbestos removed from her son's place of work, efforts, she said, that were being hampered both by her son and her son's boss. At this, one of the old women, who stood almost completely wrapped in shadow, suggested that if removal of the asbestos was the first old woman's primary concern, and her son and her son's boss were interfering, then she might simply dispose of them. There was a silence. I leaned a little closer. Yes, I'd thought of that, the first old woman said. They began to discuss methods. One of them suggested cocktails and powdered glass. Another, arson—if you did it right it could look, she said, like spontaneous combustion. After this, the conversation grew unfocused and I walked off. Just as I'd entered a nearby path bordered by a double line of flowering bushes and had begun to think about the endlessly shifting arabesques and the variety of browns and greens of the small dark leaves and stems, which would certainly be more clearly determined in the daylight, someone came up beside me and took my arm. It's a lovely night, I said. Yes, she said. I recognized the voice—it belonged to the woman who had intervened in the conversation a moment before. Should I be alarmed? I asked her. She laughed. She had a very pretty laugh, perhaps a little loud, but clear and rich in the warm evening air. I started to turn my head to look at her, but she told me to keep looking straight ahead. By now we were walking along a slightly wider path. Above us, beautifully illuminated, was the enormous eminence at the top of which stood, or in some cases barely stood, the ruins of temples or who knows what. You should take a tour, she said. I don't get out during the daytime lately, I said. An evening tour could be arranged. That's a thought. I've taken such a tour myself—the moon and starlight do wonders with polished stone. Why are you walking with me? My house is just over there. So? So that's where we're going. Is this it then? Is what it? Because I thought I had an agreement. What are you talking about? I started to look at her. She lifted her hand and placed it, firmly, against the side of my face. We walked a little farther. So this doesn't have anything to do with anything? I said. I didn't say that. What did you say? I didn't say anything, she said, squeezing my arm. I started, I thought, to get the picture. Well then, yes, I'd like to take a tour, I said. I'll arrange it. She did. A couple of nights later. No one was there but the gates were open and for several hours I wandered amidst the ruined structures. In the meantime, though, we entered a small house and then a small bedroom. I will just ask you to let me place this blindfold over your eyes. I think I'm too old for this. For what? Aren't you going to tie me up? I hadn't thought of it, do you want me to tie you up? Well, no, I guess not. Because if you want me to I will. No, that's okay. She put the blindfold over my eyes. You look much better than you used to, she said. What do you mean? Just that. Who are you? Never mind. Well anyway, I don't look better, I look terrible, I couldn't look worse. Yes you could. I was about to reply to this, when she kissed me lightly and, none too gently, shoved me onto the bed.

I am not very much bothered by the dark, as such, and in fact, under normal circumstances, I am really quite comfortable in it. I have passed many pleasant moments in the dark during my life and, if stray lines of light are capable of stimulating certain memories, so are dark closets and dark eyes and bands of curved, dark shadow and couches set in the center of completely dark rooms. So it was that, far from being disturbed by the fact that the lock turned behind her when she left, and that the room was pitch black so that it made no significant difference whether or not I continued to wear the blindfold (after attempting to check my surroundings I did), I felt quite comfortable and after a time lay down on the bed with my legs slightly spread and my hands behind my head and thought of nights gone by and the latter part of my career and my undeniable skill at certain aspects of it and my undeniable weakness at others. Before long I fell asleep. Once or twice as I lay in the dark room, I woke and, instinctively, listened for other breathing, but heard none. Then I did. Or so it seemed. A small tremor shook my skin and for half a second the hair on the backs of my hands lifted slightly. But then, after applying considerable directed attention, and with a sense of mild embarrassment, I realized that I had been listening to myself breathing, a sound no doubt much distorted by memories and dreams. Neither of which, at that moment, could be called pleasant. The breathing—I continued to listen to it—could similarly not be called pleasant and in fact seemed somehow awful, like something to be dealt harshly with, and I wished I had a gun. A few moments later, however, my breathing had come to seem normal to me again and even, strangely, to seem quite sweet or pretty, or at any rate, kind of nice and certainly useful, and I found myself turning to thoughts of the not altogether unenjoyable interaction I had had with the woman and to otherwise diverting myself in the gloom.

It was still dark or dark again when finally I rose, took off the blindfold, tried the door, and found it open. The rest of the little house was brightly lit and completely empty and after using the facility I sat a moment in the kitchen and nibbled at some fruit. It was a good thing that I did so, as it was only after I had sat there a moment that I noticed the note taped to the window above the sink. It read:

> *Arrangements have been made—the night after tomorrow—your tour.*

My tour. After all those years I was finally having one of my own. The view of the city from the battlements surrounding the eminence was very pleasing—a curiously nervous opalescence as far as the eye could see. I ran my fingers over the old stone and found that, far from smooth, it was coarse and pitted, which, if I remember correctly, was a consequence of several decades of pollution and acid rain. This put me in mind of the story about the individual who, for having stolen something, gets hammered to a rock. And as I thought of it, it was not so much the idea of the large birds that came each day to eat certain of his organs that bothered me, it was rather the thought of what the sun, wind, rain, etc., not to mention cellular decay, were doing—I ran my hands over the pitted stone—to his skin. Or to my skin. I touched it. This was depressing. But at any rate, for hours, I say, I wandered, climbing over rubble to weave in and out of columns and step through massive doorways into vaulted chambers or into chambers without roofs. Once or twice as I wandered into those starlit rooms, I thought of my recent blindfolded incarceration, if you could even call it that, you could call it that, it had been dark and the door was, at least for a while, locked, and because I didn't understand yet, and had been given no further information on the matter, I found myself slightly annoyed. Perhaps not surprisingly, such thinking brought me to my fairly recent, and far less pleasant, interlude at the bottom of the well. My legs had been further injured by the fall— despite the mud and water at the bottom. Also there was the bullet wound. So there had been pain to go along with the discomfort and hunger. On her bed in the room in the dark there had been no pain, no discomfort, only the business about the breathing and the incomprehension. Up among the illuminated columns with the view of the city and the gentle breeze, however, I found myself close to experiencing a sense of peace. Close, I say. Because just when this feeling was beginning to assert itself—I was remembering, with a small smile, certain embellished incidents from my childhood—I suddenly registered that the investigation had begun. I became convinced of this when my eye was caught by something shining among the rocks—nothing special, just a bottlecap—which reminded me of the photograph I'd found the day before in the hallway outside my door. I had come home late and, as I was pushing the door open, saw something flat and shiny and picked it up. Actually, it wasn't quite as easy as that. When I opened the door, or had partially opened it, I saw something shining a little in the light cast out into the hallway by the always illuminated handsome floor lamp and bent to pick it up, a process which took some time as I have lost a good deal of the feeling in the tips of my fingers and am far from nimble when it comes to bending over and doing things. Once or twice, I have put myself into such a position, perhaps to pick up a set of dropped keys, and have lost my balance and keeled over. On this occasion, I did not keel over, but it did take a certain amount of focus not to do so. In the end, having neither keeled over nor fainted, I picked up what I discovered was a photograph. But it wasn't until I had gone inside and shut the door and sat down directly beneath the lamp that I saw what it was a photograph of.

And now, suddenly, as I stood holding the crushed blue bottlecap—I had not keeled over in this case either—I realized what I had seen. The man in the photograph, or someone dressed like a man in a long dark trench coat and shiny leather or mock leather shoes, whose face, if face you could call it, was a pale blur, was the one I was looking for, the one I had to find. I went home and made a phone call. To them, I mean. It has started, I said. Are you asking or telling? Both. So do you need an answer? Yes. Then, yes. Is the guy in the photo the one I'm looking for? What photo? The photo I found in the hall. I was put on hold. I do not like being put on hold. After what seemed like a long time and was, I had timed it, the voice was back. Yes, it said. Good, I want a gun, I said. What kind? Large. I'll see what I can do. Ten minutes later there was a knock on the door. It was the young woman from the first day. You have a lovely figure, young woman, please sit down, I said. She said, what the fuck did you just say? I apologized. She told me to apologize again. I did. She sat down. She then took a small gray box out of her bag and set it on the table in front of me. What's this? I asked for a gun, I said. Maybe it is a gun. It is not a gun. Today, I'm just the messenger. And other days? She smiled. I opened the box. In it I found an almost impossibly tiny dagger made out of a single piece of silver with the image of a lion carved into the part of it, about two inches long, that was meant to represent a handle. What is this? I said. It looks like a bladed instrument that would probably fit nicely in someone's kidney or throat, she said, taking it from me. Or maybe into someone's eye. Or nostril. She grinned and jabbed the knife around. Interesting, I said. I kind of gave her a looking over. She winked and tossed the knife onto the table in front of me. Then asked if I had anything to eat. Aren't you the one who fills my refrigerator? I said. She didn't answer so I told her to help herself. While she was gone I looked at the knife. It really was very small. After a few minutes, she came back with a cold cut rolled tightly around a piece of cheese. Is there anything else I can do for you? she said. You can get me a gun. Or a flamethrower. Or at least a bigger knife. She swallowed then put the rest of the meat and cheese into her mouth. She left. I shut my eyes and tested the small blade against my palm, finding it worked admirably.

The next morning over a breakfast of meat (not the cold cuts—something substantial, with a little bone and fat in it) and warm bread I tried to think, now that things had started, about how best to proceed. I had slept tolerably well and the dream I could remember, if not exactly pleasant, couldn't quite be called unpleasant. In it, I had stood on the side of a rocky slope and watched as heavy dust rumbled down through a wooden sluice that seemed to have no beginning and no end, or at any rate it seemed that the beginning and end existed outside of the dream. Which did not seem, something told me, like such a bad place for them to be. I once recorded a fair amount of drivel about beginnings, pretending as I did so that I was transmitting remarks made to me by a friend. That particular friend would never, I am fairly sure, have made any comments about beginnings. He could conceivably have spoken about endings, as they were his business, and as I sat there thinking about it, about my dream and my investigation and the possibility of his having spoken about endings, the following anecdote / observation came into my head. In book III of a certain important individual's meditations, one can find the following proposition: It is one of the noblest functions of reason to know whether or not it is time to walk out of this world. A second individual, in a tract entitled, intriguingly, On Murder Considered as One of the Fine Arts (a title and precept that my former friend would have greatly admired), invites us to interpret with him that the first individual, who if I can remember correctly was an emperor, was referring to a knowledge of whether or not it was time for others to walk out of the world. He then goes on to suggest, and the reasoning seems persuasive, that murder committed in such a context is a form of philanthropy, i.e., amen, or something to that effect. Which would certainly apply in my own case. My own imminent ending. A little amen dosed with a little good riddance is what this anecdote / observation led me to think. But at any rate the dust. Pouring through the sluice in my dream. And my breakfast. And the small dagger. And the photograph. The background (a path, blurred foliage, a gleaming car bumper) looked familiar, or at least I had the feeling it did. Personally, I have never committed an act of philanthropy. That's not true. Even that isn't true. One had one's day. One's accomplishments. I looked at the knife. Amen. One might still have one or two accomplishments ahead of one. Along with one's instances of absurdity. So you can see I was thinking about it. And in this roundabout way was beginning to get somewhere. Even if only gropingly. Just like an old man, one who probably craps his pants occasionally, a typical one. Actually I don't know any old men who crap their pants, and I've certainly never done so. I'm a very neat old man. I have a full head of hair and over half of my original teeth. I always wear pressed pants and appropriate colors, don't talk too much, and can, when asked, sing at dinner parties. I have even been called presentable. Although not when they pulled me out of the well. A less-convincing form of philanthropy. Mine or theirs? The old woman — here it was — why had she blindfolded me?

But of course having thought things through I had to wait until dark before I could do anything. I passed the time sitting next to the radio. Also, I paced for a while. The apartment is not exactly what you would call spacious, but there is adequate room to make a large enough triangle or even diamond if one is given, as I have long been, to geometric pacing. When I had had enough of the radio and walking out approximations of complex shapes on the floor, and you might be surprised by how long I am able to engage in such activities, I lay down on my bed and dozed and thought some more, or, rather, engaged in repetitive thinking. I thought, over and over, and with several accompanying composite images, one of which involved small blue crabs piled in a bucket, then said crabs blackened and piled on a large plate: I should have asked for something else; I should have asked for nothing; or not nothing, but not quite something either. Frankly (and I thought this even as I attempted to gather myself), I had begun to suspect that it might not happen—that they would skip the whole thing as too expensive, too tiresome, too much. But not as too complicated—complicated they didn't mind, they had proved this time and again. And anyway it wasn't. In fact, in the end, as far as their part was concerned, it was quite simple. It is quite simple. Really. Or will be.

The old woman wasn't home. I had pocketed the dagger (imagining, as I did so, the reaction I would get if I presented it at a tricky moment—smiles, a punch in the mouth, no more teeth) and the photograph and set off through the dark streets. Without the old woman to guide me, it hadn't been easy finding the little house. It sat at the end of several tricky turns, and I think I spent the better part of an hour negotiating them. Darkness, of course, complicates any route, even the simplest one—say from bed to bathroom; actually that's a poor example; interiors are often more complex than exteriors; even the most intimate ones; I had an apartment once that seemed always to be shifting around me; or at any rate I kept banging into walls and furniture; usually with my shoulder; I'm not sure what is at the heart of this phenomenon; possibly the darkness; certainly not the walls and furniture; likely myself; but also the darkness; the darkness has some role;

fucking darkness; even if I also love it, etc. At the end I did find it, as I've already made clear. I tried the door, found it open, and went in. Little had changed. A packet of crackers, which I ate, had appeared on the kitchen counter, and there was a similar assortment of fruit on the table. The bedroom, which with the exception of the toilet, was the only other room in the house, seemed much neater than it had when I had lain there in the dark, but that was really just speculation. I wanted, insofar as it was possible, to avoid speculation. The business at hand, my last assignment as it were, seemed to merit more. I would, I said aloud to myself rather pompously, restrict myself to the evidence in making my final determination. Or course, leads were different. The pursuit of leads seemed to admit some degree of speculation. And what beyond speculation could have brought me back to the house of this old woman? I was momentarily at a loss. Fortunately, at that very moment, as I stood with my hand in a drawer full of undergarments, a voice, hers, said, don't turn around. Hi, I'm sorry about this, I said. It's just I'm making an investigation and wanted to ask you some questions. I'm hungry, she said. You can ask me your questions over dinner. This seemed reasonable, even civilized. I took my hand out of the drawer and started to turn around. Don't turn around, she said, and put your hand back in the drawer. I followed both her instructions. She gave me the name of a restaurant, told me to wait five minutes before following her, then left.

Her house was much easier to leave than to get to, and I soon found myself negotiating small streets, where wisteria spilled over balconies and hyacinth and jacaranda were in bloom. During the day, these streets were likely

THE IMPOSSIBLY

bustling, but at night there were only a few unsavory shadows and the occasional cat, and despite the flowers and stars overhead, I was not unhappy to leave them and, after following a long row of pine trees and climbing a steep flight of steps, to arrive at the restaurant. Actually, I am omitting the part where I had to stop and ask directions. The young man I interpolated was exceedingly polite and even called me sir, which was not at all unwelcome. It is only in recent years, and even now infrequently, that anyone troubles him / herself to call me sir. I have wondered if this has anything to do with the fact that for so long I was so heavy, and now I am so gaunt. I look like one of those ancient employees you come across in medium-size family-run operations—the one who, a little wobbly on his / her pins, receives the item the other more limber family members have pulled down. The comparison is faulty only inasmuch as I am, despite the above-mentioned tendency to keel over, somewhat more agile than such individuals. I'm not, in fact, quite that far along, I'm not really far along at all, only to look at.

The restaurant was extraordinarily crowded. The walls were covered in photographs, of various citizens and sections of the city, as well as with rather hideous caricatures, possibly of the owner or some other somewhat distinguished gentleman. Waiters came and went around extraordinarily encumbered tables. An individual was playing an accordion. Another was playing a guitar. I looked for the approximation I knew to be my party, but saw no one who fell within the parameters. Clearly, however, if I took a table, she would find me. I was beginning to do so when a man called to me from across the restaurant. Actually, I'm with someone, I said. She won't be coming, come over here and sit down, he said. The man, although he had nice eyes, was quite a fucking sight. It looked like he'd had an extra chin sewn onto the side of his face and also, in the throat area, a little like he'd swallowed a couple of tennis balls. It's not communicable, he said. At least not highly, otherwise they wouldn't let me in here. It's just I'm a little busy, I said. With your investigation? You know about my investigation? He smiled. I sat down. What will you eat? I've already eaten. We both know that's not true. Then I would like some boiled meat. He called a waiter over. The waiter went away. Are you . . . ? No questions please, he said. We sat there. I listened to the accordion and the guitar. I don't know what he did. The food arrived. I asked him if he would like some. He declined. He leaned forward and I could see his shoulder holster. I wondered if this was him. I'm not him, if that's what you are wondering, he said. I was. Well, I'm not. The gun has nothing to do with this or with you. Well, that's good, I suppose. Eat, now, he said. I did. The boiled meat was excellent. He poured me a glass of wine, which I quickly polished off. More? he asked. Yes, please, I said, registering that I was beginning, slightly, to enjoy myself. I was a little disappointed or disgruntled or put off or taken aback, but I'm doing much better now, I said. Good, he said. What's wrong with your face, anyway? It's a condition. I've had those. Not this one you haven't. He had very pretty green eyes and delicate eyebrows. I was about to remark that his face must at one point have been quite sympathetic, perhaps even handsome, I had even settled on a way to say this very politely, had planned to make an allusion to a book I had once heard summarized, involving a tortoise someone had covered in gold, although actually the tortoise had ended by dying badly, from the gold, ah well, I would have omitted that part, when he leaned forward and asked me if I recognized him. No, I said. I was terribly handsome before all this. I can believe it. But you don't recognize me? No. Well then let's leave it. We did, but it troubled me a little afterward. I have been told many times that the old forget, that this is part of their reward for having lasted so long, but when it happens, or when I am aware that it is happening, I derive little satisfaction from it. Usually what I forget are key words and phrases, so that I look even more foolish than usual in clever company. The unpleasant episodes, which have been legion, I remember. The pleasant episodes, such as that visit to that earlier city on the coast, I also remember, but such memories pain me. The memory of her hands and of her back and of her lovely, careful movement pains me. Just as the memory of the way I think it may have ended makes me sick. You haven't changed, he said. Someone told me recently that I looked much better than I used to. I don't agree. I thought you said we were going to leave it. We are. Good. Go over and tip the accordion player. What? Put a tip in his basket and compliment the young guitar player, he's really coming along. I stood. I had the idea that I would just walk right out of the restaurant, go home, drink a beverage, put a pillow over my head, and wait for whoever was coming for me, but when I reached the accordion player he jazzed up his tune and looked at me expectantly, and the guitar player, who really wasn't that bad, did the same. So I reached into my pocket, pulled out some bills, and made to place them in the little basket that sat between them on the table. Only I saw that

there was an envelope there. Should I take this? I asked
the accordion player. Tip me and compliment him, and
you can take anything you like. All right, I said. I
dropped the bills into the basket and paid the young
man an exaggerated compliment. The two beamed at
me and I beamed back then picked up the envelope,
turned, and discovered that my interlocutor was gone.
When I reached the table, I saw that he had left enough
money to cover my meal and also that he had left me a
note wrapped around another note. The first note read,
put this note in the envelope. I opened the envelope. It
was empty. I thought for a moment, then decided that
by "this" he was referring to the second piece of folded
paper. I put it in the envelope, which I then licked and
sealed. Then I sat down, had a sip of wine, thought a little about my interlocutor's chin (and here is when I settled on the image of the swallowed tennis balls), decided
it wasn't so bad, his chin, wondered if I had known him,
decided I had, thought about the investigation, smiled
at the musicians, then took out the tiny dagger, cut open
the envelope, unfolded the piece of paper it contained,
and read the following:

> Go home now. Digest. The boiled meat may cause prob-
> lems, I am suspicious of it. I will have a strong antacid
> put in the medicine cabinet. Three weeks from tonight at
> 11 P.M. go to the southwest entrance to the public gar-
> dens. Wait.

Three weeks from that night, I went there and waited.
Afterward, after I had stood waiting all night, I realized
it was possible I'd been given a significant clue, one that
might hold the answer or something like an answer, but

at the time, having waited three weeks for that moment, and then being involved in that moment, to use the word "moment" in its more expansive sense, I was mostly just pissed off.

But in the meantime, there were those three weeks, and it occurs to me that it might be useful to give some account of them. After all, it was during this period that I learned the identity of the old woman and heard what she had to say about a key event in my life, although this isn't to say that I believed her. Her account of that event was by no means the first I had heard, and, if you have followed any of what I have set out previously, you will no doubt have some sympathy for my attitude toward her revelations. If, in fact, you could call them that. I think it would be more accurate to call them opinions and inter- pretations, maybe even slander. After all, by her own account, she wasn't in the room when it happened, when I received the punitive portion of my first disaffirmation. Which, incidentally, was nothing compared to the second in terms of sheer excruciation. They did several things to me before they threw me down the well, and, as one of them remarked after they sent the so-called spelunkers down to retrieve me, it was curious that I had not bled to death. So you can see why, among other reasons, certain of them might have felt obliged to treat the requests I made at my exit interview with extra attention, or at least why they pretended to have done so. I think she was definitely hands-on involved, the old woman I had known briefly as a young woman told me. And do you think she was the person I encountered some time later? Do you? she asked. I'm not sure. But you said you spent a fair amount of time with her. Most of it was in the dark, and before the lights came back on, the body, if it was hers, was wrapped in tape. Couldn't you have exhumed the body? I had just buried it. So—you could have gone back later. I don't want to talk about it. Fine, what do you want to talk about? I thought for a minute. Are you a prostitute—is that what you're doing with your retirement? That's what you want to talk about? Yes. Who says I'm retired? Well, I thought you must be. Just exactly how old do you think I am? I didn't answer, as I wasn't sure, not at all. So right now, talking to me, you're on the job? I said. Is the blindfold too tight? she said. No, it's fine, but why do we need the blindfold now—I know who you are. Have you gotten a good look at me? No. That's why we need it. I don't understand. And so on. I mean my interaction with her, once the cards, so to speak, were on the table. If there was a table, if there were any cards.

Also during those three weeks I had my body manipulated. I have taken, in recent years, to having this done occasionally. I found it helped greatly, following my fall down the well, to undergo the realignment process the procedure entails, and also to lie on the comfortable matting or padded table that is provided. I am not against the use of oils or scented candles either, although in general I prefer the sort of manipulation that occurs when my skin remains relatively unsmeared and my clothes stay on. Imagine me, a dilapidated older individual, glistening with oil, lying in my poorly filled briefs beneath a towel. Perhaps when I was younger and something of a fatty this image would have possessed some charm. I was not, in those days, against applying the occasional cream to my pleasantly taut (and so deliciously abundant) outer tegument and to ingesting any number of beneficial liquids and solids. My world was not, during that epoch, without several individuals who found corporeal configurations such as mine appealing. And it was really very lovely to present to them an exterior that was as well-maintained as it was abundant. But clearly I have, without particularly meaning to, left the subject far behind. I meant only to convey some sense of a particular manipulation, one that was conducted while I lay on a comfortable mat on the floor, fully clothed. One of the old men from the benches in the gardens had given me the manipulator's name, describing her, as he did so, as highly capable. Extra to my desire to get some needed realignment, I have always, since my early days, been fascinated by individuals who are described by others as highly capable, which is exactly, one of my early keepers once told me as we were sitting in front of the television, what you are not. I did not disagree and in fact, quite interested, asked this particular individual to elaborate, which he / she did when a commercial came on. A highly capable person is one who is able to do whatever he / she wants to or is asked to or is required to by others. Which you, you fat little bastard, are not. And as I say, far from disagreeing with this assessment, I found it remarkably apt, and found the evocation of these mysterious, highly capable individuals extremely stimulating, and I have made it a point to avail myself of their company, in as much as they will have me, whenever they have been reliably identified. I don't mean to say that I found the old man's assessment entirely credible. I didn't know him that well, and he had some rather suspect, or at least overwrought, ideas on, for example (I had brought up the subject), asbestos removal. There was a curious mechanism once, he had said, built in the shape of a great bull and made entirely out of burnished bronze and silver into which up to three individuals of normal size could be placed. A fire was then lit under the belly of the bull and the individuals were cooked. The interesting aspect of the mechanism was that an elaborate system of pipes channeled the screams of the individuals and converted them into a music that, while not exactly beautiful, was beautifully strange. I don't think that ever existed, I said. It did, but, alas, I'm not sure where it would be possible to procure one, he said. Where did you hear about it? In a book I've just been reading about an unpleasant house. It was during our subsequent discussion of this unpleasant house, which apparently devoured the psyches of its inhabitants as it constantly realigned itself, that we came to the topic of manipulation and how I came to visit the individual he recommended, who indeed proved highly capable and left me utterly satisfied.

One was asked to take off one's shoes and to lie on a mat fully clothed. Then one was asked to relax insofar as one was capable of doing so. Next, one was told that one would not have to do anything except follow simple instructions, which did, in fact, prove to be very simple, although I worried about carrying them out a little. I have a poor track record with simple instructions. But I did just fine, she said when I asked her, with these, which were of the roll over gently onto your stomach kind. It was the "gently" part that troubled me. And also the question of direction (which way to roll). Once or twice I had, so to speak, and with consequences — in one case a dull burbling sound — rolled the wrong way. And as for the interpretation of "gently," I'll just say that I was told, once, to handle someone "gently" and upon beginning, as I thought, to do so, was instructed that I had gotten it wrong. You've done everything right, now pay me and you can leave, she told me after I had lain wrapped in blankets for several minutes. I did leave. I felt much better. Then the three weeks were up.

Or almost. Because as I lay there wrapped in blankets, my body realigned, my blood enjoying better circulation, my attention oscillating pleasantly between my highly capable manipulator, who sat in the corner drinking a beer, and a blood vessel that had recently burst in my eye, my thoughts turned to another occasion, some years before, when I had lain wrapped not in blankets but in towels, following a swim. I really didn't think much about this, likely it would be more accurate to say I remembered, not thought, or to say it came to mind. It also came to mind, and I don't say it did so accurately, that as I lay there, a woman came in and sat down beside me. This woman, if she was there, and if it was her, was beautiful, but also terrible, like something that should not have been, at least not in my company, and despite my exhaustion, I made an effort to sit up. Don't, she said. Thank you, I said. It was very pleasant and very frightening to lie, exhausted and wrapped in towels, with her, my love, if it was her, sitting completely naked beside me. Part of the mechanism of this memory is that I was never certain. Afterward they told me that no one had come in and sat down beside me, although I had spoken about someone in my sleep. I believed them until a few months later when I thought I saw her again. Which shouldn't matter to anyone besides me. Or should it? Clearly now I am thinking again.

But I did feel better and did for several days afterward. So much so that I even went out and took in some nightlife. In this city, apparently, much is done in the old quarries, which can be found in the oddest places—in the backs of government structures, behind a department store facade, beneath the vaulted roof of a magnificent structure into which, during the daytime, groups of individuals go to stand among the blasted rocks and, heads bowed, intone and sing. It was into something like this last that I went late one evening to witness, and in a small way to participate in, an event. It was not a nice event— there was a lot of white rock and then the white rock became splashed with red—but it was diverting. At one point, after I had, more or less symbolically, taken a turn with the mallet, I remarked to another individual that what the event lacked in subtlety it made up for in vigor. Yes, it's colorful, the individual said. I feel like I've gotten some exercise. Yes, definitely, I think the upper portion of my forehead is damp. Yes, mine too. I won't dream at all tonight. Or if you do it will be pleasant. Why is that? No one knows.

I also, in my freshly realigned state, contemplated taking a trip. The islands near this city are apparently very beautiful. Even at night. Perhaps, the travel agent told me, especially at night. She recommended some islands. On one of them an important battle had been fought. On another there had once been centaurs. They have found skeletons, she told me. One was obliged to travel by jet-foil to get to these islands if one wanted to leave at an hour of one's choosing. Traveling by jet-foil was slightly, but only slightly expensive. I told her I would have to do some research. She suggested a book shop in the vicinity.

None of the books I found, however, had much to say beyond the quality of the nightlife and the possibility of starlit strolls. Against which, I explained to the travel agent when I returned, I have nothing, in fact I enjoy looking up at the stars as I walk, though I have become accustomed to regarding them through a haze of light and suspended particles. There is very little of either of those on the islands I have recommended, the travel agent told me. Little or very little? I asked. I used the adverb for a reason, she said. Oh yes, I said. I also said, you look like someone I once knew. I think it's disgusting, she said, when people say that. Disgusting? Yes. Would you like to go out with me? Yes. We went out. No we didn't. Who am I kidding? She was definitely very pretty, and definitely not interested. Maybe this is why I then, completely changing the register of my voice, blurted out, someone is going to kill me. What? she said. Yes, that's why I'm here, in this city, I said. I got my letter, I've been retired, they're going to deactivate me. I'm not even sure I should be asking about starlit excursions. She seemed interested, perhaps even sympathetic. I quickly entertained certain relatively unadorned fantasies about escape mechanisms involving her. Can you swim? I asked. Of course, she said. Encouraged, I took out the tiny silver dagger and showed it to her. I've been given this, I said. Don't cut yourself with that thing, she said. In the meantime I'm undertaking an investigation. So far, all I have to go on is a photograph and a tip. The photograph is blurred and the tip's a little vague, but I have high hopes. Oh, she said. Or I said. I suddenly realized I was speaking rather loudly and shaking the knife in her face.

I thought it best for a time, the investigation notwithstanding, and still within this three-week time frame, to limit my contacts after that. I restricted myself to the old men in the park and, when they were out and about, to the old women in the little streets at the base of the rocky eminence. Also, once or twice, I saw the young woman with the limp and the high cheekbones. I'm waiting, I told her. We all know that, she said. She had come to change all the lightbulbs in the apartment. One evening, somewhat late, I had begun to be concerned that the bulbs in the various lights might burn out and that I might be left in the dark. I'd rather not take up the question of whether, given my earlier comments on the matter, there is some kind of contradiction involved in that admission. In fact, see above, there isn't. It's just that one night I got it into my head that my security might be seriously compromised if all the bulbs, for whatever reason, were to simultaneously burn out. So I put a note on the fridge. Why, exactly, am I doing this? she said. Start with the floor lamp, I said. She set to work and I followed her, both because I liked the way she worked—slowly, carefully—and because I wanted to make sure all the bulbs got changed. They did. I switched them all back on. Would you like a drink? I said. No, but I'm hungry. So have a snack. I can't remember exactly what she had this time, but I can remember the sound of her lips smacking softly together, or (I've just tried it) pulling softly apart. That last may be my imagination—my hearing is actually quite bad. No doubt in watching her eat I was put in mind of other meals I had shared. I was young once too you know, I said. You're not all that old now, she said. She then continued biting and chewing, making or not making the concomitant sounds. You're actually, you know, rather remarkably beautiful, I said. And I couldn't care less what you think, but thanks, she said. After a little more of this, she raised an eyebrow. You know the power could go out. I've thought of that. Or it could be shut off. Are you trying to scare me? Are you scared? Not now that the bulbs have been changed. Somehow, the prospect of having what I had envisaged happening because of the lightbulbs all burning out happen because the power had been extinguished didn't particularly trouble me. It interested me, which was problematic enough, but didn't cause that familiar feeling to radiate from my stomach around to my back — the one I experienced when I thought of the lightbulbs all going out in a simultaneous snapping of filament and the house being thrown into darkness and an individual moving forward (i.e., toward me) with, say, infrared equipment. You're right, I said, that someone could turn the power off, but that doesn't bother me. And anyway, it's too easy. How so? I mean it's too logical, in an easy sort of way. What do you mean by logical? I mean it's boring. Define boring. You're not one of these smart people are you? I'm extremely smart. So why are you the one they send to fill my refrigerator? I've already made it clear to you that I don't do that. You mean by not answering my question when I asked you before? Exactly. What would be wrong with filling my refrigerator? Nothing, except that I don't do it. Why not? you're the one they sent to change my lightbulbs. Are you looking to get smacked? Can you smack hard? She came over and smacked me. It was hard. While my ears rang I thought about high intelligence and simple tasks. The most intelligent individual I had met in recent years — or so it seemed to me, a poor judge, but she could carry off stunning calculations and do those curious and unnecessary gymnastics with the number pi — had the position of polishing the shoes of the dead, if the dead were in fact wearing shoes. Clearly, I don't mean just any dead. I mean those who, through dealings with our organization, had become dead, or almost. The latter fell into the category of the near-dead and their shoes were polished too. Once, admittedly in one of my more casual moments, I held up the leg of a member of this category so that I could look at something about my hair in the reflection I hoped might be produced. Extra to the fact that the reflection wasn't much good, it was at that moment, as I was peering at the shoe, that the individual died. I know this because the shoe polisher, still present, said, at that moment, $74 * 57 = 4,218$, there he / she goes. Suddenly it struck me, really struck me, that *I* was going to go. I'm sorry for being rude, I said to the young woman with the limp and the high cheekbones. I'm not sorry for smacking you, she said.

The old men, for their part, fell to telling me their dreams. Their dreams were not so bad, but I would have to seriously doctor them up to make them interesting enough to include here. Instead I will tell you one of my own. Because of its narrative elements and the fact that it crossed detective and ghost story genres, it was something of a success when, at my insistence that I have a turn, I told it to the old men. It helped that we were sitting on one or two barely lit benches and that the park around us, with its winding paths and heavy foliage, was lit everywhere with small round lights, so that, as one of the old men said, you never knew whether wolf or lamb or some unpleasant combination of the two was going to step out of it. Actually, I said that. And the response I got was not so positive. Shut up and tell your dream, they said. I cleared my throat and did so.

I am an inspector in an almost silent black-and-white world working to track down a noted member of "the resistance." Not for the first time, I catch up with him and unload my handgun. The bullets fly out in long thin slivers of shining lead that the wind distorts. I tell my colleagues, when they arrive, that I'm sure I hit him. They shake their heads. This scene repeats itself. One evening everyone is out making a sweep for him in a warehouse across town. On a hunch I go back to his place of work, a book shop where he hasn't been seen for weeks. And sure enough, he's there. I see him through the window, puttering around the shop—a tall man in yellow light. I call my colleagues then pull my gun and close in. Just as I am about to enter, however, I register that he keeps repeating the same movements. And then I know. My colleagues arrive and we go in. I touch one of the books. He vanishes. He's been keeping us busy chasing him, I say. He's been dead the whole time.

When I finished there was a silence, or a relative one—a couple of the old men suffered from that condition which makes one's teeth, it is unfortunate, clack together. I am happy to say that I was not one of them. Although I'm not too proud to confess that my lips sometimes make movements I don't command them to and that my hands, on occasion, shake a little. Also, my skin, from when I was fat, hangs somewhat inharmoniously and is very rough in places, and I am prone to considerable stiffness in the lower back, which makes me, at times, very slow and decrepit seeming indeed. Furthermore, I look old. In and of itself this would not be a bad thing. I actually like the look of the old, and not just the pretty, if slightly watery, eyes. For instance, I am inclined to think that the somewhat overpronounced veins on the backs of my hands are quite beautiful, and that the blunt, crooked aspect of my fingers is not without a certain charm. Sad to say that most don't share my opinion. And even if they do, even if they call you sir or madam and pay you compliments, they are still usually inclined to think you are, by dint of being old, somewhat bonkers. But my dream. Someone came up with, not bad. Another said, yeah, yeah. Someone else said, you could make a movie out of that. The discussion turned to movies. One old guy brought up a movie where a man goes out west, is given a paper flower, gets shot, and spends the rest of the movie dying. Some of those who had seen it claimed he was dead before the movie started. There was a general murmur of assent. I like cowboys, I said. Well this guy wasn't a cowboy, he was just some dead guy who got shot. There was a brief argument. Then a silence. Then someone asked me how my investigation was coming along. What investigation? I said. We've all heard about it, another said. I looked around. Everyone I could see was nodding. Because of the travel agent? I asked. And the restaurant. I heard it from my wife, she's one of the old women. How do they know about it? Oh, they all know about it. Well, do any of you have any tips? Yeah, don't speculate. How am I supposed to do that? I don't know. Great, thanks, what else? Consider the evidence. What evidence? I mean the clues. I've hardly got any. Isn't your three weeks about up? They were. In fact, the next night I stood waiting by the garden's southwest gates.

But in the meantime—it was still early—I went up into the old city to see if I could find any old women to talk to. I used the walk to think some more about my dream and about what the old men had said about it. The fact that they were all aware of my investigation, seemed somehow tied to my dream, as if the dream of an investigation had merged with the speculation surrounding the real one. I wasn't entirely sure, having formulated this last, what I had meant by it, but was strangely pleased for a moment, as in some small way I'd made a breakthrough. As soon as I was over that feeling, I went back to the dream itself. Upon waking from it I'd been very interested by the notion that the whole thing had hinged on a hunch, largely unexplained, and I had lain in my bed thinking about how, in my real investigation, I could turn this to my advantage. As I lay there thinking about it, calling to mind bits and pieces of the dream, no doubt adding patches and embroidering connective elements onto it, I remembered or created the phrase, he's been dead for weeks, and this too seemed to have some resonance. It also occurred to me to wonder whether my character, as it were, when supposedly acting on his hunch, had known all along how it would end. I don't know, I thought. And still don't. I can assure you, however, that at that point I didn't know (or was unaware that I knew) how my investigation would end and, properly speaking, still don't—I am waiting. I wait here. With all the fresh bulbs in the apartment burning. The tiny dagger on the table in front of me. Waiting for the man in the photograph to arrive.

And then I ran into the guy with the face and neck problem and the woman who had blindfolded me. They were standing or walking arm in arm beneath a trellis hung

heavily with wisteria. I can't remember if they were coming toward me, or I was coming toward them. It is a small
point, perhaps, but over the course of the investigation,
as pathetic as it was, I developed the habit of considering
such details and attempting to make some sense of them.
Likely, it seems to me, it was the former, as I often
pause—and am often bumped into from behind because
I do it pretty abruptly—and also because when I remember this part, I remember an absurd amount of motion in
the area of his face and of her bosom. This perceived
motion, however, may derive from faulty memory and my
limp, not to mention my fairly poor night vision. At any
rate, both of them stopped or started—I either stopped or
stood still. Oh, it's you, one of them said. You're the woman
who blindfolded me, I said. And you're the one I caught
with his hands in my underwear drawer, she said. Tut, tut,
the man with the fucked-up face said. Then he asked me,
presumably because she was holding up one of those masks
that have a lot of feathers and a handle on them, how I had
recognized her. The voice, professor, I said. Of course, he
said, it's just I hadn't realized you were close enough to hear
us. Well I was and, incidentally, who are you? I said. Me or
her? Both, while we're at it. If you can't recognize me I'm
not going to tell you, he said. If you let me put a blindfold
on you I'll tell you who I am, she said. Why, is there something wrong with your face too? Tut, tut, don't be rude,
said the guy. What's this tut, tut crap? I said. I understand
you're under a strain so I'll give you five seconds to apologize for your comportment. Likely there were large individuals in close proximity, and there was definitely his gun
and maybe also hers, but mainly I was feeling a little fragile, so I said it—sorry. Good, he said. We all stood there a
minute. There were night birds calling and the sound of

motors and car horns and the air was full of the scent of wisteria. Look, do me a favor, I'm not getting anywhere, tell me something, anything, I said. You'll learn more tomorrow, maybe even tonight. Just tell me something now, one thing. All right, there will be witnesses. Where? At the scene. Why? It's a new procedure—straight from the records department. The records department? I said. Yes, he said. I don't get it. Get what? What that means or why you told me that. He shrugged. So that's it? That's all you'll tell me? Yes. Well, fuck you. They looked at me then at each other then started to walk off. Hey, hold on a second, I said. But they didn't. And I couldn't blame them. As a matter of fact when I bumped into her again a little later, alone this time, I apologized without being asked to. She lifted her mask high enough for me to see her mouth, smiled, said, follow me, then lowered it again.

When the three weeks were over, I went to the southwest gates of the public gardens and hid behind a bitter orange tree. It was a small tree with dark green foliage and large inedible oranges, meaning the top half of me would not be visible to anyone approaching or leaving, was my theory. The tree was off to one side of the gates near a pair of overfilled trash bins. As I stood there, someone came over and threw something into one of them. My irritation at this gesture (whatever it was had simply bounced off the top of one of the bins, dislodging, as it did so, several other items, all of which fell at my feet) was quickly replaced by a sense of anxiety (he had walked away) that this had been the individual I was waiting for. Or hiding from. Why was I hiding? Hiding was better. I had had some of my greater successes because of hiding, or related to hiding. But did that apply in this case? Surely, simply, it was better to play it safe. I had "waited" before and paid the consequences. Having thought that through, I decided it hadn't been him, as the individual in the blurred photograph was clearly pretty large (I mean fat) and this individual hadn't been. A moment later, when I took into consideration the possibility that this individual, like myself, might recently have lost weight, possibly during the process of a disaffirmation, one that had later been overturned, this decision was in doubt again. I momentarily stepped out from behind the tree to see if I could spot him, but couldn't. For about five seconds I was at a loss, then it occurred to me (and I have no idea why this seemed plausible) that he might return, at which point I could, calling out from behind the tree, tactfully ask him if he had recently lost a great amount of weight, or, depending on my mood, and if no one else more likely had come along, leave the tree and follow him.

The life of the investigator involves a lot of waiting, as does that of the small-time gangster. One waits (or hides) and one thinks and usually this thinking is not much. As I stood there in the semidark behind the orange tree I thought, more or less, nice oranges, nice thick foliage, nice dark leaves. I thought, fucker for knocking the trash onto the ground and for possibly being my killer and, I thought, I was happier when I was fat. Fat and younger so I could handle said fat. Images of myself—fat and younger; wearing a cakeseller's apron; wearing sunglasses; standing on stage singing opera; looking fat in shorts. Now I am old and where there was once honest fat there are dubious folds. This has nothing to do with my being old. This doesn't matter. Someone approached. I stopped thinking. It was a woman. My heart went whomp! then I started thinking again. About the woman I had loved and lost and maybe, for a short while, found again. Then the oranges. Then my life as an organic asset, certain aspects to do with pay. Also with screwing up. Then I thought about hiding. About wearing infrared goggles and standing in the dark. Then about moving through the dark. Once I hid in someone's closet, someone known to carry two guns. She fell asleep, then I came out carrying a hammer. I was convinced I was dead for a time, early in my career. There was even some evidence, not to mention one or two minor out-of-body experiences, and it was during this period that I first got it in mind that I would like to carry out an investigation and even went so far as to set myself up with an office, a friend who was willing to work as my secretary, and one or two clients. For health reasons, however, I was soon obliged to return to work for the firm with which I had been previously engaged. To say anything is to complicate it. Like darkness. To remember anything. My boss in the early days liked trains. I had several friends. One in particular. We drank a lot. Clearly, here, I was remembering. Or forgetting—I am always confused which. My dream came up. I considered rearranging it to make it absolutely clear at the next telling that at the beginning my character had had no idea of the outcome. So that in a sense he, I, knew without knowing it. Which seemed a great luxury. And also utterly outside the realm of possibility. I said this out loud. I smelled something. It didn't smell good. It was me. Then birds began making noise and I realized that a considerable interval of time had passed. I came out from behind the tree and sat on a bench. I sat there for another interval. I stood. I walked in through the garden gates. I met the woman with the mask only now she wasn't wearing one.

The next day I mostly spent in bed, although one or two things happened. One of these things was that the young woman with the cheekbones knocked on my door. She was quite a mess, had been crying even, and when I let her in she wouldn't speak for a few minutes. Bastards, she finally said. She paced around the room a little. In her agitation, her limp seemed more pronounced. It occurred to me, though I didn't get a chance to suggest it, that she might be able to get one of those special shoes. None of this is real is it? she said, cutting off my thoughts. What do you mean? I said. None of this, what we're doing, right now—it's not real. I have no idea what you're talking about. I'm talking about this, for example, she said, pulling out her gun. It's got blanks in it and that stupid little knife of yours is plastic. No it's not. Yes, it is. Don't point that thing at me. She did. She fired. Then, when it was dark, I went back to the restaurant in hopes of finding the guy with the face and some explanation for the previous evening, but he wasn't there. Neither was the accordion player or the kid with the guitar. Or at least I was fairly certain they weren't. I put it that way, because there was a guy playing the accordion and another playing the guitar, but I was pretty sure they weren't the same ones as before. Whoever they were, they played pretty well, though, and I stood there for a number or two. I would have stood there longer, swaying slightly, feeling reasonably content, but the waiter started shooting me censorious looks. So I tipped them and started to leave, or did leave, got the hell out, away from everything, went to the beach, took a swim, floated on my back, and looked up at the dark sky, but then the guy in the photograph walked in the door. You will ask, rightfully, how, given the condition of the photograph, I could have been so sure that the fat guy I was seeing was the one in the photograph, and the truth is, even though it was him, and I soon confirmed this, when I saw him I wasn't entirely sure. Is this a photograph of you, fat man? I said a couple of minutes later, after he had sat down and ordered and they had brought some of his food. Fat man? he said. I made to wave the photograph around in front of his face, then, remembering the regrettable scene at the travel agency, set it down next to him and contented myself with tapping it once or twice. I'm sorry, I said, for any present or imminent rudeness on my part. Fat man? he said. I apologized some more. After a certain amount of this, he took out a pair of glasses, put them on, and looked at the photograph. Yes, that is me, he said. Where did you get it? I told him where. He told me he had a sister who lived in my building and that about a month ago he had visited her. As he was leaving, she had handed him a stack of photos from an excursion they had taken together—clearly he had dropped one of them on his way out. You mean to tell me you're not an assassin. A what? Because you can tell me if you are—I won't do anything, I just want to know. So if I were an assassin and had it in mind to assassinate you, you wouldn't do anything about it? That's right. Then why do you have a knife? How do you know about the knife? You mentioned it. No I didn't. He took a drink. Do you mind if I pat you down? I said. The waiter had been standing near the table for some time and now he came forward and put his hand on my elbow. I'm going to make a phone call and we'll see if your story holds up, I said over my shoulder, because the waiter, quite a sturdy individual, was now leading me away. And maybe I'll just pay a little visit to your "sister" while I'm at it, fat man. By this time I was out of the restaurant, lying on the sidewalk, and it was the waiter who answered. Please do, he said, but be very nice, she's a friend of mine.

The "sister" really was the sister and really was also a friend of the waiter's, in fact she had once, she said, been on exceedingly friendly terms with him. She told me many things about her brother, including certain habits of his, one or two of which I could have done without knowing, and she confessed to me that she was a little worried about how much weight he had recently gained. He can lose it, I said. I used to be a little heavy and look at me now. This reassured her—that a gentleman such as myself, as she put it, could have lost a considerable amount of weight and still retained such grace of carriage and elegance. I smiled. She smiled back at me. We drank tea on a terrace that had a much better view through the black netting than mine did, and it was pleasant to recline in one of her comfortable chairs and to sip tea spiced with bergamot and to look at her face, which was not unhandsome. In fact, for a woman not of the absolutely earliest years she was quite stunning, and as we sat there and discussed her brother, a very "sweet man," I began working up one or two compliments, which I never got the chance to use. Because the truth is, when I got home after leaving the restaurant and knocked on the only other door in the building, I found it open and the rooms it opened directly onto empty, or almost empty—in the smallest of them, beneath a single bare bulb, was a small wooden table and two chairs, in one of which sat the man with the troubled face.

I know who you are, I said. I know you do and it doesn't matter, does it? No it doesn't. So sit down. I sat. He asked me how I was doing. I told him that, frankly, I was a little confused, that I was having trouble with real and not real, and that my confusion was making me prone to outbursts and to regrettable comportment and unfortunate remarks. He said that the outbursts, etc., aside, this was probably a good thing—that it was good to be a little confused about real and not real when in the middle of carrying out an investigation. Am I carrying out an investigation? Absolutely—why wouldn't you think so? For a moment I thought I'd met my killer's sister. In this apartment? In the other room and on the terrace. But instead you met me. Yes. And because of it you're confused. And a little irritated. Stop trembling, it's all right. What's all right? Your investigation is almost over. So that fat individual is going to kill me? What do you have against fat individuals? Nothing. Well it sounds like you have something against them. Could you just answer my question? That will be for you to determine. What will? That was the answer to your question. Well it looks a little fishy. Yes it does. I suppose you already know the outcome. Not at all. I looked at him to see if he was lying. I'm not lying, he said. Well then are you insulting my intelligence? I might be. Couldn't you get that thing removed? Tut, tut, he said. If in fact he had ever said, tut, tut. I asked him if he had. Take it easy, he said. Was she lying to me? I asked. Was who? About what happened. You mean a few months back? It hasn't just been a few months. Fine, it doesn't matter, I know what you're talking about. How long has it been? A while—not too long. But was she lying? I don't know. And was it real? You'll have to answer that. I thought about it. When I was finished thinking, or rather sitting there, as he had put it, trembling, I still didn't have an answer, or only a hypothetical one—that event, the one about the paint and shelves and caged animals, had been real, but much of what followed had not. This was unsatisfying, and a bit too disturbing, so I turned my attention to another matter. Why was my second disaffirmation overturned? What? Why did they pull me out of the well? The boss ordered it. Which boss? You know which boss, you smacked her in the head with a shovel. I killed her. No, you gave her a severe concussion—when she woke up, she said, let him go. But what about all the blood at the crime scene? I don't know anything about it. You're lying. About which part? All of it. No, I'm not. I hit her with the shovel because she set me up. Everybody is aware of that, now let's change the subject. I did kill her, I said, my voice rising, I know I did. End of discussion. So you're saying she ordered that my disaffirmation be overturned—why, so she could set me up again, is all this another set-up? I won't say another word about it. By the way the thing on his face was throbbing I could tell he meant it. I took a deep breath and said, okay, let's talk about my investigation. Fine, he said. What the hell was that southwest gate of the public gardens thing? It was a clue. A clue? We sat there. In a small room off to the side a faucet had been left on and, nearby, someone was operating a jackhammer. A little daylight was coming in through one of the windows. He leaned forward and put his elbows on the table. Would you like to ask me anything else related to your investigation? Yes, why are we having this talk? Because I'm required to tell you something. Who is doing the requiring? Never mind. Okay, do I want to hear it? I don't know, do you? I thought about it. There were many things I would have liked to hear: the sound of milk being steamed, a large bird beating its wings, thousands of goats wearing bells coming down out of the hills. Another thing I thought I would like to hear was the sound of my once-upon-a-time and forever-lost sweetheart coming into a room, her feet hitting softly against the cool tiles, I think they would be cool, her dress moving, it must be moving, against her legs. I would also, I thought, like to hear the words "you were highly capable" or even, and of course I mean in reference to me, "he was highly capable," but I knew the individual sitting opposite me with his pretty eyes and awful condition, familiar, as he was, with my career, would not say them. I don't really want to die, I said after a moment, aware, incidentally, that I had not answered his question. You expressed that sentiment volubly at your exit interview, he said. I know, I said, after a while I couldn't think of anything else to say. He shrugged. I can't say I blame you, he said. Really? I don't say I approve of your approach to expressing yourself (I took it he was referring to the fact that I had broken several things, including one of my own fingers), but, to be somewhat honest, I'm not really looking forward to my own retirement either. How exactly could it be something to look forward to? Some might see it as a relief. This struck me as a pretty good answer. Have you gotten your letter? I asked him. Not yet, probably a few more years. I thought we were about the same age. Each asset's career has a different trajectory. I see, I said. I thought of my career's trajectory. I decided I would only use the word "plummet" in regards to it if I could also use the word "rocket." This made me smile. Okay, tell me, I said. You're ready? Yes. Your time is almost up. Is this real or not real? Real. How much time do I have? I can't be any more specific. So you think I should just go home and wait for that fat individual to come and get me? I'm not sure your investigation is complete. You mean it's not him? I didn't say that—I said, I'm not sure your investigation is over. So you think I should keep going? Yes. And are you going to give me any more helpful clues? You have been given excellent clues, right from the start. So that's what you've been doing, you've been giving me excellent clues? Some of them yes, others no, but the principle holds. What about hunches? You mean in reference to your dream? You've heard about the dream? We all have. Do you have an opinion? Not one I'd care to share. So are we done here? Almost. Almost how? You're about to be given another clue. How about this time you just tell me what I'm supposed to think. You're the one who wanted to undertake an investigation. I snorted. Some investigation, I said. He snorted back. Apparently in agreement. I say it that way because at that moment someone limped over and cracked me on the back of the head.

If I could imagine it might be interesting, I can't, and had the energy, I don't, I might, using some mechanism involving the number of times I've been knocked out, compose a record of my days. I can remember once reading about the consistent pattern of a saturated presence of low-grade fractures in the skull and clavicle area of ancient remains, and suspect that if by some chance my bones retain their integrity long enough for them to bear some anthropological interest if found by future researchers, the presiding scientist might draw the conclusion that he was dealing with some sort of anachronism, which is to say that, by my own reckoning, I've been knocked out—I'm not counting smacks here—upwards of a dozen times. Starting very early. Much too early. And it was of this that I thought when I came to—an image of myself, a little too small, having been struck and, some interval having passed, waking up. I woke up. It was the same room, same table, same, likely, chair, I thought. Although my recent interlocutor was gone, and in place of his chair, behind where he had sat, was a round mirror, in which, looking back, rather dull—an old man. Who regarded himself for a time. Then stood, collapsed, stood again, and walked out.

I would like to return now, in a manner of speaking, to the little house near the old part of the city where the woman lived. Follow me, she had said. It was to the little house that I followed her. On the way, though she didn't blindfold me, she did ask me not to speak, as she had a slight headache and found my voice, which is a little high-pitched, grating. You could gag me, I said. I have asked you not to speak, she said. So we walked along in silence, or in as much silence as two old people can manage in navigating poorly maintained streets—one of them, not me, wheezing a little—with curbs of varying heights and pieces of loose stone and piles of sand. Once, having nearly fallen into one of these last, because of one of the penultimate, I cursed, though remembering her injunction I did not do so loudly. We had bumped into each other some distance from her house, and I took advantage of the time to continue thinking about my dream, and also about several other things that came to mind, one of which had to do with a dark airshaft I had once lived by and another of which had to do with the advantages, first for a perpetrator and then for an investigator, of being a ghost. This last, however, devolved into an internal debate on the practicality, with regard to one-on-one contact, of such a state, i.e., would a dead individual possessed both of sentience and some means of self-propulsion, in fact be able to satisfactorily conduct investigations, i.e., interview living individuals and relate conclusions or relevant observations to them? The dead individual might only, and with great effort, be able, when the guilty party's name, for example, was mentioned in conversation, to knock over a vase, or produce some meaningful condensation, or partially appear, but who could predict how such interventions would be treated, or if they would receive any consideration at all? My sort of ghost, I concluded shortly before we arrived at her house, would most likely be the kind that, not deficient in self-awareness and some measure of intent, would lack a predictable means of locomotion, and so would have to rely, to carry out investigations, on such things as local wind currents and fluctuations in the magnetic field. Most likely, as I pictured it, my course would take on something of the aspect of an all-but-incapacitated butterfly, or a plastic bag caught in an updraft, adding dubious consistency to the air.

We entered her house and sat down at her kitchen table, where I picked up an apple and she took the mask away from her face. Oh, I said. Yes, it's me, she said. I wondered, looking carefully at her, why it seemed so easy to be certain about her identity. After all, it had been some time, and I had only known her then for a short while. Only a few weeks, she said. If that, I said. You remember because you didn't like me. That's true enough. I mean you like me now, but then you didn't like me. What does that mean? You know what it means. No I don't. Nevertheless, it is me — I asked her why she was revealing her identity now. There's no longer any reason to keep it from you, she said. What reason was there before? It was important not to influence the early stages of your investigation. Are the early stages over? Yes. Well I still don't know anything. You probably know more than you think. This seemed reasonable and even vaguely encouraging, so I changed the subject. I asked her how she had been and what she had done with herself all this time, and she said she had done very well for a while, then very poorly and that lately, largely due to her acquaintance with the individual with the face, she was doing a little better. Who is he? I said. She told me. That guy? I said — he was just some schlep who couldn't say good-bye. He's made something of himself. Unlike me is what you mean. She didn't answer. Answer me, I said. Yes, unlike you. This silenced me for a while. As I sat there, silent, listening to her light wheezing, she told me some more about her life and about some of her exploits, which I have to say I found a bit dull. And also a bit sad. Maybe more sad than dull. Maybe all sad.

When I was quite young, as I have mentioned previously, I lived in certain rural areas, as often as not surrounded by various domesticated animals, as well as various wild and even savage ones. Also in abundance, in the summer months, as in all such regions of the world, were any number of insects, which used to become intrigued by us at night or prowl in the evergreen bushes or hover above stumps in small, oblivious swarms. The wasps stung and the arachnids frightened and the horses and mules, if you got too close to them, or let them come up behind you, would bite, and although there were cats to come and gently brush against your legs and dogs to lie beside you when you had been made to lie very still facedown in the barnyard, most of the menagerie seemed to have a certain mildly ferocious aspect in common with the other—I mean not me—bipedal inhabitants of the house. With so many animals on my mind and numerous occasions to think about them, either before I fell asleep or when I was locked up, I acquired the habit of describing to myself the characteristics of various hybrid beasts. Some of these were very pretty and quite wonderful, such as the occasionally carnivorous glow-in-the dark humming-bird with the colors and patterns of the swallowtail; others were less so. It was one of these latter—a species that inhabits and is in fact engendered by the smoldering space between two openly antagonistic old people (the relatives I lived with during that period) sitting opposite each other—that I thought of as we sat there at her kitchen table. The evocation was unpleasing. Suddenly, everything was unpleasing. I picked up her mask and looked at her through it. What happened that day all those years ago? I said. You sure you want to hear it? No, but start talking.

After you dropped us off, she said, we went upstairs and, as had been arranged, found them waiting there. We also found that during our absence a great number of items had been added to the shelves, and she, as had been arranged, quickly added what the two of you had brought back from the trip. Then they carried in the animals and splashed it all with violet paint. She laughed when they splashed it all with violet paint. Especially at the monkey, he kept looking at his hands. I think it was at this point that you called. And a little while later they brought you in. After you came to they sent me into the kitchen to cook. She stayed in the room with the Stutter and the skinny woman and took her turn at burning you. Your good buddy John was there for that part. We sat in the kitchen and when the remainder of the food had cooled we ate it. Then we all left and a couple of days later they got the package you had put the wrong address on, then your pal, your hero, who, you've probably gathered, was working with us the whole time, came back to pick you up. The end.

Thanks, he wasn't my hero, I said. You're welcome, she said. So you didn't participate in the burning? I didn't say that. No, you didn't. Would you like to cross-examine me? Okay—why the shelves? The shelves? The objects and the shelves. I have no idea, the concept either came from the Central Job Committee or maybe she thought it up herself, anything else? Yes—why didn't you haul me in as soon as you knew I hadn't gone through with my assignment? Our instructions were to determine whether or not you were working alone. What did you determine? That you were. Well, anyway that's true. It's all true. No it's not. Yes it is. Where did she go afterward? Nowhere. What do you mean? I mean she didn't do very well with her next couple of assignments so she was disaffirmed. Was she recuperated? I don't think so. Of course, this was just her version of the story, even if it did, in certain details, correspond with other versions I had had, but it still wasn't definitive, as I didn't trust her, for whatever reason, never had. Or didn't want to. Maybe I did trust her, but didn't want to and was confused by that. I was certainly confused, but was still in hopes that the next day, when the three weeks were up, I would be able to move forward with my investigation, which after all was the important, even if somewhat laughable, matter at hand. Anyway I don't believe you, I said. I told them you wouldn't, she said. And what did they say? They said to ask you what you believe in. What I believe in? Yes. What the hell kind of question is that? I'm just the one asking it. Well, I'm not sure. They said you would say that. They're clearly very well-informed. Yes, they are. What do you believe in, Smarty? A certain unexamined measure of synchronicity. Well that's very clever. Thank you. And is that what this is, our meeting after all these years? No, and anyway, I said unexamined. Yeah, yeah, so what is this? This was planned. And on that—she gave me another apple and showed me out—our discussion ended. At least until the next night.

But in the meantime, I slept then spent the day more or less waiting then went to the park and waited and worried that I'd missed my killer, but of course hadn't, then went to the restaurant and saw the man in the photo, who in fact had had nothing to do with my case until they learned I had found the photograph of him—it was planted evidence for another affair in the building—and so sent him to eat at the restaurant, correctly reasoning I would find my way there in hopes of having the previous evening's exercise explained. There, I received the misinformation about the sister, which I followed up on, still, of course, under the impression that my killer was possibly the fat man in the restaurant—I'm not sure why they didn't just change the photograph—then got conked on the head, woke in front of the mirror, walked out, made

THE IMPOSSIBLY

179

a phone call, and heard the word, bingo. I won't, I said. Yes, you will, the voice said. I want to talk to someone. You are. Someone besides you. I'm the only one. Let me talk to the young woman. She doesn't talk on the phone. This is just cheap, you guys are just trying to get economical. There was a silence then—investigation over— a dial tone.

Investigation over but not an account of all incidents relevant to it. There are a couple more. After replacing the receiver, I went back down the hall and knocked on the door. Almost immediately the young woman with the high cheekbones and slight limp answered it. Thanks, I have an incredible headache, I said. I've been working on my technique, she said. Is he in? No. Any idea when he'll be back? He won't be back. You over that real / not real stuff? Yes. Good, me too, do you have any kind of a gun? Of course I do. But you won't give it to me. Why do you want one now? Because I want to get this over with as quickly as possible. Well, I'd like to help you, but the last time I allowed myself an instance of compassion, I got this bad leg and was temporarily disaffirmed. How long is temporary? About six hours. So they must like you. They do. So do I, I said. So I'll give you a tip—hit a little to the right. That way you'll be sure to achieve full unconsciousness in your subject. I winked. She looked at me. After I'd been struck and under for a while, I told her, I woke for a few minutes or seemed to and found myself lying rather unceremoniously on the floor. Several individuals were sitting at the small table and it seemed to me that they were complimenting me, and that their compliments were not at all trivial. I heard the words courage and rectitude used.

And I discerned definite traces of sincerity in one or two of their utterances, and then I fell asleep again, or rather, went under again, and came to in front of the mirror. If that's true, which I doubt, they were talking about another retired asset, she said. I knew you would say that, I said. I smiled. She smiled. I shook her hand and turned to leave, but she said, wait. She disappeared for a moment then came back with a very shiny multi-colored piece of cloth. He told me to give this to you, she said. Thank you, I said. Then she put her hand on my chest, gave me a gentle shove, and shut the door. This shove made me think about seeing the somewhat unpleasant woman from my youth the night before by the garden gates. She had shoved me too. That made three shoves. She had also punched me and kissed me and said, good-bye. This was following a continuation of our conversation on the subject of belief. She had come to the gardens, she said, to see what I had learned from my wait and I said, nothing. Not too quick on the uptake are you? Apparently not. We walked a little. I told her I had thought some more about the belief thing and that while I hadn't gotten anywhere I would keep thinking about it. I will too, she said. At least you have something you believe in. Synchronicity isn't much. No, but it's something. Yes, it is something, but not much more than nothing. That reminds me, I said. I know all about that, that was just something she made up, she said. I got it out of my pocket anyway and, hand cupped carefully, held it up in front of her. Does that look made up to you? I said. This was when she punched and kissed me. Actually, she didn't kiss me. She hadn't really even kissed me that evening in her bedroom. I don't even know why I'm going on about her kissing me at all—I never liked her. Except to look at. She *was* nice to look at. Stop now, she said. I let my hand fall to my side, and whatever had or hadn't been in it fall to the ground. And, it was interesting—after she had seen me to my apartment (the shove had occurred sometime before that), I kept hearing, over and over, the words, stop now. Which had a particular and unpleasant resonance then as well as later after the mirror, and certainly now. Good-bye, I said, to the young woman behind the closed door. Then, almost finished, as I was making my way back down the hallway, I thought, my eyes are deceiving me, then as quickly thought, no they aren't, and bent over and picked up a photograph that was lying on the floor. When I was back in my apartment, I sat down under the handsome floor lamp and set the photograph on the table in front of me. Well, that's overkill, I thought, but it's not bad. Better, at any rate, than what I had just seen in the mirror. On the back of it, in the man with the fucked-up face's willowy hand, was written the following note:

I wanted you to have this photograph of yourself. There was an error of sorts initially—the wrong photo was dropped in your hallway, or rather the right photograph was dropped in your hallway, but it wasn't for you. You've concluded your investigation within the required time frame—congratulations. I'm sorry that in the end we had to resort to the mirror, but you will understand, no doubt, given the time constraint, that it was necessary. The blindfold is a gift, a touch of flash, of color—I remember how much pride you took in your appearance in the old days. But also, of course, by way of further explanation of the blindfold, you will remember those encounters in your, I mean one's, childhood with both mirrors and blindfolds, and the ensuing, once their purpose was grasped, sense of departure and wonder. We are all of us, as children, investigators, sailing around in our imaginations like cups and saucers gone far out to sea. Never mind that cups and saucers out to sea would likely sink. The image is still rather pretty. At any rate, I expect my own letter soon and have decided I will request a similar investigation, and have no doubt many others will also follow this trail you have blazed, and that it might even become institutionalized. You were always highly capable, and what our mutual friend told you about those long ago events wasn't true—you loved and were loved in return, perhaps even more fiercely. Adieu.

Or at any rate, something like the preceding minus a few emendations appeared on the back of the photograph. But probably you won't find surprising my interest in maintaining that all of it, emendations included, was true. Could it, after all, have been possible, much less reasonable, that in the midst of our short time together, all those years ago, my love had said, in the presence of several others, myself included, that piece of shit means nothing to me? I don't think so.

Such are my thoughts on the case and, more generally, on the time I've spent since coming here. Now that the case has been, so to speak, closed, without, as it turns out, much real help from dreams or speculation or hunches, I find that I am by no means encouraged by its result. Being aware of the identity of my putative killer in no way renders more tolerable to me the imminent prospect of being killed. Though I'd like to make clear that I never seriously thought it would. I mainly wanted, as we used to say, to buy myself a little time, or at least to keep myself busy. I also wanted, once he / she was found, if not to actually injure my killer—although that would have been nice—to scare him / her a little, and now find myself, however perversely, pleased to register that this desire will be gratified. Is being gratified. It certainly is an exceedingly sharp knife. And it glistens on the table in front of me. As does the blindfold with the multicolored sequins I will soon tie on.

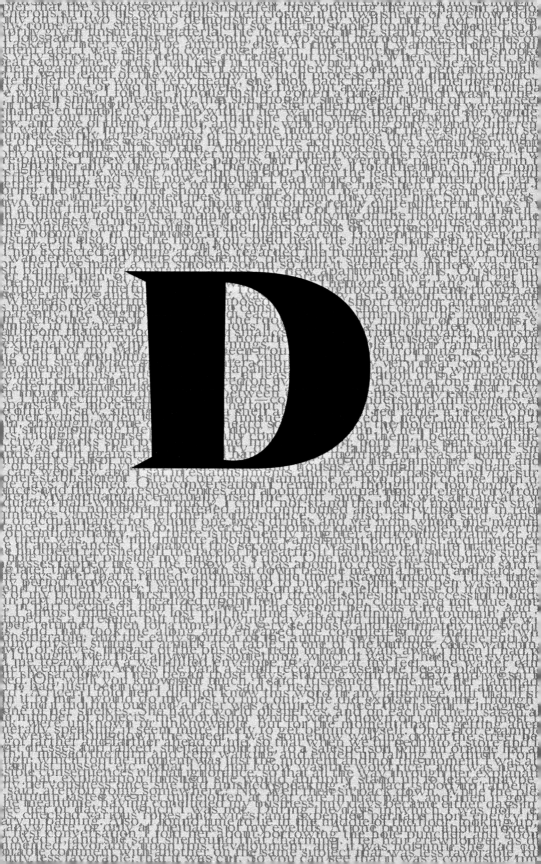

"We will be silent" "& wait," "the voice
said." "Then we were truly quiet" "& being
that," "were nothing," "really nothing."

—ALICE NOTLEY
The Descent of Alette

S O THAT, THESE SEVERAL MONTHS OR years or circumstances ago, after a certain interval, I found myself moved to rise, to go into the front room and join my friend, to sit, as it were, in company with him. This laudable ambition notwithstanding, I got no further than the handle of the door — my friend was no longer alone. He was talking to an individual with an orange hat and a cracked tooth.

Yes, he's in there, and he's feeling very lonely, my friend said.

So maybe I'll go in there and give him some company, the individual with the orange hat and the cracked tooth said. And when he stood — the door was slightly ajar — I could see he was holding a gun.

It occurred to me, of course, that I was simply, as so often, drifting again. After all, I had witnessed this scene, or one much like it, several days or weeks previously. Something, though, told me it might be important to attempt to play it safe. So I did what it had lately struck me I could do — I became barely visible.

Or thought I did.

The individual, wearing his orange hat, entered quickly, gun drawn, a smile on his face, finger on the trigger, a burst capillary in his left eye. On registering that I was not at my desk, he performed a series of deftly executed advances and pivots, which, each motion, he repeated several times. When he was satisfied that I wasn't standing out of the range of his peripheral vision, he took two quick steps over to my desk, simultaneously looking under it and pushing the curtains aside.

Where are you? he said.

He said it in a very casual, almost friendly way, which nearly caused me to become, if I wasn't already, completely visible again, or at least to attempt to answer. For a moment though, I was drawn all but irresistibly away from this line of hypothetical inertia into a moment's reverie in which I was hiding in a footlocker in a dark room and someone holding a large knife and a flashlight was looking for me.

Where are you? she said, in a very casual, almost friendly way, so that, as she stood outside the locker, I nearly answered, or began to breathe again.

Suddenly, he was standing right beside me. If I could have felt anything I would have felt his breath on the lobe of my left ear.

This is where you are, he said. He spoke now in a hoarse, half-whisper, so that it was somewhat difficult to hear him.

Yes, this is where you are, he said, tilting his head back and forth. I wonder what you've learned so far. I wonder if you have learned anything at all.

Very little, I thought, though I have learned some things. I have learned, for example, that murder was done, most certainly. Great quantities of blood and tissue and several small pieces of bone were found.

By whom? (I thought.)

The authorities.

What authorities?

Those charged with attending to this variety of incident.

And how did you come by this information?

I was part of the clean-up crew.

To clean up the blood and . . .

Yes. This was following the assessment.

After the scene had been analyzed?

There was no analysis. There was just the assessment, then the cleanup. There were some 1.8 pints of blood, 3 ounces of tissue, and 3 slivers of cranium.

I don't believe you.

Nevertheless.

Who estimated the amounts of blood and tissue? Who determined that it was cranium?

I did.

You possess the expertise?

I possess the expertise.

This was done under whose orders?

The authorities'.

Whose authorities?

The firm's.

What firm's?

I can't tell you.

What became of the body?

It had been removed.

By whom?

(No answer.)

Isn't it possible that the body, not dead, removed itself?

No.

Why not?

There were certain indications.

Such as?

The blood had spread around the body and congealed, leaving behind an almost perfect outline.

Almost perfect?

There were bootmarks, a single set, pointing inward. They interrupted several of the edges.

Was this documented?

There was a photograph of the crime scene—a damp alley, much rusted metal and garbage and crumbling brick, to one side of which stood a green door; an alley like the one I had recently visited, having left the dark woods and having, part of me that is, returned. A small man was in the photograph. He was standing off to the side, looking down at the almost perfect outline of a body.

I am small. (I thought.)

Who was the victim?

We have not yet made a positive identification.

I repeat, who was the victim?

We aren't sure yet.

Who is we?

We of the firm.

What firm?

I can't tell you.

I know what firm.

Not from me.

No, not from you.

This I had probably learned earlier during those days I spent alone as a teenager in the large farmhouse or out in the surrounding fields. I would lie in bed in the dark and look at the rectangle of light the service lamp projected through the window onto the ceiling above my bed. It seemed to me, as I lay there each night and early morning looking at it, that the world had at last been reduced, that its substance, if substance it could be called, had been sucked away, that all that was left was this poorly formed rectangle, which, in its turn, would surely begin to fizz and fade. In the fields, in the early morning, I would walk and hum and throw stones and think, there where they have fallen, there, quite silent, is where I will lie.

I stared at her astonishingly handsome face. I mean the body's.

What body?

The body that had been there. The one I had put there. When I had been there earlier, having left the dark woods, having returned to my apartment, then crept down the back stairwell and out into the alley, earlier.

How long have you been dead? I said after a time to the astonishingly handsome face.

I'm not sure I am yet.

You are.

And where is my body?

It has been removed.

It suddenly occurred to me that I had been speaking aloud, that almost all of the preceding had, in fact, been said loudly enough for the individual with the orange hat and the cracked tooth to hear.

Did you hear me? I said.

Yes, he said.

So you can see I know very little.

Not as little as you should know—one should know very little about these matters, as little as possible.

About what matters?

He laughed. A judgment has been made.

What judgment?

You've been disaffirmed.

I've already been disaffirmed.

He lifted his gun and aimed it at me.

Yes, knowing very little is best in these matters, he said.

The gun, unless my eyes were deceiving me, probably they were deceiving me, was largely transparent and glowing slightly, and though I wasn't entirely sure what a gun, or any weapon for that matter, could do to me, given my current condition, I did not feel well enough informed to make the correct decision. And in fact it was just as well that, right before he smiled and pulled the trigger, I allowed myself to fall backward through the wall, because the bullet, itself partially transparent, that issued from the gun and struck me in the neck instead of the heart, did considerable damage and hurt tremendously, as bullets, even beautiful ones, are wont to do.

Shot through the neck and falling backward then, I watched him smiling, his cracked tooth caught in some stray line of light and my friend's head peeping in through the door, until the wall I had fallen through obscured them.

For a time then I fell—through the floor of the next room then through other floors then through the earth which glowed and seemed warm and then through a shaft and the edge of a platform and onto the rails of a subway line along which I skidded for a time then lay still. I don't know how long I lay there, but many trains passed through me, causing me only a slight pain, nothing compared to the pain in my neck. It was likely this pain that held me immobile and caused me to focus my thoughts so effectively. I had often done some of my most interesting thinking when in pain and this has remained the case, even all these years later. It was just a moment ago, in fact, when they reset my leg, that several details (of the events I am now relating) both resurfaced and were seen in a fresh alignment that might have helped shed light on what had followed, if only, once the pain lessened, the alignment had not begun to seem less assured. I am still, however, in a position to relate several of these details, and will now do so.

I have killed someone.

Who?

There, on the ground.

Who is it?

My boss.

Which boss?

(No answer.)

Why?

Because of a stapler, because of a shovel and a dark woods, because she was about to have me killed, because . . .

I was in love once. Or perhaps twice—in a park, and then again on a couch.

The wind and scattered clouds and pigeons, soothing us.

But to return . . .

Yes?

To what you did.

They were waiting for me. Three of them in my apartment. My boss set me up. I escaped. Went down the back stairs into the alley. My boss was waiting there for them to finish.

So you killed her?

Yes.

With the shovel?

It was still in my hand. I'd been using it in the woods.

Using it for what?

To dig.

To dig what?

(No answer.)

And then they shot you?

A flesh wound, in the neck. Then when they found me again they broke my legs.

Such were the thoughts I had, more or less, as I lay there on the tracks and afterward, and that I have just had again, though of course they must be somewhat different. In fact, given my condition at the time and my condition now, not to mention the considerable interval, it would be irresponsible not to admit the possibility that these memories were inaccurate, i.e., that they did not substantially adhere to the real, or at least to some satisfactory approximation thereof. I learned quite early on (in the bedroom, in the fields) to content myself with approximations and have long taken comfort in them.

Taken comfort.

One comes to whisper that.

At any rate, to resume, it was the thought that I had been in love with someone, this perplexing and galvanizing premise, that caused me at last, as I remember it, the pain in my neck notwithstanding, to stir and, eventually, one or two more trains having passed through me, to stand.

Then I walked along the tracks, through dark tunnels lit occasionally by train lights and yellow soot-covered lanterns. Every few hundred yards the tunnels opened onto platforms where people, collapsed into chairs, slumped against walls, leaning on painted girders, waited in a kind of daze. They were strangely attractive to me these people waiting for trains below the earth, and once or twice as I walked I stopped and considered them. Mostly though I walked, and walked and walked, and stopped walking and rested with my cold feet in a puddle that held some special appeal for the rats. The rats, intent upon their puddle, which probably had a little oil or meat or rotten lettuce in it, paid me very little attention, although one or two of them attempted, in desultory fashion, and with no luck at all, to bite my ankles.

The city, I then discovered, was as intricately articulated below its surface as it was above, and it was not at all unpleasant to walk along, at best a pale blur, and think about love. Or about being in love. At first it troubled me greatly that I couldn't recall any further details, and that, in fact, some of what I was sure I had just remembered, had already slipped my mind. But this feeling passed quickly enough.

I love you, I said, and the words both warmed and chilled me, as if they were some strange food or drug, or the last faint traces of a dream. I walked and walked and the words "hand in hand" accompanied me, as did the words "I love" so that after a time, when I began to rise up off the tracks, through the damp ceiling and back onto the dark streets, I was not surprised. Nor was I surprised when, still walking, still wrapped in similar thoughts, my mouth making the shape of similar words, I floated up the sides of several buildings and, once, a water tower, where, as the cold wind blew both through and around me, I could just make out the gray-blue light of the approaching dawn.

THE LOST CHAPTER

Green Metal Door

(GHOST NOIR)

And as I went upon my way I was slightly glad that I had met him. A droll customer.

—FLANN O'BRIEN
The Third Policeman

THIS OCCURED QUITE SOME TIME AGO, LONG before the events I have set down elsewhere, long before, at any rate, most of them. During that period I was working, principally, in a firm of transaction specialists. I say "principally" because, at the suggestion of a colleague, I had taken on some outside work as an investigator of sorts, setting up shop, as I did so, in an office on the fourth floor of a building on the far side of town. It was not, at the beginning, particularly nice, this office. It was unsettlingly run-down, with cracked paint and exposed pipes and stacks of newspapers and a huge green sofa with a large stain on one of its arms, and it looked out onto a courtyard into which, clearly, several decades of garbage had been dumped. Still, even though at the beginning it wasn't nice, it did have a sort of anteroom where illustrations could be hung and clients could wait and where a secretary, this was the best part of all, could sit, and it had two of those terrific semitransparent plateglass doors. Once I was settled, I would stand, in fact, for considerable periods of time beside those doors — one leading out into the corridor, the other mediating between my office and the waiting room — considering, as a part of my self-imposed and, admittedly, desultory training, any number of deductive intricacies.

Often, as I stood there, my secretary would bring me small snacks.

Yo, Boss, here's another snack, he would say.

In short, I had great hopes.

The above-mentioned colleague from the transactions firm helped me rent the office.

Sport, he said. This has got to be the place.

It was. I sat down. I stood. I went over and looked at my secretary. He looked at me. I had not seen his teeth when I engaged him. I went back and sat down. Several days went by like this, exactly like this. Then one afternoon there was a knock on the door.

Send him/her in, I said.

Incidentally, when I speak of several days, I am not referring to consecutive days. Most of my time, of course, was still spent at the transactions firm or in the field, which should be taken to mean any place—dock or alley or social club—where business was conducted outside the firm's premises. The night before the afternoon of the knock on the door—there is someone knocking, Boss, my secretary excitedly said—I had been in all of those places, variously in company and alone, and have to confess that, as the events I propose to relate began, I was feeling somewhat the worse for wear, somewhat tired, not quite right. I was thinking of just that when my secretary put his head through the door of my office and said, there is someone knocking, and I said, so answer it.

The individual who came into my office and stood before me looked vaguely familiar. She had long blond hair that did a lot with the dim, yellow light dripping down from the ceiling, and she was wearing a brown trench coat that didn't do much to hide her attributes, of which, let me tell you, there were plenty.

Evening, she said.

Evening? I thought. I looked at my watch. It *was* evening, well into it. I had been under the impression, as I indicated above, that we were still dealing with the afternoon.

Come in, sit down, I said. But looking up, I saw that she had already come in, had already sat down. Clearly, something was off. I was off. I made a note to myself to get friendly with some food and take a break.

I still have that note. It is written in that extraordinarily faint, barely determined hand, that was to characterize all of my attempts at note-taking over the coming days and weeks, and that was to contribute, increasingly, along with other factors, to my inability to make consistent sense of the evidence that was put before me.

Eat burger then sleep, the note reads.

So simple. If only.

I smiled at her.

She smiled back.

Lovely teeth.

Very different story from the one I got when my secretary flashed his choppers, which looked like they'd been soaked in caramel every night for many years.

My own teeth, I don't mind informing you, were in excellent condition in those days, as were many other aspects of my person. My male colleagues at the transactions firm liked me tremendously and even went so far as to call me Champ and Sport. It will come as no surprise then that I was far from being unpopular with certain female individuals, and that I even had one or two special friends.

How can I help you? I said.

Don't you know who I am? she said.

Why do you ask?

Because that's a very, very blank look on your face.

Of course I know who you are.

Good. What have you learned?

Learned?

Yes, learned.

Her hair and the light were collaborating even more nicely now that she was sitting down, and I have to say I had a hard time keeping my eyes off it. Her eyes, too, were worth noting—they were a very pale gray . . .

Pale blue, she said. It must be the light—in a more robust light they are clearly blue. But thank you for noticing.

Did you, ahem, just say something? I said.

She frowned.

I asked you if you had followed him, hello, as per our agreement.

Of course I did, I said.

When?

Last night.

And?

And I learned some very interesting things.

Elaborate.

After a moment, I did so. I told her that at approximately 5 p.m. the previous evening I had followed him out of his office on the west side and had trailed him across town. Subject had walked briskly, one might even say, without overpresumption, purposefully.

He is purposeful.

Yes, I could see that.

Go on.

On the way across town, Subject had stopped four times. Once for a chocolate bar at a newsstand; once for a cake of heavy-duty soap at a hardware store; once outside the window of a gift shop; once in an alley where he knocked twice on a green metal door, after which I momentarily lost sight of him.

Lost sight of him how? Did he go in the door? Did someone answer?

I'm not sure.

At this juncture, she leaned forward and looked at me with a curious expression.

Incidentally, that's quite a bruise, she said.

It was. I had checked it several times over the course of the afternoon in the mirror that hung next to my desk. The bruise, above my right temple, had made its way through several colors, and now — I took a quick look — seemed to have settled into a deep violet ringed with indigo and brown.

How did you get it?

I'm not sure.

You don't seem to be sure about a lot of things.

This was definitely true, but I decided not to answer. Instead, I just nodded, noncommittally, and smiled.

She asked me if I had taken any aspirin.

I said I had.

So you must have lost him after that.

After what?

After he knocked twice on the green metal door.

The funny thing is I didn't, I said. It's true that he got away from me for a minute or two, but I caught up with him just as he was entering a private residence on the east side.

Who lives there?

I gave her the name.

So that's it.

This was not put as a question and I did not treat it like one. My assignment, and I suddenly found I remembered it all, had been to follow the individual and to provide my client with a name. I had done so. She was satisfied, and I was satisfied and, once she had paid me the outstanding portion of my fee, we would leave it at that. Clearly, as one thinks to one's self, I had a future in this business, and would soon enough find myself in a position to reduce my hours at the transactions firm. While it was true that I would miss certain aspects of the work, there was no doubt in my mind that brighter things lay in store for me as an investigator, and I can say with all surety that I was not wrong.

I couldn't be wrong.

I mean compared to the way it has worked out, which is differently. I am no longer an investigator and I would not call things bright. And yet at that moment they were. A beautiful client sat in a chair opposite me, I had a secretary, an office, and had somehow, in carrying out my duties, earned myself a bruise.

Can I offer you a drink? I said.

I don't think so, she said.

Are you sure? It's said that I have a winning personality.

How much do I owe you?

I told her.

She stood up to leave.

I think that's how it went, because at precisely the moment I asked her to share a drink with me, or thought I did, the room began to go very dark and then very light and I saw some things. I saw, for instance, that while I had been interacting with my client, someone else had come into the office and was conversing with my secretary. My secretary was not smiling. He was nodding and looking meaningfully and not altogether pleasantly at the door to my office, and the individual he was interacting with was holding a gun.

Excuse me a moment, I said.

My client was standing before me holding out a few bills. I walked quickly around her and jerked open the door to the front office. My secretary was sitting there, smiling, all alone.

Brush your fucking teeth, I said.

Are you all right? my client said.

I turned away from my secretary, bowed, and assured her that I was. I also told her that it had been an absolute pleasure carrying out her assignment, and that if she should have any future need of an investigator, she could call me.

Good, she said.

Excellent, I said.

She handed me the money, shook, I think, my hand, nodded at my secretary, and left.

I was somewhat less comfortable than I like to be after that. I stood for a time in the doorway, between my room and my secretary's, listing a little, first to one side then to the other, and all the while my secretary, apparently not the slightest bit nonplussed by my outburst, spoke to me. He spoke to me quietly and soothingly about the quality of the client who had just left—about her coat and about where, in his opinion, the coat had been purchased. He spoke to me about her hair and the line of her jawbone and about her blue eyes, which set off to such effect the large and tasteful rock she had been wearing around her neck. He spoke to me about the job, about how well I had carried it out, and about how well I had interacted with the client, and after he had gone on for some time in this vein I finally got it.

You want me to pay you, right? I said.

Yes, immediately please.

I gave him the money the client had handed me, and after counting it twice, somewhat ostentatiously licking his thumb in the process, he slipped it into his pocket, presumably satisfied. Then he went on talking for a while. He talked mostly about his mother—a favorite subject of his—and about a house they had once visited on a lake long ago. The house, which had belonged to his mother's employer, had sat on a small promontory overlooking the enormous lake, which was notable both for its color—red—and its shape—a near perfect horseshoe. Each day, he and his mother would rise early and row out onto the lake, where, in my secretary's phrase, surrounded by mist and bird song they would drop their lines. While they fished, and the fishing was excellent— they ate of it every night, his mother undertaking the bulk of the cleaning, so many small wet shapes, as my secretary put it, in the bucket, on the plate—his mother would tell him stories. Son, she would say, and she would tell him about something wonderful that had happened before he was born. She had been unusually old for a mother, so old it had always seemed to my secretary incredible that she had been able to pull it off, a point with which I, now leaning into the doorframe, or so I thought, completely concurred.

In fact, by now I had left my office and, on my way over to the transactions firm to attend to a little business, was running over the sequence of events in my head. Notable about this process was the nagging feeling that I had forgotten something, most likely something important, but I registered that this was not necessarily linked to the somewhat strange events I had just experienced, or rather to the somewhat strange way I had experienced the foregoing events; despite my relative youth during this period, I was already plagued by various failings in memory along with the concomitant anxieties this can provoke. And, my anxieties having further evolved, it troubled me to note (and this is simply the example that leaps to mind) that while I could very clearly recall telling the client about trailing her "husband," I could no longer recall the trailing itself, and firmly suspected that the events might have occurred otherwise. In which case my performance on the job would have been somewhat less than satisfactory, a hypothesis I found deeply disturbing. I had, after all, accepted money from my client, and I was in no way interested in establishing myself as some moderately hard-boiled variety of charlatan. Clearly, the matter would require follow-up, even if only to put my mind at ease.

I have done many things in my life with the idea of putting my mind at ease. Having come now to this end of it, of life, I am none too happy to report that it is a hopeless task.

Be that as it may, however, it is too early in these proceedings to dwell on that, I soon found myself back at the transactions firm sharing a pleasant drink with three or four fellow transactionists. In accordance with long-standing tradition, drinks were shared in the copy room, and, if one required additional intimacy, in the large closet therein. No additional intimacy being required on this occasion, we stood and leaned against the various machines and reams of paper and drank from bottles and dubiously washed glasses. The largest of my colleagues, an important member of the firm's junior staff, drank from a bowl. This was the individual who had helped me to set up my office and, in fact, had gotten me started in the firm. He was, as I say, quite a large individual, with much flesh to recommend him. Later—after the events I am setting down here that is—he would grow leaner, and an astonishingly handsome face would emerge from its fleshy encasement, or rather from its entombment, as he would put it, but during this period it was not his looks, or lack thereof, that distinguished him. It was his undeniable talent for transactions—far exceeding my own or that of any other member of the junior staff—that set him apart and ensured him a steady set of interviews with the boss.

It was of the boss that we were speaking as we drank. The boss, apparently something of an aficionado, had recently purchased a new line of track for the enormous electric train set that he kept in his office and which none of us, with the exception of our large colleague, or so I then thought, had seen. Later, I would learn that I had already seen the office and the boss and his train set under conditions both pleasant and less so, but at that moment I was convinced I had not, and so, despite my headache and liminal concerns, listened eagerly to our fleshy colleague's description of it.

First of all, he said, you have to understand that the office itself is much larger than the ordinary office, both in terms of area and volume, so that one is only gradually struck by the remarkable size and complexity of the boss's train set. It is quite a pleasant thing, then, to wander through the office and to discover aspect after novel aspect of that network. The mountain range and aerial bridge assert themselves only after one has considered the detailed curiosities of the tropical river and surrounding rain forest or vice versa. Just as the great city seems marvelous only after one has wandered through the desert wastes. This is perhaps a function of the track's emphatic primacy, and of the single engine, black with a beautiful red smokestack, that is forever sliding along it. It was this circumstance that struck me, in fact—the engine never stops, and he, the boss, was kind enough to confirm this for me.

The engine, he says, will never stop, even as the dust forms high drifts on the savannah, the paint wears off the mountains, and the electric bulbs burn out in the great city's miniature streetlights. It will continue along the ever-expanding network of track long after he has diverted the river, replaced the stand of rubber trees, and thrown away the plastic glacier. Those of us, he says, who perform satisfactorily, will one day be allowed to take a turn at the switchboard, to feel the curious thrill, the genuine but subtle sense of power, and of loss and bewilderment.

At this point our colleague fell silent and, as we were well along with our respective beverages, one of us suggested that it was time to see about our assignments for the evening. Assignments, in that firm, were generally posted in red marker on a white board outside the second secretary's office, and the larger part of our number set off to see what had been arranged for them. Soon, in fact, it was just myself and the fleshy colleague left in the copy room.

Well, Sport, he said.

We clinked beverages.

I'm glad it's just the two of us, I said. I had been hoping to have a moment with you before we got started.

Sure, Sport, no problem, he said.

But the truth is I really didn't have much of an idea about where to get started. There were several things I hadn't quite understood about what he had said about the boss's train set, although I had very much enjoyed his intervention. I told him as much.

Thank you, he said.

Yes, I said. While there were several things I couldn't quite grasp, I found that your description of the network made me think of deltas.

Deltas?

Not the track—the track doesn't branch off, it seems—but the visitor to the network experiences a certain measure of branching and expansion in his/her thoughts, presumably. For instance, from the great city to the mountains, but also, simultaneously to the rubber forest and the river, and the tiny lights.

Why are you talking to me about deltas?

I'm not sure.

We stood there.

He told me a joke.

He said, one more for the road?

We had one more.

Deltas, he said.

I told him that it was likely my investigation work that had led me to think of them.

That's great, Sport, he said.

It's just that both the blood system in the brain and trees look a lot like deltas if you make a schematic of them. I have been trying to determine how I might make a schematic of a crime or rather of a perpetrator's actions during the commission of a crime.

You don't look so good, he said.

I don't feel so good.

He patted me on the shoulder then pulled a very large bag of unshelled peanuts out of his jacket pocket and offered me a handful.

We put our glasses away.

Let's go check the board now, Sport.

Okay, but first tell me, where was I last night between 5 and 5:30 p.m.?

You were with me, Sport, don't you remember?

In fact, now that he mentioned it, I did remember. I could very clearly recall that we had worked together all afternoon and well into the evening. We had worked together on a very unpleasant job; or rather—unpleasant is the wrong word—it was difficult. They were sometimes. Perhaps, then, I had gotten my time frame wrong; perhaps I had trailed my client's husband the night previous to the previous one; perhaps. Perhaps, indeed, but even if that was the case, my earlier description notwithstanding, I still couldn't remember having done it. At this juncture, however, my case-related ruminations were cut short by another of my colleagues, who popped his head into the copy room and said, let's go, Champ, you're with me.

For the next few hours then, I was very much occupied in some business, a tricky but rewarding transaction for which we acquired a trunk, a razor, and thirty feet of rope. And while it is certainly true that over the course of the evening my thoughts reverted to my client's lovely bones and perfume and snug-fitting raincoat, I did not trouble myself, or rather had no time to trouble myself, with the residual time- and memory-related vagaries of the case, for which, after all, and this had to indicate an adequate measure of success, I had been quite handsomely paid.

Several days went by. I barely noticed them. In fact one or two of them I did not notice at all and what's more, when they did come to my attention, a quick inventory revealed that I had nothing in my possession that could definitively account for them.

Incidentally, this has remained a problem. Here, for example, whole weeks slip by, entire months are simply sucked away from me, and I'm left lying in bed in the middle of what should have been.

At any rate, I soon found myself back in the office, back at my desk. Since I had last been there my secretary had made several improvements, including having an intercom system installed so that I would not have to move or shout in order to contact him. I found this arrangement highly satisfactory. We both did. In fact, I quickly took to conducting the larger part of my business with him through the intercom. This was in part to cut down on the number of times I was forced to gaze upon his teeth—so medieval in their aspect—in part because I liked the sound of his voice as it came through the small speaker, and, when we talked at mealtime, the sound he made while eating the moist, warm dishes he favored, his lips smacking lightly at the soft foods. Also I liked to click down on the "communicate" button. It was lovely to do so—to speak then hear a voice in return.

In this way I learned more about the red lake and about his mother and various other things. He in his turn, if he was listening, I could not always be sure that he was, learned various things about me; for example, that I, too, in my earlier years, had gone out in the early morning with a relative onto a lake, although the lake I had gone out onto had not been red, it had been a very murky green. Mostly I would fish, but occasionally my relative, at the time sadly moribund, would instruct me to pull up my line and let go of the oars so that we would "just drift." Sometimes, as we drifted through the mist across the green lake, my relative would speak. More often, though, my relative remained silent, staring over the side of the boat or into the mist or at me.

At me was the least desirable direction.

There were cataracts involved.

My objection was not aesthetic.

My relative could barely see me: I was barely seen.

It was hard for me to remember that this condition was temporary; that my perceived half presence—"I can hardly see you—wave your arms or something"—would not extend beyond the bounds of the boat, once we had left the misty lake and returned to shore.

It wasn't.

Temporary I mean.

Are you listening? I said.

There was a silence, quite a long one, and then my secretary said, Yes.

This was true, I thought—I could see him, quite clearly, leaning over the intercom, his chin in his hands, smiling sweetly, attentive, staring at the red light that, illuminated, indicated that the line was open. I should say that since the previous occasion, I had had no such convincing visual confirmation of my secretary's or anyone else's activities as they sat in rooms other than the one I sat in. Only once, in fact, during the days that had elapsed (although clearly I do not, here, include the days I could not account for), had anything at all "curious" in this regard happened. One evening, one or two nights previously, as I had lain in bed attempting to sleep—I could not—I had very clearly heard a lawn tractor, with the mower engaged, maybe two or three feet from my bed, and above the sound of the lawn tractor, the sound of my grandmother calling out my name.

I have still not decided whether this event was connected to the predicament I was in then, the predicament I came only quite slowly to recognize, and only lately to fully accept. The business about "seeing" my secretary helped to push this process along. Which is to say that, remembering that I had seen things incorrectly the last time, I stood, crossed the room—very quietly: my secretary, as part of his improvements, had had plush carpet installed—and jerked open the door to the front room.

Hello, I said.

Sitting in one of the two chairs reserved for waiting clients was a very small man wearing a raincoat. It was hard to make out his features, as he was wearing a hat with a wide brim. I could see the end of his nose (large) and his lips (moist, thin). His chin was square and his jaw unusually heavy.

I'm sorry to have kept you waiting, I said. Have you seen my secretary?

I asked him if he wouldn't mind taking a walk down the hall, just for a few minutes, you understand.

I told him I did.

Then I asked him how long he had been sitting there.

Quite a while.

From where I stood, I could see that the intercom was still on.

Did you . . .?

Yes, everything.

About the cataracts?

It's quite a nice story. Your relative lived a very handsome life.

Yes, I said.

Yes, he said. I liked the story about the war, and the military plane, sitting next to the prince and seeing the leaning tower from the air. Have you ever seen it?

No, I said.

I have, he said. It's a nice tower, you stand on a green lawn and look at it, but it's not as nice as it would be from the air—blue sky above and around, brown and yellow fields below. And then descending at dusk on the airfield lit by gas lamps to dine with the prince while bombs went off against a backdrop of thunder.

Those were different days, he said.

Yes.

He wasn't lying, was he, your relative?

I don't know.

Because they do lie, not always but sometimes.

He was looking at me. I could see his eyes now. They were a very pretty green.

You don't recognize me, do you? he said.

No, I said.

I don't mean to imply that you should. I just find it curious—a curious result.

Result of what?

My name is Green.

Mr. Green?

No it's not, never mind, a little joke, don't call me that.

We stood there a moment. That is to say that I stood there and he sat there.

Can I help you with something? I said.

Yes, you can.

I told him that perhaps, as it was a business call, we should go into my office, that that would be more appropriate. I could sit behind my desk and he could sit in the client's chair. I could take notes on what he had to say. I had a notepad and a very nice pen.

All right, he said. He smiled as he said this and his smile, like his eyes, was very pretty, despite his lips, which were not pretty; I could not understand how they could participate in something as pretty as the smile they helped to compose.

I didn't recognize him at all.

We began to walk into my office. I motioned for him to precede me.

Please, I said. After you.

You are very polite. I am happy to be in the hands of an investigator with some manners.

He stepped ahead of me. We moved forward. And as we did so, strange to relate, it seemed to me that I passed through him, that he paused a moment and I continued and slipped straight through him, that, in fact, I continued to move, straight through what was to be his chair and through my desk and through my chair and the wall behind it and across the courtyard and out into the open air above the dark street where I stopped and floated for a time.

When I turned, however, I found that I had misperceived my situation, and was sitting in my chair, pen in hand, notebook open in front of me. Beside the notebook, several pages of which were filled with writing, was a card that read, "Mr. Smith," and gave an address—the address to which I had followed my previous client's "husband." As for my client, having presumably said all he wished to, he had seen fit to take his leave.

I found, now that he had gone, that I was very tired, and even though it was late and I would soon be expected for my shift at the transactions firm, it seemed hard to move. It was pleasantly warm in my office and the yellow bulbs gave off the kind of soft, inadequate light that lends itself to lucubration and dozing. Aware, then, that I was in my element, I depressed the intercom switch and said, Are you there?

Yes.

You're back from your little stroll.

Yes.

Don't let anyone in.

There is a woman here to see you.

Make an excuse. Send her away.

I switched off the intercom and, leaning back in my chair, let out a sigh, took up my notebook, and read the following:

> [Client]: I have a story too. It's not coming to me right this second, but it will.

We sit. I ask the client for details of the business matter he has come to share with me.

> [Client]: Ah, here it is, I knew it would come. It is of a slightly older vintage than the one you related, and while it does not involve princes and airfields, I think you will find it makes for agreeable listening.

Client's story summarized: A great-great-uncle or aunt or client, having fallen in with a certain group, burns rose at midnight and waits up until dawn for ghost of rose to appear.

> [Me]: And?
>
> [Client]: It didn't. Or so it seemed to my relative, for a number of weeks, months, or even years—the account isn't clear—and then one morning at breakfast, on a sun-flooded table, an iris, very pale, appeared and began slowly revolving, all through breakfast.
>
> [Me]: An iris?
>
> [Client]: Yes, strange isn't it? The ghost of an iris for a burned rose. My relative took to burning all kinds of flowers after that. Whole bouquets. But it is not clear whether there were any more apparitions.

[Me]:   I see.

Client falls silent. Starts to hum. Pretty green eyes. Somehow familiar. I offer him a drink. We drink. Toast relatives. I ask him if the story he has told me is true.

[Client]: Yes.
[Me]:   I see.
[Client]: But there were no witnesses. Or none have come forward yet.
[Me]:   The victim had been bludgeoned to death?
[Client]: So our sources tell us, but we haven't been able to confirm. None of our people have seen the body. It is, you understand, a very delicate matter.
[Me]:   Delicate in what sense?
[Client]: In all senses.
[Me]:   Where is the body?
[Client]: We aren't sure.
[Me]:   But you are sure the victim was one of your firm's employees?
[Client]: No.
[Me]:   So you want me to find out if it was.

Client doesn't answer. I ask client if any employees are missing. Client says it would be impossible to say.

[Me]:   You mentioned sources. How about some names?

Client gives names, places of business, phone numbers: Mr. Jones, Ms. Green, Ms. Krumpacher. Settle on fee. Reasonable. Client looks at watch. Says he has to leave. Leaves. Room is suddenly filled with flowers. Very pale. Slowly rotating. Whole bouquets.

By this time (I had been rather slow in reading), it was quite late and high time I left my office and made my way over to the transactions firm to see what they had for me that evening. Before leaving, however, I carefully copied the above-mentioned names and phone numbers onto a fresh sheet of the notepad, tore the sheet out of the book, put the book in the desk drawer, closed the drawer, locked the drawer, pocketed the key (I thought), went out and had a short conversation with my secretary, who I found in high spirits (the new client had tipped him generously), left him the names and numbers with instructions to set up appointments, felt for my pulse, couldn't find it, asked my secretary to take it, was told it was eighty, asked him if he was lying, watched him smile, shrugged, then smacked him, gently, then left.

And while it had been my intention to mull over certain aspects of the new case, especially those aspects that (even if only hypothetically) impinged upon my own person, before I could begin, before, in fact, I could begin even to be aware of my passage, i.e., down the hall, down the stairs, out the front door, along the crowded streets, then streets plural, I found myself at home, sitting on my couch with a scotch and soda in my hand.

I took a sip.

This was scotch from a good bottle, not any bottle I owned. For a moment, then, I had the pleasant thought that the entire night had slipped by, that not only had I misplaced my passage home, but also my passage to the firm, some light banter in the copy room, a welcome dose of exegesis from my fleshy friend or one of the more senior transactionists, an assignment, perhaps on one of the rooftops this time, or near a furnace, or outside the city in the wetlands, or on one of the many dark plains; at any rate, a fine night's work, it occurred to me, might have passed, been completed, been achieved, after which I might have purchased (or even been awarded) this fine scotch.

I sighed. I took a sip. As I pulled the glass away from my lips, a woman came out of the kitchen with her own glass and sat down beside me.

Now it came back to me. I had been on my way to work and, in light of the seriousness of the case I was now working on, had stopped off at home to retrieve my gun. Arriving at my door, I had met this woman, who, she had told me, had attempted to see me earlier that evening at my office and had been turned away.

I'm sorry, I said.

You've already apologized, it's all right, she said, sipping at her drink.

She, too, was quite an interesting aggregate. By that I mean that she was in possession of attributes both comely and less so, some of them simultaneously. Take for instance her legs. They were exquisitely shaped, but exceptionally short, as if she had on the legs of a much smaller person. Her hands, too, which looked as though they'd been chiseled out of brown granite, were tiny, so that she was obliged to hold her glass of scotch, rocks no water, with both of them. Her face, for its part, was gorgeous, and it was a little hard not to just stare at it, and stare at it and stare.

I'm sorry, I said. I mean for staring.

How do you like the whiskey? she said.

Lovely, I said.

She had poured it from a leather-wrapped stainless steel flask that she had taken from an inside pocket. When she had pulled it out, I had seen her shoulder holster and the small but deadly looking automatic it held.

How do you do with that thing? I had asked.

Marvelously, she had said.

At that point, I had excused myself to the bedroom where I had retrieved my own gun, a revolver, not too accurate but persuasive, had slipped it into my pocket, then returned to the living room and sat down.

I took another sip.

The apartment seemed a little cool to me.

I asked her if she would like me to turn up the heat.

She told me that she was adequately heated.

It seems cool to me, I said.

It's probably your bruise.

Probably.

Take another drink.

I took one.

Helps, doesn't it?

I told her it did.

For a while we sat there drinking.

Any particular reason you stopped by?

Yes.

We drank a while longer.

I found that most of my thoughts, though dull, had to do with her face.

The tiny hands, too, had their charm.

Sitting there, I had a vision of them—very quickly, even too quickly, sewing small items of clothing for dolls. Then I saw her fingers, wearing bonnets, walking together one fine morning along a country road.

One encounters curious physical attributes more often than one would imagine, I considered saying.

I also considered proposing to discuss my own.

For instance, I have a trick knee.

I am holding it and having it do its unpleasant trick now.

And considered doing so then.

I'm sorry I didn't see you earlier at the office, would you like to look at my knee? I said.

I've seen it, she said.

Oh.

You probably don't remember.

Of course I do.

It was some time ago.

I remember it very clearly.

That took care of me for a few minutes.

During those few minutes I rolled back my eyes and ransacked my brain.

I haven't been feeling that well recently, I said, finally, having turned up nothing, absolutely nothing.

I know.

For instance, hah, hah, I don't have a pulse. By that I mean I haven't been able to find it recently.

She looked at me.

You don't have a stethoscope do you? I said, laughing a little. A stethoscope would probably clear this up.

No, she said.

She continued to look at me. She lifted her glass and looked at it. Then she looked at my wrist then at my chest, I think, then somewhere over my shoulder, at a mirror, maybe, that hung there, then looked at her glass again, lifted it to her lips, drank, looked at me, at my eyes, my eyes are brown shot with green, like a mineral I forget the name of, I saw a sample once, in a dark hall in which only the mineral cases were lit, looked away, set down her glass, leaned back, crossed her small legs, and said, I don't either, I mean have a pulse, or anyway not much of one.

That night at work I asked for some time off. The Chief Dispatcher, an agreeable older gentleman always in shirt-sleeves and a blue fez, told me that would be fine as long as I worked my current shift. This seemed fair, so I went out into the hall and took a look at the assignment board. I found my name next to that of my fleshy colleague — I'll call him John — who I subsequently found in the copy room having drinks with another of our colleagues. This transactionist, John told me as we went out the door and onto the street, possessed a bosom he deeply admired.

Yeah? I said.

Very, very special, John said.

That's interesting, I said.

Yes, it is, John said.

I thought about this as we walked along the street toward our destination, a disused power station that was soon, our briefing note told us, to be converted into a live/work space. Which is not to say that I spent an inordinate amount of time thinking about our colleague's bosom, although I was happy enough, without having had the pleasure, to be supportive of John's position on it. Rather, I thought of John's choice of words, *deeply admire*, which made me think about my first client's attributes and my recent visitor's face and hands, then the lamentable state of my pulse, not to mention the revelations thereon my recent visitor had shared with me and the hallucinations of a sort that had both preceded and followed that interaction, all in the context of the case I was now working on, so that when for perhaps the tenth time since leaving my apartment I probed my wrist for some positive indication and found it, even if it was only very faint, very far off, very feathery . . .

There is one, or almost one, she had told me and had helped me to find and count it—eighty-five faint beats that would grow fainter, as I grew fainter, she had said.

. . . I thought of deeply admired bosoms, and of, strangely, being bludgeoned to death, even if only, and I said this last aloud, hypothetically.

You're a weird fuck lately, Sport, said John.

Then we arrived at the disused power station.

This was quite an impressive facility, with enormous brick walls and high windows and the words, carved in capital letters above the orange door, ELECTRICITY IS LIFE. We knocked and after a moment were let in. Inside it was dark, and the curious agglomeration of derelict machinery, tools, ladders, and sawhorses, lit only, as they were, by the streetlights filtering in through a few high, small windows, put us in a philosophical frame of mind.

John told me afterwards, as we walked toward the river carrying the heavy bag between us, that the spectacle had made him think of a book he had read recently on the phenomenon of decay, many of the illustrations for which had been taken from this city's archives. Quite a number of the book's pages were devoted to microscopic decay and the corruption of molecules. There is nothing that does not decay, said John, from the steel in the skyscrapers, to the flesh that wraps and hides us, to the light that bathes and burns our faces. Even ideas decompose, and the gods we once carried inside us have broken down into simpler products, many of which have, themselves, entirely wasted away.

For my part, having left aside for a moment the bosoms and bludgeonings I had been preoccupied with, as soon as we began to walk through the rows of ancient transformers, I thought of travel in deep space, and of a newly described propulsion system in which a spacecraft would generate a plasma field that would effectively function as a sail to harness the cosmic winds. It seemed to me that the majestically derelict machinery surrounding us, including the gutted turbine where the body was, must once have had something in common with the proposed plasma generator, which might someday lead us to strange and distant parts. It was along these and tangential lines (and not of decay) that I thought as we lifted the body wrapped in black plastic and deposited it in the oversize bag we had brought with us.

The individual who had let us in let us out through another door. This individual had been silent throughout our visit and seemed not at all predisposed to engage in the kind of banter that is often characteristic of these assignments. Perhaps, it occurred to me, he too had been struck by our surroundings and was engaged in musings of his own as he led us through the all but dark. (I asked him about this when some days later I had the opportunity to converse with him. He told me that he had thought of nothing, that when he was working he did not think, but that he liked the idea of decay, especially insofar as it applied to himself. How do you feel about plasma-based propulsion systems? I asked him. Why? Because that's what I was thinking about while we were there. Sorry, but I don't care too much about that.) Still, as we left, John, who at the opening of the door found, he later told me, a sense of levity returning, made a remark regarding the quality and prodigious size of our colleague's external accoutrements, which elicited the beginnings of a smile from the individual. This beginning of a smile, in its turn, when we had stepped out through a green metal door and into the dark alley beyond it, reminded me of something (see above — my first case, a certain set of minutes unaccounted for).

Are you missing part of one of your teeth, the right incisor? I asked him as he was preparing to shut the door.

Yes, he said. And as he said it, perhaps in a moment of empathy for the body we had in the bag, I found myself drifting back through the dark equipment to lie for a moment in the open turbine. Before long though I found myself back with John, walking along one dark street after another as we made our way to the river. We were discussing our thoughts on the interior of the power station and also the desirability of live/work spaces. Neither one of us had ever lived in a loft and we agreed that the prospect of so much renovated space had its appeal. My apartment at that time was a renovated space. It had once been the office of a fairly successful tailor who had returned, the housing agent had told me, to another country to die. When I moved in there were some scraps of cloth and thread on the floor behind the radiators, and in one of the closets I found a needle and a pin. Later, when John moved in with me and we became roommates, we found a bolt of blue cloth beneath one of the floorboards, and John had shirts made for each of us. This was not long after the events I am currently attempting to give some account of, that is to say after the conclusion of the present case and my retirement from the investigation business. This was not a happy moment, as you might imagine, but it seemed a necessary one. Now, of course, all these years later, I see how things might have been different for me if my speculations had been more probing and if my conclusions had been more prescient and if certain events had not unfolded as they did.

They did.

We reached the river.

John said, wait here, swung the bag up over his shoulder and walked off into the gloom.

But instead of waiting for him, as our briefing note directed, by the crates of rotten carrots, beets, and yellow squash that lined the walls of the warehouses we were now behind, it occurred to me that without actually doing so, or at any rate seeming to, I might in fact follow him, or try. I took this decision in an attempt to consciously effect the phenomenon that had lately, and as recently as the turbine, afflicted me, in light of the considerable amount of advice my earlier visitor had imparted to me, and not just concerning my pulse.

It worked. I walked beside John, I walked behind him, I walked in front.

There are other things you can do, she had told me. And if, as you say, you are currently engaged in a potential homicide case, you will find some of the modalities of your condition quite useful.

This seemed useful. John, instead of taking the bag to the river and dropping it over the side, simply, in walking, leaned his shoulder into one of the ubiquitous crates by the water's edge, causing it to fall into the dark water (a sound I would later remember having heard as I stood waiting by the warehouse for John), while he continued on a little farther, at which point he was met by a certain individual, difficult to make out in the half dark, until he smiled and showed his cracked incisor. There followed both an exchange of words and of knowing expressions, and also of the bag, which the individual hefted onto his own shoulder and set off with. Pushing my luck a little further, I fol-

lowed along with this individual as he made his way
back through the crates and into an alley not far from
where I stood waiting and where John would momentarily rejoin me.

We walked through the same set of alleys John and I
had negotiated in carrying the body to the docks and,
before long (it was necessary to be impressed by this individual's robustness) we were back at the green door,
where, instead of following the individual into the
machines and the dark, I began, light as one of the lesser
elements, to float up the side of the building into the night
sky.

One will be sure to think it possible, even necessary, to
draw certain conclusions from this episode, and I was
subsequently both willing and almost eager to do so.

1) Necessarily, for instance, something was afoot; 2)
That something involved me; 3) As well as the case I was
working on; 4) Possibly; 5) John had something to do
with it; 6) The transactions firm had something to do with
it; 7) I was a ghost.

This possibility had been presented to me by my earlier visitor, herself, she alleged, a ghost.

What do you mean you're a ghost?

I'm a ghost, I'm dead, I do things.

And yet here you are.

But then she wasn't.

Suddenly she was standing behind me.

She put her hands over my eyes.

It was possible to see through them a little.

All this means, I said, gesturing with my drink, is that
I've been feeling a little unusual lately. I see through your
hands because I'm so sleepy. I've been working two jobs
and keeping some pretty strange hours and talking to

some pretty strange customers and doing some pretty ugly things. Likely, you're not even here.

I'm not, she said. Which is to say that I am and am not. I'm also elsewhere.

Where?

I don't know.

But you've floated over here to inform me that I'm a ghost.

I didn't float. I try not to. Voluntary use of such capacities tends to overdetermine them, makes it difficult to get back.

What do you mean by "get back"?

To my body.

So you *do* know where it is.

No, I don't. All I know is it's dark—or that my eyes don't work. Which is a possibility. It happens in a pretty high percentage of cases.

And how did you learn all this?

There is literature available.

Literature?

Yes.

Listen, I said, I appreciate the scotch and you and your weird small hands and legs, but I have to get to work. I've just been having some mediocre out-of-body experiences, which a couple of pounds of food and some sleep will remedy.

You won't sleep, she said.

I have to go, I said.

But we sat and drank and she said other things.

8) She said it was akin, at times, to a dream state, that at times I would like it, that at times I would not.

Can I walk through walls? I said.

Haven't you already?

I thought about that.

And also, she said, barely there, you are divisible—can be barely there in more than one place, send off slivers of yourself. Then there are mirrors.

What about them?

A ghost sees many things in a mirror, but never him/herself.

So how come just after I got my bruise I could see myself in the mirror in my office?

It takes time for the condition to fully assert itself. Try it now.

I stood. In the mirror hanging behind the couch on the wall I saw a row of brightly colored computers, a mummified crocodile, a shotgun, a row of turnips, a display of ray guns.

What do you see? I said.

Two galaxies in the constellation Canis Major colliding, she said.

9) She also said that the visions or hallucinations I had been having could be both useful and dangerous—useful because any accurate edge on upcoming particularities was helpful; dangerous because as often as not what felt like an accurate edge was apocryphal or too vague to do anything but fuel confusion.

So how can I tell the difference?

You can't. At least not until afterwards. Maybe not even then.

Well, that's just great. Doesn't the literature you mentioned have anything to say about it?

She nodded. It says what I just said.

Can you add anything—like maybe from your own experience?

I'm an optimist, she said.

Meaning what?

She shrugged. Meaning I think it's all going to work out. Some way or other.

I took a sip of scotch and thought about it. I didn't know what to think.

At any rate, before I knew it I was no longer floating up above the buildings and warehouses, but walking back to the firm with John and discussing all manner of first-rate subjects.

John was very interested, he told me as we walked along, in the subject of big cats in general, and of cheetahs specifically. He had been doing some research lately and had learned that cheetahs, while well deserving of the title "fastest land animal," were at a considerable disadvantage when it came to weight and strength, and often lost prey. Lions, who were in many ways the scourge of the jungle, and also of the savannah, were always delighted to come across a cheetah working over a fresh kill, as there was nothing easier for a lion than to send a cheetah packing. John had never yet seen either a lion or a cheetah, but he had seen a jackal once. The little dog, as John described it, had snapped viciously at a stick John was carrying before running away.

Jackals live in dens, John told me.

Like badgers, I said.

Yeah, just like badgers, Sport.

Anyway, as you can imagine, I might well in the face of this benign but interesting conversation have come around to being convinced of the apocryphal nature of my surreptitious tailing, had not one subsequent remark struck a jarring note. After we had concluded our interaction regarding cats, jackals, and more or less related categories of animals, John said, that was some hat that guy was wearing.

What hat? I said.

Never mind, he said.

That was all there was to it. But little by little, as I sat in my office later, after my leave of absence had started, I began to consider the events that had occurred while part of me had waited for John by the warehouse. One of the things I remembered was that, unlike earlier, the individual with the cracked tooth had been wearing an orange hat, a hat that John had remarked on as they stood bantering a moment before exchanging the bag.

My secretary buzzed. I buzzed back. The first of the appointments he had set up for me came in.

This was Ms. Krumpacher—a very pleasant and intelligent individual who had, you will remember, information relevant to the case. When she had gone, Mr. Jones came. Then Ms. Green.

Ms. Green, I was somewhat surprised to note, was more or less the woman I had shared scotch with the previous evening. We had a nice chat. Then she left. After I had seen her out, I returned to my desk, hit the intercom, told my secretary to hold all calls and to tell any visitors I wasn't in.

Sure, Boss, said my secretary.

Good, I said. Incidentally, how have you been?

Not so bad, Boss, he said. A little lonely, but not so bad.

We all get lonely, I said.

Sure, Boss. Will that be all?

Yes. Although, frankly, I'd rather you didn't call me Boss.

What would you like me to call you?

Sir.

I won't call you Sir.

Then don't call me anything.

Having concluded that exchange, I leaned back in my chair and set my mind to the task of digesting the information I had just received from Ms. Krumpacher, Mr. Jones, and Ms. Green. Despite my best efforts at concentrating, however, I found that my thoughts kept returning to my secretary's remark about loneliness. No doubt it was this remark that brought to my mind images of all those days I spent alone as a teenager in the large farmhouse or out in the surrounding fields. I would lie in bed in the dark and look at the rectangle of light the service lamp projected onto the ceiling above my bed. It seemed to me, as I lay there looking at it, that the world had at last been reduced, that its substance had been siphoned away, that all that was left was this pale rectangle, which, in its turn, would surely fade. In the fields, in the early morning, I would walk and hum and throw stones and think, there where they have fallen, that is where I will lie. And much else along these lines, so that after a certain interval I found myself moved to rise, to go into the front room and join my secretary, to sit, as it were, in company with him. This laudable ambition notwithstanding, I got no farther than the handle of the door to the front room. My secretary wasn't alone. He was conversing, in a suspicious whisper, with the aforementioned individual with the cracked tooth.

Yes, he's in there, and feeling very lonely, my secretary said.

So maybe I'll go in there and give him some company, the individual with the cracked tooth said. And when he stood (the door was slightly ajar) I could see he was holding a gun.

It occurred to me, for a moment, that I was simply hallucinating again. After all, I had more or less witnessed this scene several days previously. Something, though, told me it might not be entirely illogical to attempt to play it safe. So I did what Ms. Green had lately, i.e., a few minutes before, told me I could — I became barely visible.

Or thought I did.

It worked for a time.

The individual, wearing his orange hat, entered quickly, gun drawn, a smile on his face, finger on the trigger, a burst capillary in his left eye. On registering that I was not at my desk, he did a curious dance, a kind of wheel and pivot movement, executed quite deftly, which he repeated three times. When he was satisfied that I wasn't standing out of the range of his peripheral vision, he took two quick steps over to my desk, simultaneously looking under it and pushing the curtains aside.

Where are you? he said.

He said it in a very casual, almost friendly way, which almost caused me to become visible again, or at least to attempt to answer. For a moment though, and perhaps this saved me, I was drawn, all but irresistibly, away from this line of hypothetical inertia, into a moment's reverie, in which I was hiding in a foot locker in an enormous dark room — a small dark set off from a larger dark and my own dark set off from the whole — and someone holding a large knife and a flashlight was looking for me.

Where are you? she said, in a very casual, almost friendly way, so that I almost, as she stood outside the locker, answered, or began to breathe again.

He was standing right beside me. If I could have felt anything (I could see, hear, smell, and taste but not feel) I would have felt his breath on the lobe of my left ear.

This is where you are, he said. He spoke now in a hoarse half whisper, so that, with the receptive capacities of my remaining senses much reduced, it was difficult to hear him.

Yes, this is where you are, he said. I wonder what you've learned so far. I wonder if you have learned anything at all.

Very little, I thought, though I have learned some things. I have learned, for example, I thought, from my interview with Ms. Krumpacher, that murder was in fact done, most certainly. Great quantities of blood and tissue and several small pieces of bone had been found.

By who? (I thought)

The authorities.

Which authorities?

Those charged with seeing to this variety of incident.

And how did you come by this information?

I was part of the cleanup crew.

To clean up the blood and . . .?

Yes. This was following the assessment.

After the scene had been analyzed?

There was no analysis. There was just the assessment. Then the cleanup. There were several pints of blood and three slivers of cranium.

Who measured the blood? Who determined that it was cranium?

I did.

Under whose orders?

The authorities.

Whose authorities?

The firm's.

What firm?

I can't tell you.

What became of the body?

(I was now addressing Mr. Brown.)

It had been removed.

By who?

Difficult to say.

Isn't it possible that the body, not dead, removed itself?

No.

Why not?

There were certain indications.

Such as?

The blood, of which there was a great quantity, had spread around the body and congealed, leaving behind an almost perfect outline.

Almost perfect?

There were bootmarks in the blood, they interrupted several of the edges.

At this point Mr. Jones showed me a photograph. The photograph was of the crime scene—a damp alley to one side of which stood a green metal door, an alley much like the one I had followed my first client's husband to, much like the one I had recently visited, having left the disused power station and having, part of me that is, returned. John was in the photograph. He was standing off to the side, looking down at the almost perfect outline of a small body. I am small.

Who was the victim?

We don't know.

(This was Ms. Green.)

Who is we?

We of the firm.

What firm?

I can't tell you.

I know what firm.

Not from me.

No, not from you.

We sat there. I stared at her astonishingly pretty face.

How long have you been dead? I asked her.

I'm not sure I am yet.

And where is your body?

I don't know.

Where is my body?

Not, perhaps, where you think it is.

It suddenly occurred to me that I had been speaking aloud, that almost all of the preceding had, in fact, been said loudly enough for the individual with the cracked tooth to hear.

Did you hear me? I said.

Yes, he said.

So you can see I know very little.

Not as little as you should know. One should know very little about these matters, as little as possible.

About what matters?

But instead of answering, he took a gun from his pocket and aimed it at me.

Yes, knowing very little is best in these matters, he said.

The gun, unless my eyes were deceiving me, was largely transparent and glowing slightly, and though I wasn't entirely sure what a gun, or any weapon for that matter could do to me, given my current condition, I did not feel I was adequately informed to make a safe decision. And in fact it was just as well that, right when he smiled and pulled the trigger, I allowed myself to fall backwards through the wall, because the bullet, itself partially transparent, that issued from the gun and struck me in the neck instead of, most likely, the heart, did do considerable damage and hurt tremendously, as bullets, even beautiful ones, are wont to do.

Shot through the neck and falling backwards, I watched him smiling, his cracked tooth caught in some stray line of light, my secretary's head peeping in through the door, until the wall I had fallen through obscured them.

For a time then I fell—through the floor of the next room then through other floors then through the earth, which glowed and seemed warm, and then through a shaft on the edge of a platform and onto the rails of a subway line along which I skidded for a time then lay still. I don't know how long I lay there, but many trains passed through me, causing me only a slight pain, and nothing compared to the pain in my neck. It was likely this rather severe pain, which held me immobile, that helped bring to mind promising bits of memory that emerged for a moment like pieces of some phantom jigsaw puzzle that came tantalizingly close to locking together, only to pull apart again before I could discern their pattern. Some of what I remembered as I lay there has completely vanished, but the substantive details included the following:

I had been in love with someone, someone I had walked with through a white mist.

I had, at some point, been to the boss's office, had seen the train set and had a gun held to my head.

I had been to the crime scene before the crime, had followed a well-dressed individual into the poorly lit alley, had watched him knock on then disappear through the green metal door, had myself gone through the door, where, in the dark, I saw machines.

As I lay there, stray images of my childhood came to me, years ago, years before, of myself lying dreaming in an attic room, light on the ceiling, mist in the yard. Then of a conversation with a stranger, a traveler, dead bees in his pocket, butterfly net.

Then a memory of a beautiful face set into a smile, gazing at me.

Then, again, the boss's office—lying amid the train sets, standing up, being forced up, Ms. Green being brought in. The name Lyla seemed, for a moment, to correspond to her. She had been badly beaten, couldn't stand. Her beautiful face was set into a smile, gazing at me. There was a gun at my head. The boss, who up until that moment had been hidden in the gloom, came forward, caressed her cheek, then . . .

At any rate, it was the thought that I had been in love with someone before whatever had happened to me, this perplexing and galvanizing premise, that caused me at last, as I remember it, the pain in my neck notwithstanding, to stir and, eventually, one or two more trains having passed through me, to rise.

Then I walked along the tracks, through dark tunnels lit occasionally by train lights and yellow soot-covered lanterns. Every few hundred yards the tunnels opened onto platforms where people, collapsed into chairs, slumped against walls, leaning on painted girders, waited in a kind of daze. They were strangely attractive to me these people waiting for trains beneath the surface of the earth, and once or twice as I walked I stopped and considered them. Mostly though I walked, and walked and walked, and stopped walking and rested with my cold feet in a puddle, which held some special appeal for the rats. The rats, intent upon their puddle, which probably had a little oil or meat in it, paid me very little attention, although one or two of them attempted, in desultory fashion, and with no luck at all, to bite my ankles.

The city was as intricately articulated below its surface as it was above, and it was not at all unpleasant to walk along, at best a pale blur, and think about love. Or about being in love. At first it troubled me greatly that I could call no further details to mind, and that, in fact, some of what I was sure I had remembered, had already slipped my mind. But this feeling passed quickly enough.

I love you, I said, and the words both warmed and chilled me as if they were some strange food or drug. I walked and walked and the words *hand in hand* accompanied me, as did the words *I love* so that after a time, when I began to rise up off the tracks, through the damp ceiling, and back onto the dark streets, I was not surprised. Nor was I surprised when, still walking, still wrapped in similar thoughts, my mouth making the shape of similar words, I floated up the sides of several buildings and once a water tower, where, as the cold wind blew both through and around me, I could just make out the gray-blue light of the approaching dawn.

I'm not sure how I made it home.

I'm not sure, either, how, once home, I managed to turn my thoughts away from love—I had been having visions of horned melon and strange berries and rare truffles—and back to the case, which clearly, if what I had remembered had any validity at all, related to me and Ms. Green.

It was perhaps the growing pain in my neck, which was now radiating down my throat and out along my shoulders, that helped me to make the transition. It occurred to me, in the face of this pain, that even if I was, as Ms. Green had assured me already, like she was, dead, that I might be dying again; and I have to say that the prospect held no appeal, not least because I had no idea how it would affect my handling of the investigation, which was already problematic enough. I wished I could consult Ms. Green. In fact, I wished very much that I could see Ms. Green. Very much indeed. Perhaps together, if we could think clearly and speak frankly, it would be possible to make some progress. I was of course beginning to have my own theories, but they seemed woefully inadequate, even if one subscribed to the theory that in complex cases, even partial or compromised solutions are acceptable. No doubt, when my client came to ask for an accounting I wouldn't be able to offer him much. First thing in the morning, after I had fired my secretary, I would look into contacting Ms. Green. Maybe before firing him I would ask him to try to contact her. In fact, there were several appointments he could make for me.

I'm sorry, he said when I came into the office the next day. I don't know what came over me.

Neither the fuck do I, I said.

Having passed the remainder of the night fitfully (it is true that I seemed no longer able to sleep), I had breakfasted on toast, soft-boiled eggs, pickles, and oranges, then made my way over to the office. It had been a very pleasant walk. My neck seemed to hurt less and the sun

lit the buildings and the people brilliantly. It was probably this brilliance coupled with the fact of my large and
interesting breakfast, and my decision taken during the
night not to worry too much, if I could help it, about
whether or not I was dying again, that made my step
seem firmer and my head more clear. It was certainly this
feeling of solidity (no matter how illusory) that made my
thoughts sharper, and I took advantage of the situation to
review the case and to try, even if only in speculative
fashion, to make sense of its latest developments.

I had known Ms. Green intimately, I thought as I
walked along through the bright sunlight and clean, cool
air. That was part of the case. As was John's involvement
in it. Clearly, I would have to pay another visit to the
boss.

I did (I imagined).

So you've come, he said. You could hear a faint electric whirring. See the occasional electric flash.

I've come about Ms. Green, I said. In relation to the case.

The case? he said.

I have been engaged.

By who?

By you.

Was it me?

Yes, I believe it was you.

Look at my train.

Yes, I see your train. There were others in his office.
There were always others. John was there. But John wasn't
important, not at this moment; at this moment the boss was
important. Ms. Green, Lyla Green, was important.

Tell me about your relationship with Ms. Green, Mr.
Smith, I said.

Are you calling me Mr. Smith?

I am.

Good, very good. I sent her to see you, he said.

Which time?

He laughed. He stepped out into the light beside a small mountain just as the silver train swept by.

Each time, he said.

I've been shot, I said.

I know.

Is he here too?

The boss gestured. The individual with the cracked tooth came forward. He smiled. He lifted a finger to his mouth and blew on it.

It was you I followed, I said, speaking to the boss, Mr. Smith. You were my first client's husband. I followed you to a house, your home.

The boss, Mr. Smith, nodded (I speculated).

I had reached my office.

My secretary greeted me with donuts and bandages. I accepted a donut but not the bandages.

Bandages are no good, I said.

Well then let me clean it, he said.

I allowed him to daub my neck with iodine.

This hurt.

They paid me too well not to go along with them, he said.

Who paid you?

They paid me too well to tell you.

Has Ms. Green been here this morning?

No.

Please call her.

Certainly.

Please also call John.

Why John?

It occurs to me that John may have killed me.

But of course John hadn't killed me. Or so he said when he came into my office a little later.

Come on, would I hit my best friend repeatedly on the head with a blunt instrument?

I was almost at my office and I wasn't thinking quite as clearly. My cognitive powers were fading. The pain in my neck was reasserting itself. Aware that whatever reprieve I had been granted was ending, I redoubled my efforts — this time focusing my speculations on the missing part of the evening I tailed my first client's husband.

He had knocked on the green metal door and had entered. A moment later I had followed. It took a few minutes for my eyes to adjust to the gloom and for my mind to accept the chaos of ruined machines and sickly blinking lights. When I could both see and make sense, or some sense, of what I was seeing, I made my way through the machines (I had no idea what they were for) to a point of great light, an emanation within the darkness, a lamp-lit clearing at the center of the machines. Within that emanation (I stayed outside of it, neatly hidden, or so I thought, behind an enormous coil of wire) I perceived, and the sight was horrifying . . . but even speculation couldn't take me that far.

Now, of course, I can see quite clearly what I couldn't even imagine then. But now it doesn't particularly help me to do so. Nothing, in fact, particularly helps me, so it is not at all surprising that I have so much trouble in carrying out even the smallest tasks.

Take for instance my latest assignment, which, with the aid of charts and texts, is to peer into a telescope pointed up into the night sky, and to make notes on what I see. It is information for an equation, I am told, but I have not been told what the equation is for. The equation is part of another equation, being the only explanation I have yet received. Be that as it may, I am unable, I am told, even to correctly fulfill this task. Just as, all those years ago, I was unable to correctly solve my case and later, when I joined the other organization, this organization, having been forced to leave the transactions firm, to carry out what should have been the simplest of assignments.

I have just recently had my legs broken and set. This event has sparked my thinking on this subject, these subjects.

I am recuperating. My hours in the observatory, while I do so, have been cut back. I am allowed to lie in my bed and look out the window. It is winter again. My bed has been pulled back far enough away from the window so that, lying here, I cannot see the people below on the street, though I can hear them. They are always speaking, these people, there is always sound. When I am here I am connected to several machines, which blink dully. I am not, of course, connected to any machines when I am in the observatory. Unless you count my oxygen canister. But that is a contraption, not a machine. Incidentally, all those who have not had the benefit of cool oxygen from a canister should indulge themselves. I sit by the telescope and peer into it and make my notations and, cannister on a stand beside me, breathe. I am not, you see, entirely sure what it is I am looking for, what I am meant to detect. This despite many explanations and threats of further punishment.

It is not as though I have never spent time looking at the stars. I used to spend whole evenings lying in the yard. We had dogs then. Or a dog. The dog would lie in the dirt beside me. It was as I was lying there in the dirt beside the dog looking up at the stars that they first, they claimed, found me keening. Any excuse would do. I mean for the accusations, not for the keening. I couldn't move, this was true. I couldn't speak, this was true. But I didn't keen. And my immobility was due only to the fact that I had ceased to be able to recognize what was spread above me as the night sky filled with stars. There were no stars. No sky. There was some black with imprecise white marks on it. White smudges. Nothing moved, nothing gleamed. It was as if the entire night sky had died. Or as if I had died. Am I dead? I was finally, when the sky began to seem to move again, able to ask them. Which no doubt contributed, once this remark had circulated, to the rumors.

What I am discussing now is context, clearly. Dirt and immobility and stars.

Mr. Smith, I said.

He was waiting for me on one of the chairs in my secretary's little room.

I have come, he said, to see what progress you have made on the case.

Quite a bit, in fact, I said. I've just been engaged in the most fruitful speculations. Let's go into my office and discuss it.

I ushered Mr. Smith into my office and shot my secretary, who was all smiles and insistent gestures of contrition, a meaningful look. Meaning, don't move, I'm going to come back out of this office and fire you.

Mr. Smith took his seat and I took mine and we both smiled at each other.

Shall I begin? I said.

Please do, he said.

But before I could begin talking, he had begun talking.

I see, I said. After a certain interval I said this again.

Now you, he said.

What should I tell you?

Anything you like.

So I told him about the years I had spent on the farm after my father had died, about the small bedroom in the attic, about the books, about the basement, about the blue jay that used to screech in the fruit trees.

How often did they put you in the basement?

At the end it was almost every day.

Mr. Smith spoke again for a time.

He had never been, so to speak, in the basement, but he had been buried when a building collapsed. This had been in a city built on the side of a mountain. He had been buried, along with many others, when the building had slid down the mountain in a river of mud.

Is that true, Mr. Smith?

My name's not Smith.

But the card you left . . .

Belonged to another, an associate, a certain individual with an orange hat and a cracked tooth. I wanted to let you know he was coming, to give you a heads-up.

Thanks. He already came.

I know he did.

We looked at each other.

He smiled.

It was too bad about the lips, but he had those gorgeous choppers.

Tell me about the progress you've made on the case.

I told him.

It was not, in the telling, massively impressive, and I found myself, absurdly, adding embellishments — a chance meeting with an eyewitness as I had wandered below the streets, an interesting interaction with a mysterious blond woman at a hotel bar.

But none of it seemed out of order to him, and when I had finished, he wrote me another check. Before he gave it to me, however, he said, so you haven't spoken to Ms. Green yet?

I wasn't sure why I had omitted my interaction with Ms. Green from the account I had given of my case-related activities. After all, he was the one who had given me her name in the first place. And he was such a pleasant client, with such gracious manners, thought-provoking stories, and gorgeous eyes. Still, my recent revelation regarding Ms. Green, Lyla, and my love for her, coupled with my speculation regarding my client's true identity (he had encouraged me, when I mentioned it, to pursue this line of inquiry), his overlap with my boss at the transactions firm and all the concomitant sinister possibility, not to mention his unexplained connection with the nefarious individual with the cracked tooth, contributed to my withholding.

So you think I should speak to this Ms. Green? I said.

Absolutely. I think she can and will furnish you with significant information regarding the case.

All right.

But now you'll have to locate her because she's no longer at the number I gave you earlier.

And you don't know where she's gone?

No. Although you might ask Mr. Smith. I left one of his cards with her as well.

What exactly, if you don't mind my asking, is the nature of your relationship with Mr. Smith? I asked, but unfortunately my client was no longer there.

In his place sat my secretary.

You asked me to come in, he said.

Yes, I said.

For a moment I couldn't remember why I had done so. The poor guy.

He was a good-enough secretary after all. It was true that certain aspects of his personality, not to mention the issue of his loyalty, left something to be desired, but I really wasn't paying him very well. And how much hygiene and loyalty could you expect for a sucker's salary every month?

Cash this check and go to the dentist, I said.

Then I'm not fired?

No, you're not fired.

Thanks, Boss.

Before he left I had him make a couple of phone calls. One was to Ms. Green. My client appeared to be right — the line had been disconnected. The other was to my first client, the one with the husband troubles. Once my secretary had placed the call, I got on the line and charmed my way through her perhaps only feigned surprise at hearing from me into an appointment for drinks the next day.

Then I went over to the transactions firm.

It was late evening when I arrived and most of the employees had been given their assignments and had set off for the night. It was with little hope of gratification then that I entered the copy room in search of information, and perhaps even a drink; as it happened, I got both.

Mr. Smith, I said.

I'm not called Mr. Smith when I'm here, he said. I'm called Max.

Max, I said.

Sport, he said.

He grinned and held up a bottle.

I grinned and began backing toward the door.

But he told me there was no need. What had to occur elsewhere, under other circumstances, was entirely unrelated to what would and had to occur here.

So have a drink, he said.

I have a gun, I said.

I had the gun in my hand and, as a precaution, was now holding it against the front of his cranium.

A gun is a weapon that fires a bullet, a shell, or some other missile, I said. Most guns fire by the force of a gas created by the rapid burning of gunpowder. The shells in this gun contain gunpowder, which, I said, can quite easily be encouraged to create gas.

My cranium is soft, Sport, and I'm unarmed, he said.

Are you? I said.

Actually, I could see that he was. I could see, in fact, straight through him, straight through his shoes and clothes and orange hat. I could see the black heart beating in his chest and the black brain beating in his skull. Your brain is black, Max, I said.

Ask it anything you want then have a drink, he said.

I did so.

I mean I asked then I had a drink. Then I had another then took the barrel of my gun off Max's head.

Is the boss around tonight, Max?

Yes he is.

And John?

John is probably with the boss—he's with him a lot these days.

With the trains?

There is only one train. Many tracks, one train. He insists on this arrangement.

I think I would like to go in and speak to him, to them.

Impossible.

Why?

We have work.

We?

The two of us. A body.

I'm on a leave of absence. I'm working on a case.

Check the board.

I did. I went back. Max grinned.

My neck hurts, I said. I was shot.

Yeah, I know, I'm sorry—it looks terrible. But it's time to go.

I followed him out the door and we made our way off across the city to a small apartment in a medium-size building in which we found a small pretty body, Ms. Green.

It was at this point, I should say, that I began to lose hope in my abilities as an investigator, and also in my future in that line of work. You will remember, I expect, that not so many days earlier, I had been quite hopeful and had imagined that my future would be quite bright indeed. And yet, faced with my first complex case, I was already mired in uncertainties, which seemed sure to overwhelm me at any moment.

Can we just leave it here? I asked Max.

Our instructions are to take it to the river.

But I'd like to tell Ms. Green about this.

So tell her as we're walking, he said.

I don't mean her, I said, looking at the body.

Who do you mean then?

I had to admit I wasn't sure. I mean, there she was. But there I was, too. Or at least I thought so. Perhaps I was elsewhere. I *was* elsewhere. I could see the sides of a hollowed-out turbine. Ms. Green was there. Sitting beside me.

Explain, I said.

I can't, she said. It's up to you.

I see.

This was the next day. I was sitting at the bar of a hotel listening to a stunning blonde, my first client, and she had several interesting things to say.

You really don't remember, do you? she said.

No I don't. I mean yes and no.

You don't remember the firm's annual dinner and being introduced to me and to my husband?

No, I said.

Wait, yes, I said.

I had suddenly caught a glimpse. An enormous banquet hall filled with round tables and flower arrangements and endless bottles of expensive cognac.

You're married to the boss, I said.

Yes, she said.

So you had me following the boss?

My husband.

It really was your husband.

Why should I have lied?

I raised my eyebrow.

At this my former client lifted her drink to her lips, looked at me, smiled.

Nobody imagined that you would be able to continue to follow him once you had entered the green door, she said. That was a pretty trick.

A pretty trick, I said.

She smiled.

Your husband was seeing someone, wasn't he?

He was.

Who?

You don't remember, she said, being introduced that evening to the woman sitting on my husband's right?

Ms. Green, I said.

My husband's late mistress.

The woman I fell in love with, I whispered.

Who's that? said Max.

He had the bag open and was waiting for me to pick up the body and put it in. She was lying in the bathtub, fully clothed. We had often, I had the feeling, taken baths together in this tub, and it seemed extremely unfortunate now to have to lift her up out of it and put her in a bag.

Can I have another drink first? I said.

Sure Sport, but make it snappy, the meter's running.

He dropped the handles of the bag and began rummaging around in the bathroom cabinet. I went to the kitchen and took a flask out of a drawer next to the stove.

Tell me everything, I said.

Lyla was sitting next to me, in the turbine.

I don't know everything, she said.

Then tell me what you know.

We were lovers.

Yes.

Then we got caught.

Yes.

Then we got killed.

You want a glass and some ice with that?

Max. Standing in the bathroom doorway looking out at me.

You had enough? he said.

What do you mean?

I mean have you had enough — dead honey in the bathtub, slug in your neck, head injury, incertitude.

What do you mean by incertitude?

About the case. You don't quite have it yet, do you? Still got things to figure out. Not getting there.

You mean there's more?

There's always more.

I thought you told me it was best not to know too much about these things.

Not me.

I thought you said I shouldn't know too much then you put this slug in my neck.

Sorry, even if I did say that I don't know what you're talking about, Sport.

Lyla's dead in the other room. Is she the only one? Am I lying dead in a turbine right now?

You're getting out of my league there, Sport.

What is your relationship to my employer?

To the boss?

To my employer. The one who is paying me to make sense of this case.

I don't know your employer.

Does Mr. Smith?

Couldn't say.

How many people are dead? One or two?

We got one in there Sport, dead as we're all gonna be.

And me?

And you Sport, I don't know. I know what they tell me. They tell me you have incertitude. They tell me you're having trouble making headway. They tell me you're getting distracted and taking leaves of absence and thinking about stopping work at the firm. They tell me to take you here. I take you here. We get the body. We take the body.

Help me out a second, I said.

You've had your second, Sport. You've had your second and now I need you in the bathroom.

I went to the bathroom. The attendant asked me if I was aware that I was bleeding, ever so slightly, from the neck. I asked him if he would be willing, if he could, to stop it, as I had a lady waiting for me at the bar and I didn't know her well enough to tell if blood was her cup of tea.

Oh it might be sir, said the attendant.

Nevertheless, I said.

So he ran hot water onto a towel and began daubing my neck and placing pressure on it. While he did so I looked in the mirror. Curiously, what greeted me there was the most beautiful scene. It was a breeze-swept olive grove with an old farmhouse off in the distance. Here and there were butterflies and cypress trees.

Happy, I tipped the attendant a twenty and walked out.

Grab a handle, Max said.

We used to have dinner here, I said. After we would get off work.

I heard about that.

I looked at him.

Everyone heard about it.

From who?

Who do you think?

I don't know.

Maybe it was her, he said. She spent her time tossing them back in the copy room.

No way, I said.

But for a second I could almost see her, laughing, belting one back.

And it was, interestingly enough, in this image of her, troubling as it was, that I found the key I had been looking for, or part of one. This is not to say, I should hasten to add, that I was finally able to solve the case, I was not, I've already said that, but I was able to imagine that, having once walked into the copy room and seen her, in company, drinking, not necessarily laughing, likely not, but drinking and observing and smiling slightly and perhaps, in some way, participating, a moment of jealousy had awoken, and I had told John afterwards to make sure that he and the others kept the fuck away from her. So that, as I imagined it, it was John, perhaps out of irritation, who had let it slip in the copy room, laughing and belting one back—my buddy is getting delicate with the boss's mistress—and John who later, out of guilt, helped me into my then-current situation as investigator, in which capacity I would investigate one case in toto, the first and second having turned out to be one and the same—the first and only—and who helped me again, when somehow it was over, to close my office, to say good-bye to my secretary, and to regain at least a glimmer of my former self.

I say maybe it was John who had let it slip. Obviously, however, I mean it was me.

It was me, I said. Maybe someone else inadvertently passed the message along, but it was me who couldn't keep his damn mouth shut.

Never spill the beans, Sport, said Max.

Thanks for the advice, I said.

But at any rate, having in my possession something approximating a key, and a concomitant chain of images now at my disposal, that is to say, a reservoir of talking points, something to say, a hypothesis to offer my client, to close out our account, as it were, I made my way back over to the firm.

The early afternoon was quiet time at the firm, most of the transactionists were either asleep or hoping to be. So I wasn't surprised to find it all but deserted. The dispatcher's office was locked and the copy room was empty; even my faint footfalls echoed in those empty halls. After some minutes of trying locked doors and drifting through them into empty offices and storerooms, I began to despair of finding anyone who could direct me to the boss's office. No doubt, it seemed to me, I had been there before, and even recently, but some aspect of my condition prevented me from calling to mind the particulars of the itinerary. Fortunately, I eventually found someone—at the documents counter. This was the documents assistant, who was in charge of preparing documents for distribution throughout the firm. I had interacted with this gentleman on several occasions, and had always found him quite helpful, and I had no reason to be disappointed this time. He was able, in fact, to provide me with a map of the building, and I soon found myself knocking at the boss's door. Before doing so, however, the documents assistant and I had a short chat. As I've said, we were on very friendly terms, and it was not at all unusual for us to exchange the occasional word. He was an old individual, and he loved to keep me abreast of his latest discoveries relative to his great passion—beekeeping.

I've got some with me, he said on this occasion.

Some what?

Bees.

Where?

In my pocket.

What he had with him were dead bees. Several of them. He lined them up on the counter—three drones and four workers—then scooped them back up in his hand. He then spoke to me at some length about the honey stomach and the chemical makeup of its lining. This makeup, as one might readily gather, was a key factor in the eventual consistency of the honey, or at any rate this was his idea.

You've been shot in the neck, friend, he said.

And hit on the head. I'm actually dead at the moment. Just like your bees.

I see.

He then told me one or two things about the forelegs of the worker bee. As he spoke I let myself drift for a moment, and it seemed to me as I did so that, once again, I slipped away from myself, drifted down the many halls and straight through the boss's door without knocking.

I'm glad you've come, he said. It's good to see you again.

I've come to tell you what I've learned about the case. I've come very close to a solution, perhaps not all the way, but close.

Excellent. Make your report.

I did so.

He agreed that I was getting close, very close.

He suggested a couple of emendations, one or two variants, two or three different avenues to explore. Perhaps nobody at all, he said, spilled the beans in the copy room. Perhaps a syringe was, at a certain stage, involved, or a line of the miniature tracks that you see spread around you. Perhaps my wife, as you say she has described herself to you, had slightly more to do with it than you have yet envisaged. Perhaps, in fact, you weren't set up in the alley by me. Perhaps my putative wife set you up. What you saw when you went through the green metal door you were not, perhaps, supposed to have seen. So that perhaps you can imagine that you were not murdered, as you have put it, in the alley for what you referred to as your trespass against me with Ms. Green. Or that perhaps, at that juncture, you had not yet been murdered at all.

Tell me about the syringe, I said.

I could only offer you the wildest conjecture, he said.

So is there any way to reverse my condition?

Hmmm, he said, then raised an eyebrow and shrugged.

I asked him if he wanted me to continue with my investigation.

He said he was expecting it.

When I have to report should I call on you here?

Absolutely.

And if I have nothing further to report?

My door will always be open for you.

So it seemed to me somewhat strange that when, having just a few minutes later taken my leave of the documents assistant, I presented myself at the boss's office and knocked, and knocked and knocked, no one came to the door, not even to tell me that he wasn't there.

Afterword

AFTERWORD

I WROTE THE BULK OF *THE IMPOSSIBLY* DURING ENFORCED leaves of absence from the United Nations, where I spent five years working, in various related capacities, in the Department of Public Information. The absences were enforced because I was, effectively, a contract worker and had to be off the payroll for a certain amount of time each year to avoid being considered a permanent employee, with all the rather extravagant benefits that standing entailed. Given that during the eleven-odd months a year I was on the work was often quite exhausting, I welcomed these obligatory furloughs and did my best to fill them to the extent possible (life, as it tends to, often making its curious interventions) with writing. *The Impossibly* got started, the first day of the first of these breaks in 1997, out of the conjoined impulse to write a love story and to write something long. Taking inspiration from the three books I happened to be reading at the time (*The Oulipo Compendium, The Autobiography of Alice B. Toklas,* and *The Great Gatsby*), the thing was launched. Three years and three breaks later I had three linked novellas. Or thought I did.

On a trip to Athens, where my wife Eleni was on a Fulbright, I reread the most recent quarter and decided it didn't work at all. I liked it, which was something, but it didn't work with the rest of the manuscript. I mean, what did I know, I was young, I'd never published a novel or a series of long linked anythings, but this didn't, this third section I had written, hmmm, feel right. So I drank too much ouzo and wandered the streets of Athens' old Turkish section for a few days then decided to write something new. There was a table, which had a view of the Acropolis, on the roof of Eleni's building. I had a notebook with me. I wrote. I ate Greek yogurt, Greek salad, grilled meats. Vast quantities of meats. We took long walks through Athens. We traveled to Delphi and on to the Peloponnese. I kept writing. By the time I went back to New York, back to my work at the UN, the draft was done.

Or probably it didn't happen quite that way. There was ouzo. There was a table with a view of the Acropolis (not to mention of an intervening [insert some sea-like word that is not *sea* here] of tangled wires, dusty awnings, and concrete rooftops). There was also yogurt and meat. In quantity. The yogurt came in little clay pots and was wonderfully aerated. But I'm not sure there was ever any conscious decision to start over. Even though I did start over. It sort of just happened. I see myself, badly blurred, starting to rewrite. I took a walk in some hills overlooking Athens while Eleni was at a Greek language class and when I came back down I had started up again. The notebook I used was a blue, quadrilinear, medium-size French Lafontaine: I know this because I still have the notebook. I had a Scheaffer fountain pen. I know that because I just know, even though the pen is now lost. Speaking of other things I know, most days during my stay I walked by a building that was completely shrouded with dark mesh. Such buildings were all over Athens, but this one took the cake. And devoured it. So that went into the new thing. As did the grilled meat and the ouzo and the Acropolis, though I didn't call it that.

A year or so later, back in New York, I realized two things. The first was that what I had written was a novel (not an Austerian or Beckettian or Flaubertian or Steinian trilogy), and the second was that if I borrowed a bit from the end of the abandoned, original third section, the one that I rejected in Greece before eating the already overdiscussed meat and yogurt, not to mention buckets and buckets of the inevitable, inimitable Greek salad, the novel would be more and/or less complete. Which is how it remains. Perhaps now even more so since the amputated section, which long ago grew its own name and lived its own brief solo life on Amy Fusselman's *Surgery of Modern Warfare,* before serving for some time as a sample text in a series of long letters called *Dear Laird Hunt, Author of "The Impossibly,"* has come back to sit with its confrères in uneasy company.

Readers may be charmed or not to know that for a time after I had written the first section of *The Impossibly,* my idea was to continue the book by writing, in the mode of Kafka's great story "The Burrow," the story of a clownfish who has strayed into, and cannot find his way out of again, a submerged Louvre. The clownfish, who would narrate, was to swim through the vast, watery halls, perch unhappily behind support girders in the space at the small of the back behind the Winged Victory of Samothrace, visit the still-shimmery cases of preclassical Greek statues, gaze with a longing it doesn't understand the source of at Durer's autoportrait, the one where he is young and holding thistles.

This section was to be followed by the third-person study of a man who has been locked into some devilishly accurate recreation of the Luxembourg Gardens. Each day meat and old crepes would be thrown over the bars to him. The idea wasn't at all developed and says perhaps more than I would like about its positor's state of mind in the late 1990s. As does, I suppose, the thing about the clownfish. Which is really the same story. Just as it, the thing about the clownfish, is more and/or less the same story as the first section of *The Impossibly*. Which ends up repeating itself in its subsequent sections anyway.

Albeit differently.

COLOPHON

The Impossibly was designed at Coffee House Press, in the historic
Grain Belt Brewery's Bottling House near downtown Minneapolis.
The text is set in Cochin with Metropolis titles.

COFFEE HOUSE PRESS

The mission of Coffee House Press is to publish exciting, vital, and enduring authors of our time; to delight and inspire readers; to contribute to the cultural life of our community; and to enrich our literary heritage. By building on the best traditions of publishing and the book arts, we produce books that celebrate imagination, innovation in the craft of writing, and the many authentic voices of the American experience.

Join us in our mission at coffeehousepress.org

FUNDER ACKNOWLEDGMENT

Coffee House Press is an independent nonprofit literary publisher. Our books are made possible through the generous support of grants and gifts from many foundations, corporate giving programs, state and federal support, and through donations from individuals who believe in the transformational power of literature. Coffee House Press receives major operating support from the Bush Foundation, the McKnight Foundation, from Target, and in part by a grant provided by the Minnesota State Arts Board, through appropriation by the Minnesota State Legislature from the Minnesota arts and cultural Heritage fund with money from the vote of the people of Minnesota on November 4, 2008, and a grant from the Wells Fargo Foundation of Minnesota. Coffee House also receives support from: three anonymous donors; Suzanne Allen; Elmer L. and Eleanor J. Andersen Foundation; Around Town Literary Media Guides; Patricia Beithon; Bill Berkson; the James L. and Nancy J. Bildner Foundation; the E. Thomas Binger and Rebecca Rand Fund of Minneapolis Foundation; the Patrick and Aimee Butler Family Foundation; the Buuck Family Foundation; Ruth and Bruce Dayton; Dorsey & Whitney, LLP; Mary Ebert and Paul Stembler; Fredrikson & Byron, P.A.; Sally French; Jennifer Haugh; Anselm Hollo and Jane Dalrymple-Hollo; Jeffrey Hom; Stephen and Isabel Keating; the Kenneth Koch Literary Estate; the Lenfestey Family Foundation; Ethan J. Litman; Carol and Aaron Mack; Mary McDermid; Sjur Midness and Briar Andresen; the Rehael Fund of the Minneapolis Foundation; Deborah Reynolds; Schwegman, Lundberg & Woessner, P.A.; John Sjoberg; David Smith; Kiki Smith; Mary Strand and Tom Fraser; Jeffrey Sugerman; Patricia Tilton; the Archie D. & Bertha H. Walker Foundation; Stu Wilson and Mel Barker; the Woessner Freeman Family Foundation; Margaret and Angus Wurtele; and many other generous individual donors.

ART WORKS.
arts.gov

MINNESOTA
STATE ARTS BOARD

TARGET.

To you and our many readers across the country,
we send our thanks for your continuing support.